AN IMMODEST PROPOSAL

The Earl of Langham had never appeared more breathtakingly handsome—or heartbreakingly cold. His silver-gray eyes seemed to glitter like ice as he made his proposal to Susanna.

He agreed with her that until her sister was safely wed no breath of scandal should affect the family. Therefore he was quite willing to play the part of a devoted husband to Susanna in public.

All he asked in return was the perfect freedom to do what he wanted with whom he wanted in private. Susanna did not need to be told that the "whom" referred to the beautiful widowed Lady Julia, whom Langham had adored once and now sought again.

In short, all Susanna had to do to save her social standing was surrender the man she loved. . . .

COMING IN OCTOBER
A Signet Super Regency
"A tender and sensitive love story ... an exciting
blend of romance and history"—*Romantic Times*

THE GUARDED HEART

by
Barbara Hazard

Passion and danger embraced her—but one man
intoxicated her flesh with love's irresistable promise ...

Beautiful Erica Stone found her husband mysteriously murdered in Vienna and herself alone and helpless in this city of romance ... until the handsome, cynical Owen Kingsley, Duke of Graves, promised her protection if she would spy for England among the licentious lords of Europe. Aside from the danger and intrigue, Erica found herself wrestling with her passion, for the tantalizingly reserved Dike, when their first achingly tender kiss sparked a desire in her more powerfully exciting than her hesitant heart had ever felt before....

Buy them at your local bookstore or use this convenient coupon for ordering.

NEW AMERICAN LIBRABY,
P.O. Box 999, Bergenfield, New Jersey 07621

Please send me the books I have checked above. I am enclosing $_____
(please add $1.00 to this order to cover postage and handling). Send check or money order—no cash or C.O.D.'s. Prices and numbers subject to change without notice.

Name_____

Address_____

City_____State_____Zip Code_____

Allow 4-6 weeks for delivery.
This offer is subject to withdrawal without notice.

A BREATH OF SCANDAL

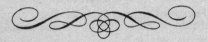

by
Diana Campbell

NAL BOOKS ARE AVAILABLE AT QUANTITY DISCOUNTS WHEN USED TO PROMOTE PRODUCTS OR SERVICES, FOR INFORMATION PLEASE WRITE TO PREMIUM MARKETING DIVISION, NEW AMERICAN LIBRARY, 1633 BROADWAY, NEW YORK, NEW YORK 10019.

Copyright © 1987 by Diana Campbell

All rights reserved

SIGNET TRADEMARK REG. U.S.PAT.OFF. AND FOREIGN COUNTRIES
REGISTERED TRADEMARK—MARCA REGISTRADA
HECHO EN CHICAGO, U.S.A.

SIGNET, SIGNET CLASSIC, MENTOR, ONYX, PLUME, MERIDIAN and NAL BOOKS are published by **NAL PENGUIN INC.,** 1633 Broadway, New York, New York 10019

First Printing, October, 1987

1 2 3 4 5 6 7 8 9

PRINTED IN THE UNITED STATES OF AMERICA

Chapter 1

SUSANNA CLOSED the front door, trudged wearily back up the staircase, and paused at the drawing-room entry to peer inside. As she had expected, she found Nancy indelicately sprawled on the Hepplewhite sofa—her slippers off, the hem of her skirt drawn halfway to her knees, her long stockinged legs stretched upon the couch. Lady Hadleigh had obviously settled in for a lengthy conversation, and Susanna stifled a sigh. It had long been Nancy's custom to linger at Susanna's weekly salons after the rest of the guests had departed, and Susanna had come to anticipate these cozy chats with her closest friend rather more than the glittering soirees themselves. But she was oddly out of spirits tonight, and she did not believe her inexplicable depression was wholly attributable to the circumstance that her guest of honor had failed to appear.

"How very rude of Byron not to come!"

Nancy might have been reading her thoughts, and Susanna started, hurried on into the saloon, and sank into the Adam armchair.

"Any other poet in England would have been *thrilled* to grace your first salon of the Season," Lady Hadleigh continued warmly. "Indeed, I'll warrant there's not another public figure who would dare to cut you so discourteously. Not a single writer or artist or actor or politician . . ."

Nancy rattled on in this indignant vein, but Susanna's mind soon began to wander. In her present dark humor, she was compelled to wonder whether Lord Byron was merely the first of her guests of honor to recognize that Lady Langham's celebrated soirees much resembled a circus. Susanna had never intended to create such an atmosphere, of course; she had not set out to exploit the "public figures" she invited into her home. But she sometimes feared that her salons differed only in form and content, not in purpose, from the performances at Astley's Royal Amphitheatre or Vauxhall Gardens. *Tonight, in lieu of Madame Saqui's descent by rope in a shower of Chinese fire, we shall feature Mr. Coleridge reciting his latest poems . . .*

So perhaps the astonishing thing, Susanna reflected, was that none of her honored guests—until tonight—had declined to display his or her talents before the assembled company in Lady Langham's Grosvenor Square mansion. No, she amended, the astonishing thing was that her soirees, which had begun quite by accident, had become a fixture of London society.

Susanna's eyes drifted to the wall above the mantel and came to rest on the portrait Papa had commissioned just prior to her marriage. Though she often glanced at the painting, she rarely *studied* it; and whenever she did, as she did now, she did not know whether to be glad or sorry that she had changed so little in the three and a half years since she had sat for Thomas Lawrence. On the one hand, or so she supposed, she should be grateful that she had not visibly aged. Apart from the fact that her face had thinned a bit—emphasizing her already prominent cheekbones and creating interesting hollows below them—she looked, at four and twenty, precisely like the twenty-year-old girl in the picture.

On the other hand, her exotic coloring had not moderated with the passage of time; and Susanna was well aware that her black hair, coal-colored eyes, and olive complexion had produced all manner of outlandish *on-dits*. The most widely circulated rumor was that her father—the infamous Simon Randall, who had amassed an immense fortune during his long residence in India—had wed (or simply bedded, depending on the particular story) a native woman and brought the offspring of this liaison back to England when he returned. The truth was that Papa had been very dark before his hair went gray and Susanna's late mother had been a perfectly ordinary Englishwoman.

But legends were made of such stuff, Susanna thought philosophically, dropping her eyes from the painting to the empty fireplace, and perhaps her social success was due in part to her allegedly mysterious background. At any rate, when she had removed to London three years since, the hanging of her portrait had reminded her of Mr. Lawrence, and she had impulsively invited him to attend a small dinner party at her new home and meet a few of her friends. She realized only belatedly—after Mr. Lawrence accepted her invitation—that she had no "friends," but only a host of casual acquaintances she had encountered during the Season of her come-out.

Since there was nothing for it at that juncture but to blunder ahead, Susanna dashed off invitations to the two dozen people she knew the best, and to her amazement, all but one agreed to come to her impromptu salon. She did not imagine for a moment that any of her guests was passionately eager to attend the young Countess of Langham's soiree; she well recognized that she had merely filled a hole in the social calendar. She had, fortunately, scheduled her party for a Thursday night at the very beginning of the Season, and those of the *ton* who had arrived in London had nothing better to occupy their time.

However, to Susanna's further amazement, the evening was an unqualified success, and upon its conclusion, Mr. Lawrence announced that he had had such a splendid time that he hoped to return in the near future and bring several young artists of his acquaintance. Since the following Thursday night was free as well, it was agreed that Susanna would conduct a second salon then; and at the end of the festivities, the guests universally concurred that they would much prefer to spend their Thursday evenings in the witty, cultured atmosphere provided by Lady Langham than at one of the crowded balls or "at homes" so prevalent in London during the Season. Susanna obligingly invited them all to return the next Thursday, when they were entertained by Elizabeth Billington, the opera singer.

Throughout the first spring Season, Susanna limited her guest list to the original coterie; but as a number of them did not come to town for the Little Season that autumn, she was compelled to invite substitutes in order to reach a contingent of two dozen, which she had determined to be the optimal size for her soirees. She shortly learned, via the ecstatic gossip of her servants, that an invitation to Lady Langham's salon had become one of the most coveted in London; and the following spring— after considerable soul-searching—she decided to capitalize on her inadvertent fame by varying her guest list from week to week. By the end of that Season, or so Susanna was advised by several reliable sources, Lady Jersey was peevishly remarking that a few misguided souls appeared to revere a summons to Lady Langham's more than a voucher of admission to Almack's.

Whether this was true or not, Susanna couldn't say; she had not set out to compete with the formidable Countess of Jersey either. But there was no denying that her soirees were immensely popular: virtual strangers frequently approached her in hopes of soliciting an invitation, and the *un*solicited invitations she issued were declined only in the event of dire emergency. Furthermore, the honored guests she asked to Grosvenor Square seemed equally eager to come. Over the years, her salons had featured such widely diverse figures as Grimaldi, the clown; the radical writer Leigh Hunt; pious Hannah More; and—two Seasons ago—the same Lord Byron who had been so conspicuously absent tonight. These various notables had never been invited simultaneously, of course; the mere notion of Byron and Hannah More in the same room brought a twitch to Susanna's lips.

"You find it amusing?" Nancy said sharply. "That Byron should consent to attend your soiree and then leave you in the lurch?"

In truth, Susanna did not care a whit for Lord Byron's unprecedented slight, but she was at a loss to explain her peculiar apathy even to herself, much less to Nancy. "I daresay everyone was sufficiently entertained without him," she murmured aloud, transferring her gaze to Lady Hadleigh. "And I fancy Byron is preoccupied by his recent marriage."

"Humph," Nancy sniffed. "He is more likely preoccupied by his affair with Lady Melbourne. Or his liaison with his sister Augusta. You did know that, I trust? That he has added incest to his already extensive catalog of sins?"

Susanna had, in fact, heard the *on-dits* concerning Lord Byron and his half sister, but not in words so raw, and her cheeks warmed with embarrassment. It was hardly the first time Lady Hadleigh's frankness had set her to blushing, she reflected wryly. To the contrary, she was hard pressed to recollect a single hour during the whole course of their acquaintance when Nancy had not shocked her with some sort of horrifying pronouncement.

Indeed, Susanna often wondered how she, conservative by nature, could possibly have been attracted to the wildly unconventional Countess of Hadleigh. Nancy's appearance alone was forbidding: she was taller than many men and so generously endowed that she seemed always at the point of spilling out of the excessively low-cut gowns she favored. Her hair was a flaming, uncompromising red, her eyes a vivid green; and a great sea of freckles splashed from one of her ears to the other—quite inundating her broad cheeks and the bridge of her incongruously short nose.

As if these physical deficiencies were not sufficiently damaging, Lady Hadleigh was encumbered by a host of scandalous rumors. Chief among these was the *on-dit* that her husband, the Earl of Hadleigh, had been recalled from his post as governor of Jamaica because of his young wife's untoward conduct. Since Lady Hadleigh's precise sins were never enumerated, Nancy was able to tell an altogether different tale: in her version, the aging Lord Hadleigh—who was some thirty years Nancy's senior—had voluntarily resigned his position for reasons of health. Specifically, according to Nancy, the unfortunate earl suffered from severe gout, and it was this malady that kept him confined to their seaside estate in Exeter while Nancy herself gaily flitted among the finest drawing rooms in London.

The intimate details of Lady Hadleigh's present life were as unclear to Susanna as the circumstances surrounding her departure from the Indies. She spent by far the greater part of each year in her elegant Bruton Street townhouse, visiting her ailing husband for only a few weeks during the summer and a month or so at Christmas. Nancy had given Susanna to understand that these conjugal visits were strictly a formality, Lord Hadleigh having long since grown so ill as to reduce their marriage to a union in name only. Nancy claimed to compensate for the earl's debility by conducting more or less constant *affaires de coeur* with various gentlemen of her acquaintance; but as none of the *partis* she identified ever granted her a moment of public attention, Susanna was inclined to take these claims with a considerable grain of salt.

Though perhaps, she occasionally owned, she was deliberately deluding herself. Despite the great difference in their characters, she had become so fond of Nancy, so dependent on their friendship, that perhaps she didn't *want* to believe anything that might diminish her good opinion of Lady Hadleigh. Anything that might once have diminished her opinion, Susanna amended: two or three years earlier, she would have been genuinely shocked to learn beyond doubt that Nancy was involved in an illicit liaison. As the months went by, however, she was coming increasingly to comprehend how a married woman could be driven into the arms of another man.

"Well, do not tease yourself about it," Nancy said soothingly. "About Byron, I mean. It is only the fourth of May, and you'll have many splendid salons before the Season is over."

"I wasn't teasing myself about Byron," Susanna muttered. She paused, casting about for the words to describe her vague listlessness. "I was teasing myself because I am starting to find my soirees rather . . . rather . . ."

"Dull?" Lady Hadleigh supplied.

No, not exactly dull, Susanna thought; not in comparison to the rest of her dismal existence. Even without the mercurial Lord Byron, tonight's salon had been vastly more amusing than the interminable winter evenings she had sat alone in front of the library fire. But she could conjure up no better adjective, and she sighed and bobbed her head.

"I notice that Percy was the last to leave this evening," Nancy said.

This was scarcely a startling observation inasmuch as Colonel Percy Fordyce had been the last to leave Susanna's soirees *every* evening for above a year.

"He remarked," Nancy went on, "that his uncle's condition has deteriorated most alarmingly in recent weeks. Naturally, Percy was too discreet to speculate just how long the old man might survive, but I collect he cannot last beyond the end of the summer. Whereupon Percy will, of course, become Viscount Grafton. You could make a far worse match, Susanna."

"You are overlooking one critical point," Susanna reminded her dryly. "The factor that I am wed already."

"You are beginning to try my patience," Lady Hadleigh snapped. "How long do you intend to await your husband's return? You told me when we met that he was expected back at any time."

"I did expect him back at any time," Susanna protested. "Ned initially planned to be in the United States only a few months, just long enough to inspect Papa's American properties. And then he decided to stay a few months more—"

"A few months which have now expanded to a few *years*," Nancy interjected. "But you have always sought to excuse him, have you not? You eagerly seized on our war with America as the justification for Ned's failure to return. His failure even to *write* you."

"Wars do tend to disrupt one's lines of communication," Susanna said stiffly.

"Disrupt but not necessarily destroy. As I have previously mentioned, Lady Perdue's sister resides in New York, and Lady Perdue received letters from her throughout the war. Letters sent through Canada."

In fact, Nancy had mentioned this at least a dozen times, and Susanna had yet to devise a satisfactory rejoinder. She bit her lip and said nothing.

"Be that as it may, I am curious what rationalization you are employing now the war is over. Or do you think to wait for him forever?" Nancy gazed at the wall above the mantel. "I shall grant you that he is prodigious well-looking," she said, her voice softening a bit.

Susanna's eyes followed Lady Hadleigh's to the portrait which hung beside hers. Yes, she reflected, Edward Sutton, the fifth Earl of Langham, was prodigious well-looking indeed. Since Mr. Lawrence had posed both his subjects in a seated position, it was impossible to ascertain from the twin paintings that Ned was well above the average in height—towering nearly eight inches above Susanna, who was herself fully five and a half feet tall. However, one could readily see that the earl was excellently proportioned: his legs, encased in evening breeches and silk stockings, were long and slender, his waist narrow, his shoulders exceedingly broad. Above the shoulders, the artist had accurately captured Lord Langham's fair complexion and strong chin, his longish nose and high cheekbones, his remarkable silver-gray eyes and thick blond hair.

The portrait would have been perfect except for the circumstance that Papa had instructed his daughter's fiancé to appear "suitably serious" for his wedding picture. As a consequence, Ned stared eternally unsmilingly across the drawing room, and this was not the way Susanna remembered him at all. No, her recollection was that the Earl of Langham generally wore a wry, somewhat crooked grin, which exposed a tiny gap between his upper front teeth. And though those small blemishes—his lopsided smile and the space between his teeth—should have detracted from his handsomeness, they served, instead, to enhance it.

"Yes," Nancy said, a note of bitterness creeping into her voice, "your father is to be commended for choosing you such a strapping young buck of a husband. Would that I had been so lucky."

Lady Hadleigh had expressed this lament dozens of times before as well, and, as she had on every prior occasion, Susanna wondered how she would have reacted if she had been thrust into Nancy's place. If her papa, too, had arranged a match with an unattractive man much older than she. She preferred to believe she would have rebelled, as she had briefly rebelled even against his selection of Ned, but she suspected that Papa would ultimately have bent her to his will. Especially since he had made it clear from her early childhood that he was determined to wed her to a peer . . .

"Titles, titles, titles!" Papa would rant at least once a week, clanging his silverware angrily on his plate and quite ruining everyone's appetite for the meal in progress. "I am persuaded that one could possess all the money in the British Empire, and without the so-called proper connections, one still would not be accepted in society. Apparently the only solution is to *buy* one's way into the *ton*, and you may be assured that when Susanna and Alicia are of age, that is precisely what I shall do."

Papa would punctuate this pronouncement with a furious glare at Mama and then, for good measure, small irritable scowls at his two young daughters.

In the beginning, Susanna had no notion what Papa was talking about, but as the years passed, she deduced from other scraps of conversation the nature of Simon Randall's predicament. Papa, she learned, was the son of an impecunious Tonbridge merchant, and rather than waiting to inherit his father's foundering enterprise, he had gone out to India in hopes of accumulating a modest nest egg of his own. In the event, this "nest egg" swelled to a fortune of almost grotesque proportions: Papa returned to England twenty-one years later with so much money that—had they been available in neat blocks—he probably could have purchased several counties.

As it was, he initially contented himself by buying only a substantial portion of Kent—a sprawling estate near his hometown of Tonbridge, seaside properties in Margate and Ramsgate, the principal businesses in every town and village between the western border and the Channel coast. Among the latter was a thriving inn in Ashford, and shortly after Papa's purchase of the establishment, he wed the former landlord's comely daughter.

Susanna was born barely the prescribed nine months following her parents' marriage, but, via some peculiar twist of nature, Alicia did not arrive until six and a half years later. By then, Papa's holdings extended the length and breadth of Britain: from a hunting lodge in Scotland to a castle in Warwickshire to splendid country manors in Cumberland, Norfolk, and Dorset; from mills in the Midlands to mines in Wales to ships plying the seas out of every major port. Indeed, by then, Simon Randall's financial interests spanned the world; he had extensive investments in the West Indian colonies and North America, and he was eagerly exploring opportunities on the newly discovered continent of Australia.

And by then, Papa had come to realize that his vast wealth would not give him the thing he coveted most—a preeminent position in British society. One of his earliest acquisitions was a London townhouse in Mount Street, and the spring after Susanna's birth, he and Mama spent the Season there. Many years elapsed before Susanna collected that their months in town had been an unmitigated disaster: they were not asked to a single important ball or rout, and when they conducted their own at home, only a handful of the several hundred invited guests appeared. His millions notwithstanding, Simon Randall was the son of a lowly shopkeeper, now a vulgar nabob; and, in either case, not fit to associate with the *ton*. He sold the townhouse at the end of the Season and did not visit London again for twenty years.

Papa could not buy respectability, could not buy himself a peerage. However, he *could* purchase titles for his daughters by wedding them to desperate, impoverished aristocrats, and by the time Susanna reached adolescence, he had formulated the gist of his plan. He would, somehow, locate an acceptable sponsor to bring his elder daughter out; and when it became known (as Papa would be certain it did) that Susanna Randall was the premier heiress in England, any number of out-at-heels noblemen would be eager to offer for her hand.

Since good fortune had dogged Papa all his life, it was scarcely surprising that an "acceptable sponsor" materialized literally upon his doorstep. Shortly after Susanna's eighteenth birthday, an elderly, childless local countess—Lady Elwood by name—called at Randall Manor; and inasmuch as she was the first representative of the neighborhood gentry ever to darken the portals of the house, Susanna could not resist the temptation to eavesdrop on her conversation with Papa. She watched from the dining room as Papa ushered her ladyship into the library and, when the door had closed behind them, slipped across the vestibule and planted her ear to one of the walnut panels.

Following the mandatory exchange of pleasantries, Lady Elwood revealed that she had found herself in a most distressing situation following her husband's recent demise. She had understood, of course, that the bulk of Lord Elwood's estate was entailed and would pass, along with his title, to his horrid cousin in Shropshire. But dear late Horace had assured her that his villa in Deal and all his independent income would be willed to his beloved wife. And while dear Horace had technically fulfilled his promise, Lady Elwood had discovered that the villa was mortgaged to the proverbial hilt and her income would hardly cover the payments. Much less such niceties as food and clothing and the salaries of the two or three servants required to operate the household. As she had further discovered that Mr. Randall held the mortgage, she had come to plead for a reduction in the payments, which she really did judge a trifle exorbitant . . .

After subtly interrogating Lady Elwood and establishing that the new earl was not only married but had numerous children and several grandchildren, Papa graciously proposed an accommodation: he was prepared to write off the *entire mortgage* if her ladyship would consent to launch his daughter into society during the forthcoming Season. Naturally, he would meet all the expenses requisite to the debut, including a splendid new wardrobe for the countess, who—if she would pardon his boldness in saying so—was still a monstrous handsome woman.

Lady Elwood was evidently so relieved and delighted by Papa's largess that she elected not to question why Mrs. Randall, also a "monstrous handsome woman," could not bring Susanna out herself. At any rate, she readily accepted Papa's terms, and Susanna had barely scurried back to the safety of the dining room when her ladyship emerged from the library—a happy smile on her wrinkled face and the canceled mortgage clutched to her bosom.

With this precious document in hand, a less honorable woman might have devoted only the most minimal attention to her part of the bargain, but Lady Elwood entered into the planning of Susanna's come-out with an enthusiasm rivaling Papa's own. Though the Season was still more than six months in future, she traveled to Randall Manor every few weeks to plot the campaign, leading Papa to growl that had England's allies been so dedicated, Napoleon would have been defeated long since. As the time of the debut grew closer, both the frequency and duration of her ladyship's visits increased until, by the beginning of April, every detail had been arranged even to Simon Randall's satisfaction.

Soon after that, however, Papa's historic good luck deserted him. Although he had engaged Lady Elwood to be Susanna's official sponsor, Papa had intended from the outset that he and Mama would accompany their daughter to London: if nothing else, he must be available to negotiate the particulars of Susanna's dowry with her many competing *partis*. And during the last week of April, their scheduled departure mere days away, Mama developed a blinding headache which none of Dr. Nolan's mysterious nostrums seemed able to dispel. Insisting that there was no compelling reason for her presence in town, Mama begged Papa and Susanna to proceed without her; but Papa, to his credit, refused to leave his wife behind. No doubt, he said optimistically, her health would be restored by the first of June—the date of Susanna's come-out ball—and Susanna's prospects would hardly be ruined if she missed the first few weeks of the Season.

But Mama's health was not restored by the first of June. To the contrary, her headache relentlessly worsened, and she shortly lost the ability to walk, then to feed herself, then to talk. Dr. Nolan eventually diagnosed her illness as some sort of growth in the brain and sadly pronounced himself powerless to treat it. Mama died on Susanna's nineteenth birthday, but she was unaware of this tragic coincidence, for she had lost consciousness several days before.

In view of her mother's death, Susanna could not be brought out the following Season, and her debut was consequently postponed till the spring when she was twenty. And by then, or so Papa declared, her prospects —if not ruined— had been severely damaged.

"I had thought to permit you to choose among a number of available peers," he reiterated after summoning her and Lady Elwood to the library. "However, the ones I had in mind have wed since we initially planned your come-out. Wed the daughters of wealthy manufacturers in the North."

He concluded this report with a glower of vexation, but it was a pathetic shadow of the fearsome glares and scowls he had summoned forth in the past. Cold and cunning as he was, Simon Randall had not yet recovered from the loss of his wife—whom he had sincerely loved—and Susanna wondered if he ever would.

"Fortunately," Papa continued heavily, "a new candidate has arrived on the scene. 'New' in the respect that he unexpectedly succeeded to his title following his elder brother's death in a hunting accident. His title and little else, it appears: I am given to understand that the young Earl of Langham hasn't sixpence to scratch with."

"The Earl of Langham!" Lady Elwood bolted up in her chair. "I am familiar with the family, Mr. Randall; the first wife of the present Lord Langham's grandfather was Horace's cousin. And it's true that the Suttons are destitute. Indeed, it was Horace's cousin by marriage—Lord Langham's grandfather—who gambled away their fortune. But poor as he is, I fear Lord Langham is not a candidate for Susanna's hand. He has long been engaged to Sir Walter Murray's daughter—"

"No, he has not," Papa interposed smoothly. "I explored that very point with Lord Langham during our recent correspondence, and he assured me that his attachment to Miss Murray was nothing more than a childhood *tendre*. They grew up on neighboring estates in Norfolk, and I daresay they did exchange some meaningless pledge of devotion." He sketched a tolerant smile. "But there was by no means a formal betrothal."

"Formal or no," Lady Elwood protested, "it has always been assumed that Lord Langham would wed Julia Murray—"

"That will be enough, Lady Elwood." Papa's smile had vanished, and his words were edged with ice. "Whatever their previous relationship, Lord Langham has also assured me of his willingness to sever his connection with Miss Murray, and I wish to debate the matter no further. Susanna will marry the Earl of Langham, and I am in hopes the wedding can take place before the end of the summer. Let us proceed with that objective in mind."

Her ladyship obediently fell silent, and Papa went on to discuss Susanna's come-out ball, which—via another ironic coincidence—had once more been scheduled for the first of June. It was not until he had dismissed his coconspirators and they had repaired to the privacy of Susanna's bedchamber that the countess cleared her throat and returned to the subject of Lord Langham.

"It is not my place to come between you and your father," the old woman began. Though she was now nearing five and seventy, her voice was still astonishingly steady. "However, I have grown prodigious fond of you over the years, Susanna, and I should hate to see you make an unhappy match. I consequently judge it my duty to . . . ah . . . correct Mr. Randall's misapprehension about Lord Langham and Miss Murray. While there may not have been a formal betrothal, I was under the distinct impression that he was firmly committed to wed her."

Susanna nodded; she had formed this distinct impression as well.

"And I am persuaded," Lady Elwood continued, "that a man who would abandon his lifelong *parti* for the promise of a great fortune would prove a most unreliable husband. I must therefore counsel you, despite your papa's wishes, to steer clear of Lord Langham. Handsome as you are, and—let us be candid —*rich* as you are, you will shortly have a multitude of other suitors. Suitors whom Mr. Randall, distracted by his grief, has understandably overlooked."

Susanna bobbed her head again, for she had independently reached the same conclusion during the conversation in the library. She wanted nothing to do with a man of such dubious character as that Lord Langham had displayed, and as Papa bundled her and Lady Elwood into his traveling carriage for the journey to London, she vowed to grant the perfidious earl only the barest modicum of courtesy.

But that was before she met Ned Sutton, and after she did, she was prepared to forgive him almost anything. No, not *almost* anything: had he confessed, with his crooked grin, that he was the current earthly incarnation of Satan, Susanna would have found some way to excuse even that. Ned was immensely attractive, inordinately clever, infinitely charming; and Susanna fell hopelessly in love with him at the very moment of their introduction.

She often relived it—the moment of their introduction. Awake and in her dreams, she remembered trailing Lady Elwood into Almack's; remembered her presentation to the patronesses; remembered that, after this ordeal, Lady Elwood tugged her on into the ballroom. And at that juncture, Susanna most particularly remembered, a tall blond man in his middle twenties hurried forward to greet them.

"Lady Elwood?" He bowed to the countess. "Miss Randall?" His second bow was directed to Susanna. "I hope you will not count me too presumptuous if I take the liberty of introducing myself. I am the Earl of Langham."

"So I surmised," Lady Elwood snapped. "You bear a keen resemblance to your grandfather. But how . . . ?"

Her question expired in a sniff of annoyance. Since even the Countess of Elwood's considerable influence had proved insufficient to procure Papa a voucher of admission to Almack's, she and Susanna had agreed that—if only for this one night—they could totally avoid Lord Langham.

"How did I recognize you?" the earl finished.

He smiled, and Susanna noticed that the left side of his mouth curved well above the right. And that the planes of his face were most arresting and his hair unusually thick . . .

"It was really quite simple."

Lord Langham's grin broadened, and Susanna observed the tiny space between his teeth. It lent him the engaging aspect of a mischievous schoolboy.

"Mr. Randall advised me to seek out an excessively handsome woman of middle years accompanied by a dark, beautiful girl. What other party could have fitted that description?"

He waved one long lean hand around the ballroom, and Lady Elwood visibly preened.

"*Middle years*," she echoed with a smile of her own. "Yes, I well comprehend how you identified us, Lord Langham. And I am sure I speak for Susanna as much as myself when I say how pleased we are to make your acquaintance."

"Your pleasure cannot approach mine, Lady Elwood." He swept another bow. "I trust you will not object if I ask Miss Randall to stand up?"

"Of course not," the countess cooed. "Although," she called sternly after them, apparently recollecting the duties of her chaperonage, "you must not dance with Susanna more than twice, Lord Langham."

They did not dance more than twice. They stood up for a quadrille and the ensuing boulanger, then repaired to the refreshment parlor, where they each consumed a portion of stale cake and a glass of lemonade. Following this unsatisfactory repast, the earl escorted Susanna to one corner of the ballroom, and they sat—not stirring again—and talked until the end of the assembly. Or, to be more accurate, Susanna later supposed they must have talked; she could actually recall nothing but Ned's lopsided grin and the spell of his silver eyes.

As the Season progressed and Susanna's initial fascination faded to mere adoration, she began to register the details of their conversations; and thus it was that she well remembered Ned's explanation of his relationship with Miss Murray. More than the explanation itself, she recalled the circumstance which prompted it: after maneuvering her out of Lady Elwood's still-sharp eyesight, Ned kissed her for the first time and proclaimed that he, too, had fallen over head and ears in love.

"And lest you doubt the sincerity of my emotion," he whispered, his breath stirring the curls at Susanna's temple, "I should like to clarify a . . . er . . . situation which may have come to your attention. You may have heard that I was once quite fond of Julia Murray, and I shan't deny that I was. I daresay you were also fond of your previous *partis*."

In point of fact, Susanna had never had a previous *parti*, but she could not have told Ned so had she wanted to. His kiss had left her mouth burning, had snatched her breath away, and she could only bury her face in his shoulder and inhale his rich masculine scent.

"At any rate," Ned went on hoarsely, "I realized, once I met you, that my feeling for Julia was nothing more than a youthful infatuation. And I pray you will not allow it to be an obstacle between us."

Susanna frowned in puzzlement, distantly recollecting Papa's statement that Ned had recognized the nature of his feelings for Miss Murray well *before* their meeting. But the discrepancy was so very minor, Susanna so very happy, that it didn't seem to signify. Her brows relaxed, and she burrowed deeper into Ned's broad shoulder.

"No," she said, her own voice raspy, "I do not view Miss Murray as an obstacle between us."

"Then"—Ned's lips brushed her hair—"would you do me the great honor of consenting to become my wife?"

Susanna did so consent, and her come-out ball was speedily converted to an engagement celebration. The Season ended, and the summer flew past: Lady Elwood —half in love with Ned herself—helped Susanna select her trousseau, and Susanna and Ned spent endless hours posing for Mr. Lawrence. On the last day of August in 1811, a week after Susanna's twenty-first birthday, they were wed in the parish church in Tonbridge; and following a sumptuous banquet at Randall Manor, they departed for Maidstone, en route to Papa's house in Ramsgate.

Lady Elwood had warned Susanna that the married state entailed certain physical "duties," but her ladyship's subsequent discussion of the subject had been oblique in the extreme. Susanna did succeed in collecting that the carnal side of matrimony—whatever it consisted of—was enormously pleasant for the husband and decidedly *un*pleasant for the wife. But she was so mad for Ned by then that she judged a few minutes of unpleasantness scant price to pay for her eternal happiness, and she climbed gamely, if somewhat apprehensively, into their nuptial bed.

A natural optimist, Susanna had hoped that the "duties" might not prove too distasteful after all, but she was utterly unprepared for the reality of her wedding night. She had never imagined that Ned's lips on hers—lips now freed of constraint—would unleash a wild response deep within her; never expected that his hands on her body would tease that response to a fever of longing; never dreamed that when he possessed her, he would carry them both over the brink of ecstasy. And it could never happen again, she thought, curling against him like a contented cat. She had been granted one magic moment—one perfect moment in the whole of her life—and she must savor the memory the rest of her days.

But it did happen again. It happened the next night, after they reached Ramsgate, and every night thereafter for the duration of their honeymoon. And it continued to happen when they returned from their wedding trip and took up residence in Randall Manor. Sometimes the force of their desire was such that they were hard pressed to excuse themselves from the dinner table and make their way—giggling—up the stairs and through all the confusing corridors to the bedchamber Papa had discreetly provided in the western wing of the house.

They were absolutely content for two blissful months; and then Ned, claiming a need to be "useful" to his father-in-law, volunteered to go to the United States and inspect Papa's American properties. And he had now been gone for three and a half years . . .

"Would that I had been so lucky," Nancy repeated, jarring Susanna from her reverie. "If Cuthbert were as appealing as Ned, I fancy my life would have been altogether different." She tendered a wry smile, then sobered. "But it is long since time for you to accept the probability that Ned is dead."

Probability, Susanna silently echoed; there was the rub. She sometimes wished she would receive word that Ned *was* dead and her life could go on. It was the uncertainty that gnawed at her, the possibility that her husband had perished in the American wilderness and she would never learn the time or the place or the circumstances of his demise. An uncertainty which inevitably perpetuated the fading hope that he was still alive—

"Even if he is not dead"—Lady Hadleigh might have been reading her mind again—"it appears monstrous unlikely that he will return. He wouldn't be the first man to go abroad and conveniently forget he had left a wife behind. To take a second wife and father a new family . . ."

Her voice trailed provocatively off, and Susanna once more bit her lip. She had contemplated this possibility as well and—from a purely selfish standpoint—judged it somewhat more distressing than the prospect of Ned's death.

"In either case," Nancy resumed, "you can afford to wait no longer. Much as Percy loves you, I cannot suppose his patience is inexhaustible. And if you lose him, you will be hard put to find a better husband."

Susanna could not but concur in Lady Hadleigh's opinion. She did not reciprocate Colonel Fordyce's deep *tendre*, but she didn't count this a particular problem, for she did not expect ever to love another man as she had Ned. Indeed, she often thought love to be a vastly overrated emotion, leading as it did to so much pain. Perhaps it was preferable merely to *like* one's husband, and she had grown extremely fond of Percy since their meeting a year and a half before.

Percy was another distant relative of Lady Elwood's, and though her ladyship was now crippled by rheumatism and confined to her home in Deal, it was she who had indirectly brought Susanna and Percy together. The son of Horace's niece, one of the countess's weekly letters explained, had suffered a severe leg wound during the Battle of Vitoria and subsequently been invalided out of the army. Fortunately, dear Percy had since recovered from his wound (except for a slight limp), but after more than twenty years of distinguished military service, he was quite without friends in England. Perhaps, if it would not be too much trouble, Susanna could invite him to one of her "little parties."

Lady Elwood was clearly unaware that the foremost peers in Britain were begging for invitations to her former charge's "little parties." However, since Susanna had come to regard the old countess almost as a second mother, she was more than willing to grant her erstwhile sponsor such a small favor. She consequently dispatched an invitation to the London address her ladyship had provided and hoped that "dear Percy" was sufficiently polished not to make an utter cake of himself.

To Susanna's surprise and relief, Colonel Fordyce—far from making a cake of himself—proved to be the most interesting guest at her soiree. He was a tall, attractive man, approximately forty years of age, with prematurely gray hair and exceedingly fine blue eyes. Apart from his limp, which was, indeed, very slight, his only physical deficiency was that he was a good stone and a half too plump. This, he confided dryly to Susanna, was the result of the enforced idleness he had endured since the termination of his military career.

It was that—his military career—which rendered Colonel Fordyce so interesting. After the featured guest, a young sculptor, had delivered a rather uninspired lecture contrasting Greek and Roman sculpture to the modern art, the conversation turned to the war; and Colonel Fordyce showed himself a master of his previous profession. His discussion of tactics, during which he also compared Wellington to various ancient generals, was positively enthralling, but Susanna sensed a great sadness beneath his descriptions of counterattacks and outflankings and other brilliant maneuvers. Colonel Fordyce had dedicated his entire life to war, she reflected, and now he had been dismissed from the army, he was like the proverbial fish out of water. And maybe it was for this reason—because she pitied him—that she invited him to attend her salon again the following week.

The following week and every week thereafter. Percy had come to all of her soirees since the first, and as he, too, resided in London the year around, he generally called in Grosvenor Square each Thursday evening during the summer and winter as well. Susanna had recognized almost at once that he was in love with her, and for months, she had feared she was leading him on —creating the erroneous impression that she was prepared to forsake her marriage vows and embark upon a liaison with a retired colonel who had nothing to offer but his devotion and the fact that his uncle was a viscount.

Lately, however, the situation had dramatically altered. To begin with, Percy now had a great deal to offer: following the sudden death of his only male cousin, he had become the heir to his uncle's title and considerable estate; and soon after the cousin's demise, Percy's uncle had fallen gravely ill. Though Percy was— as Nancy had pointed out—too discreet to speculate just how imminent his inheritance might be, he had hinted on several occasions that he would shortly be in a position to wed virtually any peeress in the realm. Meanwhile, much as she tried to deny it to both herself and Lady Hadleigh, Susanna had grown increasingly persuaded that she was a widow or an abandoned wife—

"Percy wants to marry you." Nancy once more shattered Susanna's thoughts. "And I advise you to have your present marriage annulled before he changes his mind."

It was hardly a revolutionary suggestion; Susanna had toyed with this very notion for the better portion of a year. But she had invariably put it aside because to seek a dissolution of her marriage was to admit that—dead or alive—Ned was never coming back. So she had manufactured a host of imaginative excuses for her failure to act, and she tendered the best of these to Lady Hadleigh.

"I doubt an annulment would be possible," she murmured. "Inasmuch as the marriage was . . . ah . . ."

"Consummated?" Nancy said bluntly. "I assure you that presents no difficulty. One of Cuthbert's brothers is a bishop, and Harvey has never been one to put too fine a point on technicalities."

Between them, Susanna reflected wryly, Lady Elwood and Lady Hadleigh must be connected to everyone of importance in the British Empire. But her amusement was swiftly drowned in a flood of panic, for Nancy's words had created a gaping hole in her defenses.

"It will take some time, of course," Lady Hadleigh continued. "Much as he would like to believe otherwise, Harvey cannot perform miracles. But if he initiates the proceedings immediately, I daresay he can have your marriage nullified within a few months. By the end of the year at latest. In the interim, lest Percy become too discouraged, you would be wise to . . . Let us say to *demonstrate* the joys which await him in the nuptial bed."

"Nancy!" Susanna's cheeks began to flame again.

"I am merely being realistic, dear. As I indicated, Percy's patience, unlike yours, is not infinite." Lady Hadleigh lowered her long legs to the Aubusson carpet, shoved her feet in her slippers, and stood up. "Promise me you will at least consider the matter."

There seemed little harm in such a promise; to the contrary, it offered the prospect of a respite from Nancy's incessant pinching. "Yes, I promise," Susanna muttered, rising as well.

"Excellent." Nancy strode toward the drawing-room entry. "I shall come tomorrow afternoon to hear your decision."

"Tomorrow . . . !" Susanna's protest died in her

throat as she remembered, now with a flood of relief, that she would be away. "No, I shan't be here," she said. "Evidently I neglected to mention that I am traveling to Randall Manor tomorrow to fetch Alicia. I'm to bring her out this Season."

"Bring your sister out?" Lady Hadleigh spun around, her brilliant red brows knitting a frown. "Why is that? I thought she was already engaged to a viscount. Which would seem to be in perfect accordance with your father's plans."

"Hugh is the *son* of Viscount Calthrop," Susanna corrected. "And though he and Alicia have been in love since childhood, they aren't formally engaged. However, I did collect at Christmas that a betrothal was imminent, and Papa appeared quite delighted by the match . . ."

She paused and wrinkled her own forehead. "In short, I am as puzzled as you, but Papa's last letter was most urgent. He insists Alicia must have a debut before the Season is over, so I shall drive down to Kent tomorrow and escort her to town. I expect to return on Monday."

"Then you will have the whole weekend to contemplate your situation," Nancy said crisply, "and I shall return *Monday* afternoon to hear your decision."

She whirled back round and, before Susanna could compose another protest, sailed out of the saloon and disappeared. When the distant slam of the front door reached her ears, Susanna plodded across the drawing room and into the corridor, up the stairs to the second story, and down the hall to her bedchamber. She stepped inside, and her eyes instinctively darted to the Sheraton writing table in front of the window. Both of Ned's letters from America reposed in the center drawer of the desk, but it would have been gratuitous to retrieve them. They were so creased and smudged by endless unfoldings and foldings, readings and rereadings, that they were virtually illegible; and, at any rate, Susanna had long since memorized their contents.

Such contents as there were, she amended dismally,

for both messages had been brief in the extreme.
Indeed, the first, written in December of 1811, consisted
of only two sentences. He had landed at Baltimore
without incident, Ned reported, and was preparing for a
tour of Papa's properties in Virginia, the Carolinas, and
Georgia. And while he greatly missed Susanna and
would miss her even more during the forthcoming
holiday season, he derived some comfort from the
knowledge that they would be reunited early in the
spring.

But Ned did not return in the spring. Not in March or
April or May, and during the first week of June—with
spring nearly gone and summer fast approaching—
Susanna received a second letter. She closed her eyes
and clearly saw the fresh, unfaded black ink in her
mind:

April 2, 1812

My dear Susanna,

I trust you have not been unduly alarmed by my failure to write; the fact is I have been quite busy. Though I have discovered your father's estates to be in good order, it has come to my attention that America offers many additional opportunities for investment. I am particularly interested in the territory called Louisiana, which the United States recently acquired from France and which is shortly to become an American state. I therefore intend to leave for Louisiana immediately and sail from New Orleans back to England. I am in hopes my journey can be completed in a few months' time.

E. S.

Shortly after the letter's arrival, the United States
declared war on Britain, and for a full year after that,
Susanna attempted to persuade herself that Ned's
silence was solely due to this conflict. But as Lady

Hadleigh relentlessly pointed out, other English residents of America managed to communicate with their relatives at home; and eventually Susanna purchased and studied a number of books about the United States, hoping to gain some clue to her husband's fate. Several of the books included maps, and she observed at once that it was a very long way from the eastern coast of the country to New Orleans. Much of the land between was as yet uncivilized, she learned, and Ned might well have met with hostile Indian savages or a band of renegade white men. Or perhaps he had succumbed to nothing more dramatic than a fever. Or maybe he had reached New Orleans safely and settled himself with a beautiful Creole belle . . .

But it no longer signified, Susanna owned, forcing her eyes back open. She pulled the door to behind her, and she could not but interpret the click of the latch as the end of a chapter in her life. As Nancy also pointed out, it was long since time to accept reality. Time to recognize that, whatever his circumstances, Ned was prodigious unlikely to return. Time to confess that the famous salons she had conducted in his absence were just another shallow entertainment—utterly inadequate to serve as the center of her life. Time to have her marriage dissolved and wed Colonel Fordyce, soon to be Viscount Grafton.

Susanna crossed the room, stripped off her clothes, and hung her dress in the mahogany wardrobe. She proceeded to the bed, which had been turned down, donned the nightgown laid neatly on her pillow, crawled beneath the covers, and extinguished the lamp on the bedside cupboard.

The Grosvenor Square mansion had been Simon Randall's wedding gift to his elder daughter and her new husband. However, the property had required extensive repair, and the work—a part of Papa's present—had still been in progress at the time of Ned's departure. As a consequence, Ned had never occupied the house, never slept beside Susanna in the canopied bed, and she now tried to imagine Percy there in his stead. Tried to envision the two of them locked in passion, later waking in one another's arms . . .

But she could not, and when, at length, she fell asleep, her dreams were haunted by Edward Sutton's silver eyes.

Chapter 2

"WHAT A HAPPY SURPRISE," Papa growled as Susanna paused in the library doorway. "I am delighted you could bestir yourself sufficiently to come and fetch Alicia. I was beginning to suppose I should have to escort her to London myself."

Susanna clenched her hands. She had received Simon Randall's letter only three days since, but patience had never been one of Papa's transcendent virtues.

"I came at the earliest opportunity," she rejoined as politely as she could. "Your message did not arrive till Tuesday—"

"You miss my point," Papa snapped. "My point is that I should not have been compelled to send a message at all. I put myself to a great deal of trouble and expense to secure you a place among the *ton*, and I assumed you would reward my efforts by conducting yourself in an appropriate fashion. Instead, you remain in the city year-round and associate with all manner of radical reformers and vulgar theatrical personalities and immoral writers . . ."

His voice expired in a snort of disgust, and Susanna ground her fingernails into her palms. She had not—could not have—missed Papa's point, for he launched a similar attack every time they were together. In the past, she had elected to maintain some semblance of peace between them by changing the subject, but her humor today was such that she could no longer hold her tongue.

"What would you have me do?" she demanded. "Pine away in the country while my husband remains abroad? The husband *you* chose for me?"

"I would have you behave as other young women of your station do!" he roared. "I should be quite content if you went to town for a few months in the spring and fall; indeed, I should be dismayed if you did not. But you ought to be here with your family the rest of the year." Lest Susanna misinterpret the esoteric word *here*, he slammed his fist on the cluttered surface of his writing table. "As it is, I am required virtually to seek an audience with my own daughter."

There was an excellent reason for Susanna's decision to reside permanently in Grosvenor Square, and she parted her lips to explain it to Papa. She had calculated that when Ned returned, he would land somewhere on the western coast of England, and from there, he would naturally proceed to his and Susanna's London home. And if he found the house deserted, he would.... Would what? Sail back to America rather than traveling three more hours to Randall Manor? She admitted the absurdity of her logic and hastily closed her mouth.

"I shan't deny that I chose your husband," Papa continued coolly. "However, I was under the impression that you thoroughly approved my selection. Or did I misread the nightly drama at our dinner table?"

He raised his brows, and Susanna flushed.

"No, I thought not. It is scarcely my fault that Ned proved so irresponsible."

"It might be construed as *entirely* your fault," Susanna retorted, embarrassment fueling her anger. "In fact, Lady Elwood warned me of just such a possibility. She was most concerned that a man who would abandon his lifelong *parti* would be equally inclined to abandon his wife."

Susanna realized that her paraphrase of the countess's actual words was so liberal as to border on fabrication, but fury drove her on. "And inasmuch as you were the one to . . . to *steal* Ned from Julia Murray and entice him to marry me, I fancy you might well be held accountable for all the ensuing suffering."

"Suffering," Papa echoed. "You are a countess and

—if I am to believe the *on-dits* I hear—quite the belle of Britain. I can hardly view your position as one of great suffering. Nor does it appear that Miss Murray suffered unduly from the change in her situation. As I recall, she wed a viscount shortly after your own marriage. A very wealthy viscount."

A wealthy *old* viscount, Susanna thought, who had died within a year of the nuptial ceremony. Indeed, Nancy had recently mentioned that Lady Thornton was now out of black gloves and would be reentering society during the forthcoming Season. As a rich young widow, Nancy had added, the former Miss Murray should have no difficulty contracting a splendid second match.

So perhaps Papa was right, Susanna conceded. Miss Murray had not been harmed by his machinations, and in the end, Susanna had married Ned of her own volition. And she could not blame Papa for her husband's disappearance; the trip to America had been altogether Ned's idea. In fact, to be perfectly fair, Papa had suggested that she accompany Ned abroad, but the earl had rejected this proposal. The journey he planned was far from being a holiday excursion, he'd said stiffly. Conditions in the rural areas of the country —where the bulk of Papa's properties were located— were likely to be primitive at best, perilous at worst . . . She shook her head.

"Miss Murray did *not* wed a viscount?" Papa said.

"No," Susanna murmured. "That is, yes, she did, but I was thinking of something else. I am sorry for my remarks, Papa. I've been a trifle out of spirits."

"Humph," he sniffed. "Come in and sit down."

He stood and beckoned her across the room, and Susanna observed, as she often had before, that he was still a fine figure of a man. He was tall, nearly as tall as Ned, and though every year seemed to add an excess pound or two to his frame, the clever tailoring of his coats and pantaloons served to disguise his ever-expanding waistline. No amount of artifice could hide the increasing plumpness of his face, of course; but his black eyes were so penetrating, his gray hair so luxuriant, that one tended to overlook his fleshy cheeks and jowls. Susanna wondered if Ned would be equally handsome at five and sixty. Indeed, she wondered what her husband looked like now, at thirty. If he was still alive . . .

She sank into the chair in front of the desk, and Papa resumed his place behind it and closed the ledger he had been studying when Susanna arrived. Although he paid numerous agents and a brilliant man of business to handle his financial affairs, Simon Randall had never been able to adjust to a life of leisure; and Susanna was confident he could personally account for every cow grazing in his pastures, every lump of coal brought up from his mines, every box of cargo carried on his ships.

"I'm glad you are here," he reiterated, somewhat less sarcastically, "because I truly was beginning to fear I should have to take Alicia to town myself. Hugh left for London only yesterday morning, but one would infer from your sister's mopes that he has been away for several years."

As Ned had been away for several years . . . But it was time to put Ned out of her mind, and Susanna shook her head again.

"I don't understand why Hugh or Alicia either one should go to London," she said. "Well," she amended, "I presume they are going for Alicia's come-out, and that is what I do not understand. Why she must have a debut, I mean. I collected that both you and Lord Calthrop were prepared to announce her engagement to Hugh."

"So we were," Papa agreed grimly, "but we reckoned without *Lady* Calthrop. I trust you are aware that she has his lordship squarely under her thumb."

Susanna doubted that anyone in western Kent could fail to be aware of this, for Lady Calthrop's domination of the viscount had assumed literally legendary proportions. The most frequently told tale was that Lord Calthrop had once offended his wife to such a degree that she had forced him to sleep in the coach house for a full week. Susanna was inclined to judge this story apocryphal because it was never explained why her ladyship had not simply banished the hapless viscount to one of the guest bedchambers, of which Calthrop Hall boasted an abundance. But the report of Lord Calthrop's ignominious exile might be true, Susanna owned, for it was certain that the formidable viscountess did, indeed, have him firmly under her thumb.

It was also certain that Lord and Lady Calthrop and their son, the Honorable Hugh Dickinson, had long subsisted in a state which might delicately be described as "genteel poverty." Calthrop Hall, for all its great size, was in a shocking state of disrepair, its staff reduced to only a handful of elderly servants. The Dickinsons' London townhouse was in slightly better condition, but Susanna attributed this to the circumstance that they had been compelled to let it out during most of the past decade and had utilized the rental income to keep the property from falling totally to pieces. Lady Calthrop naturally held her husband responsible for their dismal financial situation; Susanna had heard her bitter insinuations to this effect on more than one occasion. But whatever the source of the Dickinsons' problems, Susanna had supposed her ladyship would welcome Papa's fortune as a solution.

"What conceivable objection could she have?" Susanna voiced her conclusion aloud. "The Dickinsons obviously need your money."

"There are some people who believe that money is not the most important thing in life." Papa shook his head, as if genuinely astonished by the absurdity of such a notion. "And apparently Lady Calthrop is among them. She is prodigious reluctant to wed her son to the daughter of a nabob." He negotiated one of his scowls, which had begun to improve of late. "However, she is prepared to consent to the match if Alicia can— and I quote Lady Calthrop directly—*demonstrate her social acceptability*. Evidently Alicia must prove that she knows which fork to use and comprehends that a duke outranks a baronet . . ."

He scowled again and began to drum his fingers on the cover of the ledger. "At any rate, that is why Alicia must have a debut; if she comports herself to Lady Calthrop's satisfaction, her ladyship will approve the betrothal. I am sure I need not add that no breath of scandal can attach to Alicia's conduct. Her conduct or your own. You must both behave with perfect propriety until the engagement is announced."

Simon Randall had missed his calling, Susanna reflected wryly: he was so very adept at issuing orders that he really should have pursued a military career. He would speedily have become a general or an admiral . . . But they had quarreled enough for one day; she would not challenge his latest command.

"I collect you will not accompany us to town?" she said instead.

"No, I shall not. I perceive no advantage in reminding Lady Calthrop that she might soon be connected to the son of a shopkeeper. I should much prefer her to remember that Hugh stands to marry the sister of a countess."

Throughout the drive from London, Susanna had debated how best to inform Papa of her decision, and she doubted she would be granted a more convenient opening. "That could pose a problem," she said carefully. "I hope Lady Calthrop would not withdraw her consent if I should cease to be a countess."

"Cease to be a countess?" Papa's fingers stopped their tattoo on the ledger. "What the devil do you mean?"

"I mean . . ." She had rehearsed a dozen clever ways to present the subject, but none of them now came to mind, and she gulped and stumbled on. "I mean that I am contemplating remarriage. There is a gentleman of my acquaintance, a Colonel Percy Fordyce—"

"You think to wed a *colonel*?" Papa's horrified tone suggested that she might have proposed an alliance with a beggar she had encountered on the streets of London.

"He is related to Lady Elwood," Susanna said defensively, "and he will not be a colonel for long. His uncle is Viscount Grafton, and Percy will shortly succeed to the title . . ."

She briefly explained Colonel Fordyce's circumstances, trying to read Papa's reaction as she spoke, but his plump, handsome face remained impassive.

"That is all well and good," he said when she had finished. "Except for the slight complication that you are married already."

"Am I, Papa? I count it highly probable that Ned is dead. And if he is not, I must conclude that he has, indeed, abandoned me. In either event, it's monstrous unlikely he will return to England."

"The likelihood of his return is immaterial. The material fact is that you are legally wed."

"But I can be legally *un*wed." Susanna wriggled to the edge of her chair. "Nancy's brother-in-law is a bishop—"

"Nancy?" Papa wrinkled his forehead.

"Anne Addison. The Countess of Hadleigh."

"Ah, yes." He emitted another sniff. "The brazen middle-aged redhead I met when I was last in town."

"Nancy is scarcely middle-aged," Susanna protested. "She is only two and thirty. Nor is she brazen. A trifle unconventional perhaps—"

"She is *entirely* unconventional," Papa interposed, "as is her notion of dissolving your marriage. At least I assume it was she who concocted the scheme."

"It is not a *scheme*," Susanna said furiously. "And the possibility of an annulment occurred to me well before Nancy mentioned her brother-in-law's position."

"Then—if I may borrow your dubious phraseology—the possibility had best *un*occur to you at once. Inasmuch as you and Ned lived as man and wife for several months, I daresay Lady Calthrop would view an annulment as tantamount to divorce."

"And am I to live my life for Lady Calthrop?" To Susanna's further fury, tears of frustration had begun to well from her eyes and trickle down her cheeks. "I am nearly twenty-five, Papa, and Ned has been gone for three and a half years. Would you have me wait forever?"

She stopped to brush the maddening tears away, and Papa extracted a handkerchief from one pocket of his coat and passed it across the desk.

"Has it been so long?" he said gruffly, his black eyes uncharacteristically gentle. "Forgive me, Susanna; time passes very quickly when one is an old man. I daresay you are justified to seek a dissolution of your marriage."

Susanna dabbed the last drops of moisture from her face and returned his sodden handkerchief.

"But justified or no," Papa continued, "such a course would send Lady Calthrop fairly flying into the boughs. I beg you to be patient and give Alicia her chance for happiness."

To say nothing of giving Simon Randall his second title, Susanna thought uncharitably, but she was still sniffling a bit, and she swallowed the words.

"As I indicated," Papa went on, "Lady Calthrop will agree to the engagement as soon as Alicia has had a successful debut. In fact, her ladyship is holding a house party the last weekend of the month, and I suspect she has it in mind to announce the betrothal then. If all goes well in the interim," he added darkly. "In the interim, you must conduct Alicia's come-out ball and ensure her good behavior."

"And after that I may petition Bishop Addison for an annulment? After the engagement is announced?"

"Not immediately after that." Papa shook his head again. "You must wait till Alicia and Hugh are safely wed, but how long can that be? You and Ned were engaged in June and married in August, and I fancy Alicia's wedding can be scheduled in similar fashion. In short, you need maintain appearances only a few months more. You have waited three and a half years already; is a few more months too much to ask?"

To the contrary, Susanna was peculiarly relieved. She could tell Nancy in all honesty that she had firmly decided to dissolve her marriage, had even secured Papa's approval; but Lady Hadleigh would readily understand why the annulment must be delayed. It was such a perfect solution to her dilemma that Susanna was hard put to affect a look of disappointment as she nodded her consent.

"Yes," she murmured. "That is, no; a few more months is not too much to ask."

"Excellent." Papa, for his part, seemed hard put to repress a triumphant smile. "Permit me to stress that your comportment during those months must be beyond reproach. You must take care to treat Colonel Forsythe as nothing more than a friend. A very *casual* friend."

Another splendid solution: Papa had provided a superb excuse to avoid the affaire Nancy counseled. Susanna was so pleased that she elected not to correct his distortion of Percy's name.

"Yes, Papa," she promised. "My conduct will be beyond reproach."

"Excellent," he repeated. "If we are in agreement then, pray do go up and advise Alicia you are here. I truly cannot abide her mopes a moment longer."

This was his second reference to Alicia's mopes, and Susanna left the library and proceeded warily up the marble staircase to her sister's bedchamber. She had fully expected to find Alicia collapsed on the bed, staring miserably at the canopy above it; but she saw, when she paused at the open door, that the counterpane was virtually buried in clothes. The several chairs in the room were equally heaped, and Alicia was standing in the middle of the Brussels carpet, apparently inspecting the surrounding sea of fabric.

"Good afternoon, Alicia." Susanna stepped over the threshold.

"Susanna!"

Alicia spun around and hurtled toward her, and Susanna suffered a familiar shock of recognition. Papa had commissioned numerous portraits of Mama over the years, and though none of these had been painted by an artist of Mr. Lawrence's talent, all were reasonably accurate representations of the late Margaret Randall. And if one mentally erased the tiny lines in Mama's face and overlooked the telltale styling of her gowns, one might well suppose that every one of the portraits was a picture of Alicia, painted only yesterday. The dark brown hair was the same and the enormous blue eyes and the pale heart-shaped face, splashed with rose at the cheekbones—

"Thank God you are here." Alicia panted to a halt and seized Susanna's hand. "I could not have lived without Hugh another day."

"Then I fear you will die at midnight," Susanna said dryly, "for I do not intend to return to London till Monday."

"Monday!" Alicia wailed.

Susanna bit back a sharp retort, reminding herself of the time, now so long ago, when she had been unable to bear a single hour away from Ned. "I just arrived," she pointed out, "and I'm much too tired to undertake another journey today or tomorrow. And I am sure you'll concur that it would be excessively unwise to drive back to town on Sunday. Lady Calthrop would view Sunday travel with a very jaundiced eye indeed."

As she had calculated, this argument proved persuasive: Alicia sighed and reluctantly bobbed her head.

"Yes, I fancy you are right." Alicia spoke through another sigh, but she soon brightened and tugged Susanna across the bedchamber. "And at any rate, I haven't yet started to pack because I wanted you to see my come-out wardrobe before we left." She stopped in the center of the rug again, dropped Susanna's hand, and waved proudly about. "There! Did Miss Mooney not make me the most *wonderful* clothes?"

Susanna glanced at the bed and the chairs and stifled a sigh of her own. The dresses were piled so haphazardly that it was impossible to determine whether they were "wonderful" or not, but it was clear that the local mantua-maker—from ignorance or greed or a combination of the two—had created a number of garments totally unsuitable for a young girl's debut.

"I daresay they are lovely," she said kindly, "but you won't be able to take the half of them to London. You are only eighteen and just entering society. You can't wear"—she peered back at the bed—"gowns of sapphire satin and black crepe. Fortunately, Miss Mooney appears to have made enough simple muslin dresses to rig you out for the Season."

"Simple muslin dresses!" Alicia protested. "The blue satin is my favorite—"

"Listen to me, Alicia," Susanna snapped. Her patience had evaporated, and she fixed her sister with a quelling glare. "If you want to marry Hugh, you must demonstrate your acceptability to Lady Calthrop. I am quoting Papa, who claimed to be quoting Lady Calthrop herself. He stressed to me, as I am certain he has stressed to you, that your behavior over the next few months must be beyond reproach. You can't parade around London in a sapphire satin gown."

Alicia gnawed her lip and gazed down at her shoes.

"I shall do everything I can to assist you," Susanna went on. "I shall give you the grandest come-out ball of the Season, and I shall hold it on the Thursday evening immediately preceding Lady Calthrop's house party. Her memories of your magnificent debut will thus be fresh, and she should be *eager* to announce your engagement during the weekend."

She paused, but Alicia continued to stare at her feet.

"In short," Susanna concluded sternly, "I am prepared to pledge my complete cooperation, but you must cooperate with me as well. I shall entertain no further objections about your clothes or any other aspect of your come-out. Do you understand me?"

"Yes," Alicia whispered.

She looked up at last, her blue eyes bright with unshed tears, and Susanna bit her own lip. She was beginning to sound like Papa, she reflected: grumbling and growling and issuing peremptory commands.

"It is only for a few months,' she said, awkwardly patting Alicia's shoulder. "If you and Hugh become engaged at Lady Calthrop's house party, you can be wed by the end of the summer. And after that, you can wear your sapphire gown every night if you wish."

And after that, Susanna thought, her marriage could be annulled, and she might well be wed to Colonel Fordyce before the year was over. Alicia blinked her tears away and assumed a sunny smile, and Susanna wondered why she herself judged the future so very bleak.

Chapter 3

HAD THE DECISION been left to Alicia, they would have departed for London at one minute past midnight Monday morning—certainly no later than dawn—but after considerable argument, Susanna persuaded her sister that she could not hope to see Hugh much before noon. They consequently set out at eight and reached Grosvenor Square shortly after eleven, whereupon Alicia insisted they must call on the Dickinsons *immediately*.

As it happened, this was roughly in accordance with Susanna's own plans, for she recognized that it was imperative to treat Lady Calthrop with the utmost courtesy. She would much have preferred to delay the visit an hour or two, but since she lacked the energy to argue with Alicia any further, she consented to her sister's proposal. They agreed to freshen up a bit and meet again in the vestibule, and they were just donning their bonnets when the doorbell rang. Inasmuch as Putnam, the butler, was supervising the unpacking of Alicia's voluminous luggage, Susanna opened the door herself and found all three Dickinsons arrayed upon the doorstep.

"Good morning!" she said, attempting to inject a warm note of welcome into her voice. "What a fortunate coincidence! Alicia and I were just at the point of setting out for Berkeley Street. Well, setting out to call on you," she amended. "Are you staying in your townhouse?" She had neglected to ask Alicia.

"Where else would we be staying?" Lady Calthrop snapped.

Susanna bit her lip, berating herself for her ill-chosen

question. Evidently the Dickinsons' London home was temporarily vacant, but her ladyship would not care to be reminded that it was normally let out.

"Where else indeed?" Susanna said brightly. "At any rate, we should have come earlier, but we arrived in town only a few minutes ago."

"I am pleased to hear it." Lady Calthrop nodded her approval. "When Hugh called on Friday, your butler advised him you had gone to Kent to fetch Alicia and were expected back today. Hugh fancied you might drive back yesterday instead, but I assured him you would *never* travel on a Sunday."

Susanna cast Alicia a triumphant sideward look, but it was quite wasted because her sister was staring—utterly enraptured—at the Honorable Hugh Dickinson. Could he possibly be as handsome as Alicia thought? Susanna wondered, returning her eyes to the party on the porch. Though he wasn't the sort she personally favored, she realized that she might, unfairly, be comparing him to Ned. Hugh was somewhat below the average in height and rather stockily built, but since the same could be said of Alicia, they were perfectly matched in respect to size. He had pleasant, if unremarkable, features; a great shock of curly, sandy hair; and large, truly magnificent hazel eyes.

So if not handsome, Hugh was undeniably attractive, and Susanna was at a loss to conceive how he had come by his good appearance. She discreetly studied Lord and Lady Calthrop, hoping to unearth some previously hidden clue; but the mystery remained unresolved, for the viscount and his wife were both most *un*attractive. Indeed, they looked astonishingly alike: their hair was gray, their eyes were gray, even their complexions were gray. They were also precisely the same height, and Susanna believed that were they to be clad in some sort of sexless garment, their coiffures covered, they would be distinguishable only by the circumstance that Lady Calthrop was much too plump while Lord Calthrop was thin to the verge of emaciation. In fact, Papa often conjectured that her ladyship's historic domination of the viscount was the result of her superior physical bulk.

"Pray do come in," Susanna said quickly, aware that her scrutiny had continued too long. "I shall ring for tea—"

"That will not be necessary," Lady Calthrop interrupted, preceding her husband and son into the foyer. "I shan't take much of your time, Susanna; I merely wished to convey my opinion about various aspects of Alicia's debut. You young people may stay here." She waved Hugh and Alicia peremptorily toward the library, which was situated on the left side of the entry hall. "Remain with them, Walter."

"Yes, dear."

Lord Calthrop obediently trailed Hugh and Alicia into the library, and her ladyship sailed on across the vestibule and up the staircase. Susanna had no doubt she would have proceeded to the saloon had she known where it was located; as it was, she was compelled to wait at the first-floor landing until her hostess could catch her up. She must not lose her temper, Susanna reminded herself, ushering Lady Calthrop along the corridor and into the drawing room. However sorely she might be tried, she must remain infinitely polite. It was, as Papa had pointed out, only for a few months.

"Will you sit down?" Susanna gestured round the saloon.

"Umm."

Her ladyship peered critically about, as if attempting to judge whether any of the furniture was worthy of such an honor. At length, she chose the Adam chair, and Susanna sank onto the couch and set her hat on the sofa table. She was spitefully pleased to note, as Lady Calthrop smoothed the skirt of her walking dress, that the flounce around the bottom was flapping loose in several places. She transferred her attention to the viscountess's face and discovered her now peering at the portraits above the mantel.

"You still display your husband's picture, I see," Lady Calthrop said. "I met him only once, on the occasion of your wedding. As I recall, he left the country shortly thereafter."

"So he did," Susanna murmured.

"And he has been away for half a dozen years."

"Three and a half years," Susanna corrected.

"The difference between six years and three scarcely signifies." Lady Calthrop dropped her eyes from the portrait and leveled them on Susanna. "Let me not hide my teeth. I find your peculiar marital situation most distressing."

As do I! Susanna thought furiously, but she swallowed the words. Polite; she must be excessively polite. "My personal belief," she rejoined aloud, "is that Ned was killed en route from the eastern coast of America to New Orleans."

"I certainly hope so." Her ladyship sniffed. "I should hate to suppose he *abandoned* you." She scowled at the picture, then looked again at Susanna. "At any rate, I do derive some comfort from the information that you have conducted yourself with a reasonable degree of propriety in his absence."

Susanna, for her part, derived *no* comfort from the information that Lady Calthrop had apparently been investigating her activities. She clenched her hands in her lap, her fingernails biting painfully into her palms.

"Yes," her ladyship went on, "I am sorry to say that many women in your position might have embarked upon an immoral liaison with another man. I am prodigious comforted indeed that you do not fall into that shameless category."

Angry as she was, Susanna drew a tiny sigh of relief. It was extremely lucky, she reflected, that she had not yet revealed her intentions to Percy. Had she done so, he would surely shower her with such attention as to arouse Lady Calthrop's suspicions.

"Therefore," the viscountess said, sketching what she no doubt fancied to be a kind smile, "I am prepared to overlook your marital bumblebath and help you bring Alicia out. Permit me to be frank in that regard as well. I have scheduled a house party at the end of the month, and my tentative plan is to announce Hugh and Alicia's engagement then. If, of course, Alicia has had a successful debut in the interim."

She raised her gray brows, and Susanna nodded.

"I understand." She congratulated herself for the wonderfully courteous tone of her voice. "And I believe you will be quite pleased by Alicia's come-out ball. *My* tentative plan is to hold the assembly two weeks from Thursday evening."

"That is the very night before my house party!" her ladyship said.

"Really?" Susanna affected an expression of delighted surprise. "How convenient. Be that as it may, I selected a Thursday because I normally conduct my salons on Thursday evening. And since most of the *ton* keep their Thursdays open in hopes of receiving an invitation to my soiree, I expect virtually everyone of importance will attend Alicia's ball."

"Your salons."

Lady Calthrop cleared her throat, and Susanna belatedly chided herself for having introduced the subject. If her ladyship demanded an invitation, Susanna would be forced to comply, and the viscountess *would* make a cake of herself—

"That is another matter I wanted to discuss," Lady Calthrop continued primly. "When I stated that you have behaved with a *reasonable* degree of propriety, my qualification was directed to your salons. You are naturally entitled to associate with whomever you choose, even should your choice embrace the very dregs of society. Lord Byron, for example." She made a moue of distaste. "However, *I* certainly do not choose to mingle with such people, and I shouldn't wish Hugh to be exposed to them either. And I should hope you would protect your innocent sister from Byron and his kind."

Susanna had already resolved not to ask the infamous baron to her home again, but she perceived no harm in pretending to succumb to her ladyship's advice. "Yes, you are right," she said humbly. "I shan't . . . er . . . *expose* Hugh or Alicia either one to Lord Byron." They might have been discussing some dread and fatal disease.

"I was confident you would concur." Lady Calthrop once more nodded her approval. "Now, insofar as Alicia's come-out is concerned, I shall do everything I can to assist you."

Susanna was hard put to imagine a more dismal prospect than her ladyship's "assistance," and she cast about for a polite avenue of escape. "That is very good of you, but I have already selected a florist and a caterer and an orchestra." This was not exactly a lie, she assured herself, for she did know which vendors she would try to engage for the assembly. "And I plan to employ a printer this afternoon. However"—she glimpsed a splendid sop—"you could help me address the invitations when they are ready."

"Oh, I shouldn't dream of it, dear." Lady Calthrop tendered another frosty smile. "No, if you have arranged the ball to your satisfaction, I shouldn't want to interfere."

Evidently, Susanna thought wryly, her ladyship's pledge of assistance did not extend to any actual *work*. But she was far too relieved to offer an objection and more relieved yet when the viscountess rose, signaling an end to the interview. Susanna sprang up as well and followed Lady Calthrop out of the drawing room, down the stairs, and across the vestibule to the library doorway. The scene within was one Mr. Lawrence might have painted: Alicia and Hugh—seemingly riveted to the striped upholstery of the couch—were gazing into one another's eyes; and Lord Calthrop was slumped in one of the shield-back chairs, sound asleep and audibly snoring.

"Walter!" her ladyship screeched. "I appointed you to *watch* them!"

It was unclear to Susanna just what sort of sinful activity Lord Calthrop had been assigned to prevent: the library was awash in sunlight, the door open, and a dozen servants were patrolling the house. But the viscount, Hugh, and Alicia leapt guiltily to their feet—as though her ladyship had, in fact, witnessed some shocking breach of conduct—and Susanna felt a stir of alarm. Lord Calthrop had long lived in terror of his wife, and it was understandable that Alicia would fear to offend her prospective mother-in-law. But Hugh was two and twenty years of age, a man grown, and Susanna could not suppose Alicia's life would be a happy one if her husband was prepared to bow to his mother's every whim.

But that was not her concern, Susanna owned, and she managed a last polite smile as the viscountess shepherded her husband and son through the foyer and out the front door. Alicia floated up the staircase, restored by her brief visit with her beloved, and Susanna glanced at the long-case clock in the entry hall. She had told Lady Calthrop the full truth in one respect—she did have to order the assembly invitations today—and she decided to forgo lunch and visit the printer at once. She had left her hat in the saloon, she remembered, and as she started toward the stairs to retrieve it, the doorbell pealed again.

"Is Putnam ill?" Nancy inquired cheerfully when Susanna threw the door open. "No, I observe that you are dressed to go out."

Undeterred by this observation, Lady Hadleigh stepped over the threshold, and Susanna closed the door behind her. Nancy had promised to call this afternoon, she now recalled. Or threatened, as the case might be. And whichever verb best described Lady Hadleigh's intent, she had wasted no time, for the clock was just chiming twelve.

"I was going out," Susanna confirmed, "but if you'd care for some tea—"

"No, I can't stay." Nancy shook her head, and several unruly red curls escaped the confines of her French bonnet. "I am engaged to lunch with Lord Illingworth."

She punctuated this report with a suggestive smirk,

and Susanna stifled a sigh. Nancy had recently identified the Marquis of Illingworth as the latest of her lovers, but, as usual, Susanna did not know what to believe. Lord Illingworth, a notorious rake, might well have initiated an affaire with a conveniently available countess. On the other hand, since he was distantly related to Lord Hadleigh, the marquis might merely have invited his cousin-by-marriage-much-removed to share an innocuous meal. Or Nancy might not be lunching with Lord Illingworth at all; she might be bound for her mantua-maker or her milliner or her corsetier. One could never be sure what Lady Hadleigh was at, and Susanna elected not to respond to her statement.

"I can't stay," Nancy repeated, sounding rather disappointed that Susanna had failed to rise to her fly. "I only wanted to advise you that I spoke to Percy in your absence. I told him you had agreed to have your marriage annulled."

"Agreed!" Susanna protested. "I agreed to *consider* an annulment—"

"So you did," Lady Hadleigh interposed soothingly. "But I was certain you would decide to proceed, and I judged Percy much in need of encouragement. And I was right, Susanna. During the course of our conversation, he confessed that he is most eager to wed and was beginning to consider other matches. Fortunately, now he's aware of your intentions, he is willing to be patient a few months longer."

"Fortunately?" Susanna snapped. Nancy had finally gone too far. "To the contrary, you've put me in a wretched coil. I learned during the weekend why it is Alicia must be brought out . . ." She explained Lady Calthrop's obsessive concern with propriety and her own pledge to Papa to maintain appearances until her sister was safely wed. "But since you have let the cat out of the bag," she concluded, "I very much fear that Percy will drop some hint of my plans."

"I'm sorry you feel I created a problem," Nancy said stiffly. "But if you think on it, you will realize your fear is groundless. You know how discreet Percy is. When you inform him of your circumstances, he'll be far from dropping any hints. Indeed, I daresay he will go out of his way to *avoid* you the rest of the Season."

Despite its stiffness, Nancy's tone was unmistakably contrite, and Susanna relented. Lady Hadleigh's inveterate meddling was sufficient to drive a saint to madness, but there was no doubt she meant well, which set her dramatically apart from most of the alleged ladies of the *ton*. And what real harm had been done? As Nancy pointed out, Percy was prodigious discreet: once apprised of Susanna's situation, he would take great care not to compromise her in the slightest degree. Perhaps more care than if he had been left to press his suit in ignorance, so Nancy's intervention was probably for the best. Except that Susanna was now committed to dissolve her marriage and wed Colonel Fordyce . . .

But she had been committed to that, in principle, for some days, and she squared her shoulders. "It is all right," she murmured. "I shall invite Percy to dinner tomorrow evening and tell him the annulment must be delayed."

"You see?" Lady Hadleigh flashed a triumphant smile. "Everything has worked out perfectly." She turned away, opened the door, spun back round. "But I shan't interfere in your life again, Susanna."

Not until the next time she counted it necessary, Susanna thought dryly.

"However, I shall be delighted to *counsel* you," Nancy added. "Should you wish my advice, you've only to ask. And since you might wish to seek my advice after your conversation with Percy, I shall call Wednesday morning to hear what occurred."

With a final swipe at her errant curls, she strode through the doorway and slammed the door to; and Susanna proceeded up the staircase, shaking her head with fond exasperation. Though Lady Hadleigh was quite incorrigible, she was a true friend, and Susanna suspected she would be much in need of a friend during the difficult months ahead. She must survive the Season

and then—before the year was over
—the dissolution of her marriage and her wedding to
Colonel Fordyce . . .

Not that the latter would be *difficult*, she hastily
amended; her wedding to Percy would be a very happy
occasion. She hurried across the drawing room and
snatched her leghorn hat from the sofa table, but when
she straightened, her eyes involuntarily flew to the
portrait above the mantel.

For years, Susanna had entertained the absurd notion
that if Ned were dead, his picture would somehow tell
her so: the paint would crack, or the colors would run
together, or the portrait would fall from the wall and
come to rest among the ashes in the fireplace. Nothing
of the sort had ever happened, of course; but she now
conceived the equally ludicrous idea that if he were
alive, he would signal his disapproval of her plan to
annul their marriage.

She stood very still for several minutes, carefully
watching the picture. But the Earl of Langham continued to stare sightlessly over her head, and at length,
Susanna whirled about and sped out of the saloon.

"Shall we repair to the library?" Susanna laid her
napkin on the table, and Putnam bounded forward to
assist her from her chair. "I daresay you would enjoy a
glass of brandy."

"Oh, indeed I should." Alicia sprang up before any
of the attending footmen could reach her.

"Not you, Alicia," Susanna snapped. "I was
addressing Colonel Fordyce."

She regretted her sharpness at once, but the preceding
hours had rubbed her nerves quite raw. Which was
hardly Alicia's fault, she conceded, leading her
companions toward the vestibule, for she had frankly
forgotten her sister's presence when she invited Percy to
dine. Upon recognizing her oversight, she'd briefly
thought to banish Alicia to her bedchamber for the
evening, but she soon decided that this course was
fraught with peril. If Alicia suspected that Susanna had

a *parti*, she would no doubt confide her suspicion to Hugh, and he, in turn, might well inform his mother.

So they had sat at table for two interminable hours—Percy and Alicia devouring their food with great enthusiasm, Susanna cutting hers into tiny pieces and pushing the pieces round her plate. Between bites, Percy had enthralled Alicia with his war stories, all of which Susanna had heard a dozen times before . . .

But that wasn't Alicia's fault either, and Susanna stopped in the middle of the foyer and tendered her sister an apologetic smile. "You are far too young to drink strong spirits," she said kindly. "Lady Calthrop would not approve at all."

The mere mention of her formidable ladyship erased Alicia's nascent pout, and with a subdued good-night to Colonel Fordyce, she retreated up the staircase. Susanna beckoned Percy into the library and closed the door behind them.

"You . . . you would like a glass of brandy, I trust?" she stammered.

"If it would not pose too much trouble."

Susanna shook her head and proceeded to the bow-fronted commode beneath the window. Her "strong spirits" were normally stored in the liquor cabinet in the drawing room, but she had desired Putnam to bring a few decanters to the library. She could not talk to Percy in full view of Ned's penetrating silver eyes . . . She poured the colonel's brandy and a glass of Tokay for herself, spilling a few drops of each on the top of the commode. She was initially at a loss to explain her clumsiness, but as she picked up the filled glasses and turned around, she saw that her hands were trembling. She paused to regain her composure and studied Percy from beneath her lashes.

One of the first things Susanna had noticed about Colonel Fordyce was that he held himself almost stiffly erect—a habit she attributed to his long years in the army. But his leg must be paining him tonight, she surmised, for he was leaning against a chair, and his abnormal stance revealed that he had gained another half a stone since their first meeting. Half a stone at least: the lower buttons of his waistcoat were straining against the buttonholes, and his pantaloons had grown so snug as to verge on the indecent.

Susanna quickly raised her eyes and observed that Percy's gray hair had begun to thin. Was this a recent development? she wondered. If not, why had she previously failed to remark the obvious recession at his temples? Within a decade, he would probably be left with the merest fringe of hair, surrounding an otherwise bare scalp.

But she was being unfair again, Susanna chided herself; she could not compare Percy or any other man of his years to Ned. Ned would be forever young and handsome—in his portrait and in her memories. Had he attained the age of forty, his hair would doubtlessly have started to thin as well. Her trembling had subsided to an invisible inward quiver, and she walked carefully across the Axminster carpet.

"Please . . . please sit down," she said, extending the brandy glass to Percy. Though her hands had ceased to shake, she couldn't seem to stop stuttering.

Percy nodded and sank gratefully into the chair, and Susanna perched on the edge of the sofa. She had been planning this moment for upward of four and twenty hours, but now it was here, she discovered herself reluctant to say any of the words she had composed.

"How . . . how is your uncle?" she murmured instead.

"Gravely ill indeed. In fact, I received a letter from his solicitor in today's post. Mr. Ransom stated that Uncle Charles is no longer competent to manage his affairs."

"Umm," Susanna grunted.

Percy sipped deeply from his brandy, then set the glass on the Pembroke table beside the chair. "Let me dissemble no longer." His voice was rather high-pitched for a man of his size, and tonight, for some reason, it grated on Susanna's ears. "I have tried not to speculate just when Uncle Charles might . . . ah . . . be taken, but I quite understand your interest in the matter."

"I am not in the least interested!" Susanna protested. "Well, I am *concerned* for your uncle's health, of course—"

"Please, Susanna." Percy waved her to silence. "You need dissimulate no longer either. I never supposed that a countess would surrender her title to wed a retired colonel. I permitted myself to hope that you might return my . . . my affection"—he was stuttering a bit himself—"but I realized marriage was out of the question. Until I became Uncle Charles's heir."

"That was but one factor—"

"Pray allow me to finish."

He smiled, and Susanna noted, as she had before, that his teeth were perfectly even. There was not the slightest space between them—

"So it is altogether natural," Percy continued, "that you should wish to know my precise situation before you seek to have your present marriage dissolved. And I can virtually promise you that Uncle Charles will . . . er . . . depart by the end of the summer. Therefore, with any luck, your annulment and my inheritance will coincide very nicely."

"The end of the summer." Susanna's mouth had gone dry, and she moistened it with a sip of Tokay. He had granted her a splendid opening, and she could, in truth, dissimulate no longer. "That is what I wanted to tell you, Percy. I can't obtain an annulment by the end of the summer."

"We shall see about that," he said smugly. "With all due respect to Lady Hadleigh, I, too, have influential relatives. One of my cousins on Papa's side of the family is the vicar of a large parish near York, and he's quite close to the archbishop—"

"I fear you misunderstood." Susanna judged it her turn to interrupt. "I cannot even *seek* an annulment until the end of the summer."

"Then I did most seriously misunderstand." Percy's

smile faded. "Lady Hadleigh indicated that you were prepared to proceed immediately."

"So I was." Susanna nodded, uncertain whether she was saying the truth or not. "However, that was before I learned of Alicia's situation. Do you recollect my mention of Lady Calthrop?"

Colonel Fordyce frowned, then bobbed his own head.

"Alicia wishes to marry her son—Lady Calthrop's son, that is—and as Lady Calthrop is monstrous proper—priggish, one might say . . ."

Susanna stumbled on, her words falling all over one another; but apparently she succeeded in making some sense, for Percy inclined his head again at all the appropriate points in her narrative.

"And that is the reason I cannot dissolve my marriage till Alicia and Hugh are wed," she concluded. "Immediately thereafter, I shall petition Bishop Addison for an annulment."

"Or perhaps my cousin," Percy reminded her.

"Yes, perhaps your cousin. At any rate, I must ask you to wait a few months more—"

"Ask?" he interposed indignantly. "You have far too little faith in my devotion. Of course I shall wait a few months more. Indeed, now I am confident of your ultimate intentions, I should wait a few *years* more should such a sacrifice be required." He clenched his jaws with noble determination. "And I shall be excessively cautious not to alert Lady Calthrop to our plans."

"Thanks you," Susanna muttered. She had attained her objective, and she wondered why she felt so empty.

"So I fancy I should depart at once." Percy extracted a gold watch from his waistcoat pocket and peered down at it. "Yes, it is almost ten o'clock, and I shouldn't want Alicia to think I had stayed too long. Minutes are of scant consequence when our whole lives are in the balance."

Our whole lives, Susanna silently echoed. She had pledged to spend the rest of her days with Colonel Percy Fordyce, soon to be Viscount Grafton . . . He stood, and she crashed her glass on the sofa table, leapt up, and trailed him out of the library. He limped across the foyer, opened the front door, and Susanna followed him outside.

It was a beautiful night, unseasonably warm for early spring and bathed in the silver light of a brilliant half-moon. Percy gazed at the sky a moment, then turned toward her and cleared his throat.

"I am far from being a poet"—he emitted another cough—"but I wish to say that this has been the most memorable evening of my life. You have rendered me extremely happy."

"Thank you," she said again. But that wasn't the right response at all, and she cleared her own throat. "That is, you . . . I . . . I am very happy as well."

"My dear Susanna."

He sighed and—before she could guess what he was at—reached forward and pulled her into his arms. Her instinct was to jerk away, but she realized even as she stiffened that this wasn't the proper response either. Lady Elwood had advised her long ago that one did not embrace a man until one was engaged, but she and Percy *were* engaged, unofficially at least . . . Her mind was still spinning when he lowered his head and touched his lips to hers.

Susanna had not been kissed by anyone but Ned, but she remembered his kisses with painful clarity. Remembered the flood of warmth that had spread all through her and the delicious ache in her midsection, the crashing of her heart and the melting of her bones. She waited for Percy's mouth to create the same sensations, but her body remained frozen. Yes, *frozen* was an excellent adjective. She did not find his kiss unpleasant; she simply felt nothing.

Percy raised his head, deposited a second small kiss on her forehead, and released her.

"My dear Susanna," he repeated, beaming down at her. "Pray do not be alarmed. I should never have behaved so indiscreetly had there been anyone to see. I shall henceforth conduct myself with *perfect* propriety until your sister is safely wed."

"Umm." Her lips now seemed frozen as well.

"In fact, much as the prospect distresses me, I judge it best not to call on you privately so long as Lady Calthrop and Alicia are in town. If we meet only in public, there can be no possible breath of scandal. I shall therefore bid you good night and remain away till Thursday evening."

"Thursday evening?" Somehow she forced her mouth to move.

"You are as delirious with joy as I am." He chuckled and fondly patted her shoulder. "I was referring to your salon."

"My salon. Yes, I shall see you at my salon."

Percy executed a gay little bow and descended the steps to the footpath. His limp was miraculously improved, Susanna observed as he strode toward South Audley Street; evidently she had, indeed, rendered him extremely happy.

And she was also happy, she assured herself, retreating into the house. She closed the door and sagged against it. Percy's kiss had merely taken her by surprise. In time—after her marriage was annulled and she had grown thoroughly accustomed to the notion of another husband—her body would thaw, and she *would* be delirious with joy.

Susanna drew herself up and trudged back toward the library to extinguish the lamps. She was halfway across the vestibule when the peal of the doorbell caught her up, and she stopped and turned warily around. It could only be Percy, come to retrieve some article he had left behind, and she was in no humor to converse with him again tonight. But since she had instructed Putnam to retire as soon as dinner was finished, she perceived no convenient escape; and she plodded back across the foyer, assumed her brightest smile, and threw the door open.

A tall blond man stood on the doorstep, and Susanna's vision began to blur. It could not be; it absolutely could not be. But it was, and she swayed against the doorjamb as she recognized the unmistakable glitter of Ned Sutton's silver eyes.

Chapter 4

SUSANNA HAD PICTURED Ned's homecoming every day since his departure. In the beginning, she had imagined that he would stride eagerly through the door, seize her in his arms, and demonstrate in no uncertain manner how much he had missed her. As the months and years passed, she altered the scene a bit: he would still bound over the threshold to embrace her, but between kisses, he would murmur abject apologies for his lengthy absence and the alarm he had caused her. The one circumstance she had never anticipated was that he would continue to stand on the doorstep, gazing silently, unsmilingly down at her.

"Good evening, Susanna," he said at last. "I trust I am not intruding?"

She had never supposed that these would be his first words either. Nor that his voice—like his demeanor—would be one of frigid courtesy.

"N-no," she stammered. "I had not yet retired. I . . . I had a dinner guest."

She had predicted her own actions as inaccurately as his, she thought distantly. She might have been speaking to some lady of the *ton* who had called at a slightly inconvenient time.

"Then may I come in?" Ned said coolly.

Susanna nodded, but he remained motionless, and she realized that she was still collapsed against the doorjamb, effectively blocking the entry. She drew herself shakily up and backed into the vestibule, fearful that if she averted her head, he would disappear. She did not turn until he stepped inside and closed the door, and even then she crept sidewise toward the library, watching him over her shoulder.

"Is your guest planning to return?" he snapped, glancing over his own shoulder.

Susanna's shock had begun to subside by now, and she felt a stir of anger. He was obviously vexed to learn that she had entertained a dinner guest, overset by the notion that she was able to amuse herself without him. Had he expected her to live like a cloistered nun while he gaily disported himself in the farthest reaches of America?

"No, my guest does not plan to return," she muttered aloud.

She whirled on around and stalked into the library, attempting to swallow her annoyance. Their reunion was not proceeding at all as she had scripted it, and though the fault was entirely Ned's, matters could only grow worse if she responded in kind to his unreasonable hostility. She drew a deep breath and turned once more to face him.

"Would you care for some refreshment?" she asked. "A glass of brandy perhaps?"

"I believe not."

He began to peer around the room, and she took the opportunity to study him. Her initial impression was that he had aged dramatically: fine lines radiated from the corners of his eyes, and his hair seemed abundantly threaded with gray. Upon closer inspection, however, she perceived that these changes were a function of climate rather than age. His fair skin had been burned quite brown by the sun, and the lines were superficial— spidery white webs produced by years of squinting against the relentless tropical sunlight. The same light had bleached the streaks in his hair, she surmised; the strands she had fancied to be gray were actually a paler shade of blond.

So Ned had not visibly aged, Susanna concluded, and she wondered why he looked so different from his portrait. She mentally made allowances for his tan and the peculiar coloration of his hair, but there was still some nagging discrepancy. His clothes? Yes, his clothes were decidedly different. Ned had posed for Mr. Lawrence in evening attire, and he was now wearing black pantaloons, a charcoal tailcoat, and a dove-gray waistcoat which very nearly matched his eyes. And while none of his garments could be termed unfashionable, they were all cut a trifle oddly, betraying the work of a foreign hand.

But the variance transcended his clothing, and at length, Susanna found the adjective to describe it. *Hard*; the man in the library was subtly yet unmistakably harder than his painted image. Ned had always been slender but not unusually strong; like most English gentlemen, he had spent rather too much time in the drawing room and at the gaming table. Now he was somewhat leaner than she remembered, and she conjectured that his body had turned to solid muscle. Even the muscles in his face seemed more pronounced, but that, she owned, was probably an illusion. His jaws were set with a strange, firm determination, and there was an unfamiliar sternness round his mouth . . .

She became aware that he was reciprocating her scrutiny and hastily dropped her eyes to his boots.

"You have furnished the house very handsomely," he said.

"Thank you," she murmured.

"I could not be certain you were still residing in Grosvenor Square. In fact, I couldn't be sure you had ever occupied the property. I consequently went to Dickie's to inquire your whereabouts. He informed me that you were not only living in London but have become quite the belle of society."

"You went to Viscount Buckley's?" Susanna felt another spark of anger, and her eyes flew back to his face. She had stayed in London specifically to await Ned's return, and he had gone first to his closest male friend. "You called on him before you came to me?"

"As I stated, I could not be certain you were here."

He waved about the library, and she noticed that his hands were also lean and brown.

"I should not have supposed that would signify," she said stiffly. "I should have thought you would be sufficiently eager to see me that you might have elected to take your chances."

"And what would that have availed me?" He raised his eyebrows—brows which looked nearly white in contrast to his darkened skin. "You would have been entertaining your guest, would you not?"

There it was again: the arrogant implication that she had no right to an independent existence. Ned could remain abroad as long as he liked, then come home and chat at his leisure with Dickie Washburn, who possessed considerably less sense than the average goose. But Susanna was expected to wait, patiently wait, until her husband condescended to grace her with his presence . . . Her spark of anger exploded to a blaze of rage.

"Where the devil have you been?" she hissed.

"Did you not receive my letters?"

"Yes, I received two letters." She could not seem to raise her voice above a furious whisper. "One sent shortly after you arrived in Baltimore and the second just before you set out for Louisiana. The latter, if I may refresh your memory, was written more than three years since."

"Then you did not get any of the messages I dispatched from New Orleans." Ned nodded, as if the situation had been explained to his entire satisfaction. "I consigned three more letters to Europeans who were sailing back to the Continent. Two Spaniards and a Prussian; I no longer recollect their names. They promised to forward the letters, but evidently they did not."

"You no longer recollect their names?" Susanna echoed incredulously. "You entrusted a task of such importance to casual acquaintances? Did it not occur to you to seek a more reliable means of communication?"

"What means would you have suggested, Susanna?"

He answered question with question. "If I may refresh *your* memory, the United States and Britain were at war. I could scarcely post a letter and expect it to go out on the next ship bound for England."

"You could have sent a message by way of Canada." After all the years of denial, she borrowed Nancy's argument. "As Lady Perdue's sister did. She lives in New York, and Lady Perdue received letters from her throughout the war."

"Louisiana is a very long way from New York. Indeed, it requires twenty-four days for mail to travel from New Orleans even so far as Washington. And I knew no one on the eastern coast who might pass my letters on to Canada."

"Then you should have traveled to the east yourself and located some sort of courier—"

"Good God, Susanna!" His icy calm disintegrated so abruptly that she started. "What do you think I was at in Louisiana? Do you fancy I was on an extended holiday, free to leave and wander about the country whenever I pleased? I was—"

"I do not *care* what you were at in Louisiana!" she interposed shrilly. "I should merely have liked to know you were there! As it was, I believed you dead."

"Or wished to believe me dead." His tone was once more edged with frost. "My demise would justify all manner of indiscretions, would it not?"

"In-dis-cre-tions." Susanna acidly repeated each individual syllable. "If you are referring to my salons, pray be advised that Viscount Buckley is speaking from the most abysmal ignorance. He has not been invited to any of my soirees."

"So he confessed. With considerable regret, I might add, which is surely a tribute to your reputation as London's premier hostess."

Ned sketched a glacial smile, and angry as she was, Susanna anxiously examined his mouth. He was so different in every other respect that she would not have been surprised to find his smile changed as well. But the left side of his mouth still curved above the right, and though his teeth also seemed whiter against his sun-bronzed skin, there was still a space between them.

"However, I was not referring to your famous salons." Ned's smile vanished as suddenly as it had appeared. "I was alluding to your . . . ah . . . Shall we call him your *parti*?"

Susanna had forgotten Percy until that instant, and her mind churned in calculation. Could Lord Buckley possibly have surmised her intentions? He rarely ventured into society, much preferring the macao tables at White's. So he could know very little of Percy, she decided; he could only have related some vague *on-dit* about a gentleman who regularly attended Susanna's soirees. She was momentarily inclined to deny the rumor altogether, but she feared an outright lie would inevitably return to haunt her.

"Colonel Fordyce, you mean." She essayed a cool smile of her own.

"Colonel?" Ned affected a look of astonishment. "Your father couldn't locate another titled suitor? Or is Simon even aware of your liaison?"

"It is hardly a liaison," Susanna snapped. "And if Viscount Buckley told you differently—"

"No, he did not. To the contrary, Dickie assured me that your conduct has been beyond reproach."

"*Assured* you?" she said furiously. "You asked a . . . a . . . ?" She groped for a suitably devastating description of Dickie Washburn. "You asked an utter wastrel to vouch for *my* good behavior?"

"You've grown very clever, Susanna." Ned granted her a nod of sardonic admiration. "Your indignation is most convincing. I should be quite persuaded of your innocence had I not chanced to witness the tender scene on your doorstep."

He had spoken so mildly that she did not immediately register his words. Not until his eyes began to glitter with triumph, and then she slumped against the Pembroke table. She should have guessed, she chided herself: should have perceived at once that Ned had observed her with Percy. It accounted for his hostility, his irrational resentment of her dinner guest . . . She tried to moisten her lips, but her tongue was equally dry.

"What you saw," she croaked, "was—"

"You needn't tell me what I saw." His eyes narrowed to the merest silver slits. "I saw my wife in the arms of another man."

"Yes, but the circumstances were not as they appeared—"

"I daresay I should count myself fortunate that he was departing rather than arriving." Ned flew heedlessly on. "I initially fancied I should be compelled to slink back to Dickie's and report that your lover had come to spend the night."

"Spend the night?" Susanna gasped. "You glimpsed *one kiss* and assumed I had taken a lover?"

"What assumption would you have preferred?" He raised his brows again, as though he were sincerely curious. "I was attempting to give you the benefit of the doubt. I should hate to learn that you seal every idle flirtation with a kiss."

Susanna detected an odd sound, a wheeze like that of a winded horse; and at length, she realized she was hearing herself—that she was literally breathless with rage.

"Attempting to give me the benefit of the doubt?" she choked. "What right have you to judge my conduct? I cannot suppose you've been scrupulously faithful to our marriage vows these three years past."

"I never thought to claim I was," he said coolly. "But I came back."

"And am I to be thankful for that?" Susanna tried to stand away from the table, but her knees were weak with fury as well. "What did you expect? Did you imagine you could . . . could *abandon* me for years on end and return to find everything exactly as you left it? Did you fancy our lives could go on as though nothing had changed?"

"No. No, I hoped—"

"Hoped I would unquestioningly forgive you?" Her anger turned cold, as cold and bracing as a winter wind, and she drew herself erect. "Then you hoped in vain because I'm no longer the obedient little wife you deserted. You were quite right to assume that Percy is more than an idle flirtation. He's been courting me for many months, and I recently consented to wed him."

Even as the words emerged, Susanna wondered whether she had intended to say them. But pride would permit no retraction, no amendment; and she was distantly gratified by the brief, almost invisible tightening of Ned's jaws.

"Then I certainly shan't stand in your way," he said politely. His jaws had relaxed again; he might have been remarking some odd quirk of the weather. "I collect you have arranged to . . . ah . . . dispose of me?"

"I plan to seek an annulment of our marriage. My closest friend is connected to a bishop."

"An annulment might prove difficult now I've so inconveniently reappeared." He flashed another crooked grin, but, like the first, it was devoid of amusement. "I daresay it would be easier to obtain a divorce. You may recall that Dickie's father is one of the foremost figures in the House, and prior to my departure, I was not without influence myself. I fancy that between us, we can secure rapid passage of a bill of divorcement."

"Yes," Susanna muttered. Her anger had evaporated, and nothing came to take its place. No sense of victory or regret or even relief that her long ordeal was over; she felt as empty as she had when Percy kissed her.

"Naturally I shall accept full blame," Ned said. "As you pointed out, I did desert you."

"Yes."

"Then I perceive no reason to delay, do you? I shall urge Lord Wrentham to introduce the bill at the earliest opportunity."

"Yes," she whispered.

"Well, that is it then, and I shall trouble you no further. Good-bye, Susanna."

He bowed, the pale strands in his hair gleaming silver

in the lamplight, and strode out of the library. What had happened? Susanna wondered wildly as his footfalls tapped across the foyer. How could their reunion have gone so terribly awry in such a short expanse of time? The long-case clock chimed twice, and she estimated she had been with Ned for well under half an hour. So very brief a time that were it not for the inevitable scandal of their divorce, no one would know he had returned. Not Papa or Nancy or Alicia . . . Alicia!

"No!" she cried. She raced into the vestibule and caught him up just as he reached the front door.

"No?" He spun around, his eyes strangely alight. "You do not wish me to seek a divorce?"

"You can't," she panted. "Not yet, at any rate. I forgot about Alicia."

"Alicia?" He frowned. "What has Alicia to do with us?"

"She is at the point of becoming engaged to Hugh Dickinson—"

"Engaged?" His mouth fell open with genuine amazement. "Alicia is barely more than a child."

Did he honestly fail to recognize that the adolescent he remembered would have grown to womanhood in his absence? His remark fanned the coals of Susanna's wrath.

"She *was* barely more than a child when you left," she corrected warmly. "She is now eighteen and desperately in love with Hugh, and his mother—Lady Calthrop, whom you may recall from our wedding . . ." She explained the viscountess's intense concern for propriety, including her reference to Susanna's "peculiar" marital situation.

"I consequently promised Papa I should behave with perfect discretion until Alicia is wed," she concluded. "He believes Lady Calthrop would be excessively overset by the prospect of an annulment, and I can scarcely conceive her reaction if she learned you were seeking a divorce."

To say the truth, Susanna could conceive her ladyship's reaction very well, and she could not quell a small shudder of horror.

"So you did not intend to request an annulment before Hugh and Alicia were married," Ned said.

"No. That is, yes; I intended to wait till then."

"And you are proposing I similarly delay the introduction of a bill of divorcement."

"Yes."

"And what do you suggest we do in the interim?"

He arched his brows again, and Susanna stared at them with fascination. Was this a new mannerism? she wondered, or had the startling contrast between his sun-bleached brows and sunburned skin merely brought an old habit to her attention?

"Have you considered how we can deceive Lady Calthrop?" he pressed.

In point of fact, Susanna had lacked the time to consider this complication, and she dragged her eyes from his face to the marble floor of the foyer. She belatedly observed that they were standing very close, the toes of her slippers almost touching those of his boots. His nearness inexplicably clouded her mind, and she was compelled to step away before she could ponder his question.

"Granted my choice," she replied at last, forcing herself to look back at him, "I should ask you to keep your return a secret. But I fear it's too late for that. Even if Lord Buckley held his tongue"—which she judged prodigious doubtful—"his servants would circulate the news. So I fancy the only feasible course is to pretend that we have reconciled."

"Live together, you mean?"

His brows shot into the fringes of his hair, as though to indicate that this was by far the most cockleheaded notion he had ever heard. As it probably was, Susanna owned grimly.

"I see no alternative," she rejoined aloud.

He hesitated a moment, his forehead now furrowed in thought. "Very well," he agreed. "Inasmuch as I created your bumblebath, I daresay I should help you resolve it."

"Thank you," she murmured, not at all certain he was entitled to her gratitude.

There was another moment of silence; she could hear his breathing, her breathing, the rhythmic tick of the clock.

"Indeed, a reconciliation might be most pleasururable."

His lopsided smile shattered the hush as much as his words, and before she could guess what he was at, he stepped forward and laid one finger on her cheek. After all the years, all her rage, his touch still had the power to dissolve her bones, and she willed herself not to sway against him.

"I did miss you, Susanna." His voice was hoarse, and he cleared his throat. "In the . . . confusion surrounding my arrival, I had no chance to say it, but I missed you every day."

His eyes retained their old power as well, she reflected distantly. The power to cast a silver spell, to hold her in thrall; she was seemingly unable to move.

"So I fancy our reunion, however brief, could prove most enjoyable indeed." His finger traveled down her cheek, across her jaw and her chin and her opposite jaw, and back up the other cheek. "I fancy we could have . . . Shall we term it a reverse affaire? Yes, it would be unique: while engaged to your future husband, you could conduct a liaison with the husband you are about to shed."

He took another forward step, wound one arm around her waist, lowered his head; and at the last instant, before she melted quite away, Susanna dodged out of his grasp.

"No!" Her throat was clogged as well, and her protest expired in a great cough. "No," she repeated when her coughing subsided. "Our reconciliation will be solely for the sake of appearance; pray be clear on that head. I shall ring for Putnam to show you to one of the guest bedchambers."

She whirled around and walked shakily to the bellpull beside the pier table, but her hand froze as it approached the knob. She had given the butler permission to retire as soon as dinner was finished. And though Putnam was an excellent servant—the sort who responded with relatively good grace to an unexpected summons—Susanna was in no mood to explain her husband's miraculous resurrection.

"Never mind," she muttered, largely to herself. "I shall take you up."

She began to mount the staircase, not turning to see whether Ned followed, but she soon detected the tattoo of his footsteps behind her. Her inclination was to settle him in the remotest and smallest of the guest rooms, but as she sped along the first-floor corridor, she realized that such an arrangement would generate all manner of gossip among the staff.

"Lady Langham is acting happy to have his lordship back, but did you notice where he's sleeping? In the bedchamber at the eastern end of the house, that's where. Well, maybe the swells are different from us. I'll mention it to Lord Seagrave's coachman . . ."

No, it wouldn't do at all, and when Susanna reached the second-floor landing, she reluctantly turned right and proceeded to the bedchamber adjoining her own. Actually, she amended, opening the door and glancing inside, this room was supposed to be hers: she had decorated the house with the presumption that Ned would occupy the master bedchamber and she the slightly smaller one beside it. As a result, the main bedroom—hers by default—was done in masculine shades of beige, dark blue, and brilliant gold; and the adjacent chamber was a rather frilly concoction of peach and pale green.

But beggars could not be choosers, she reminded herself, crossing the Axminster carpet. And despite the difference in their decors, the rooms contained beds of equal size. Susanna had deliberately planned this feature, anticipating that she and Ned might wish to sleep one night in his bedchamber and the next in hers . . . Her cheeks warmed, and she hastily shifted her eyes from the bed to the canopy above it.

"What a pleasant room!" Ned said. "You have furnished this part of the house very handsomely too."

"Thank you." Her blush had subsided, and she turned to face him. "I have decided not to advise the servants of your presence until tomorrow morning, so should you need anything during the night, you will have to knock me up. My room is just there." She nodded to the connecting door beside the painted wardrobe.

"That is extremely kind of you," he said solemnly. "However, you have indicated that the service I most particularly need is one you are not prepared to provide."

Susanna detected the threat of another flush and counted it best to ignore his comment. She gazed studiedly about the bedchamber—an inspection worthy of Putnam himself—and eventually bobbed her head with approval. "As everything appears to be in order, I shall bid you good night. I trust you'll be comfortable."

She hurried to the connecting door and threw it open, then paused on the threshold, entertaining a vague inkling that something was amiss. At length, it came to her, and she turned back round.

"Where is your luggage?" she asked. "Did you leave it outside?"

"No, I left it at Dickie's. I shall retrieve it tomorrow."

"But what of tonight? What will you sleep in?"

"How quickly we forget." He shook his head with mock despair. "Do you not recollect that my habit is to sleep in nothing? I don't recall that you posed any objection when we were sharing a bed."

Susanna spun around again, stumbled into her room, and crashed the door to behind her. Her face was aflame, and she sagged against the door, praying that Ned had not noticed her discomfiture. But she was dismally certain he had, for a rich, derisive peal of laughter floated through the door behind her.

Chapter 5

THE MANTEL CLOCK was striking six when Susanna woke, and she turned her head on the pillow and gazed nervously at the door connecting to Ned's bedchamber. As she had done at least a dozen times during the night, she calculated. Her eyes had flown open every half hour or so, and she had peered into the darkness, fancying she heard a tap on the door or the telltale click of the latch or the squeak of the hinges. At one juncture, she had even fancied she heard Ned's breathing, but that was impossible, for—whatever his multitudinous other deficiencies—the earl did not snore.

At any rate, his room was silent now, and Susanna squirmed upright in the bed, propped a pillow behind her back, and tried again to puzzle out why their reunion had gone so dreadfully awry. She had accused Ned of expecting their lives to proceed as though nothing had happened, and she belatedly wondered what she herself had expected. He was certainly entitled to be—she groped for the right word—to be *curious* about the life she'd led in his absence. Particularly when he observed her in the arms of another man . . .

But he was not entitled to assume she had taken a lover, and Susanna ground her teeth against a new flood of rage. He had drawn that conclusion without permitting her a single word of explanation, she recalled. Which really didn't signify because he had made it abundantly clear that he would not have believed her anyway. Yes, he had soon proposed that she conduct a liaison with *him* before she married Percy.

In short, Susanna concluded furiously, Ned obviously

viewed her as a . . . a lightskirt. The very sort of woman he had dallied with in Louisiana, no doubt. And though she might have been able to effect an uneasy reconciliation if she had begged him to hear her out, he would have regarded her with suspicion for the rest of their days.

But the "might haves" and "would haves" were quite academic, for she would never *beg* the arrogant earl for anything. Susanna flung the bedclothes aside, leapt out of the bed, and stalked across the Turkey carpet to the wardrobe. No, she would perpetrate the fiction of a joyful reunion until Alicia was safely wed, and then—to borrow one of Ned's sardonic words—she would "shed" her husband and happily plan her own wedding to Percy.

Susanna opened the wardrobe and scowled at its contents. Though she was reputed to be one of the most fashionable women in Britain, she suddenly found herself unsure of what to wear: she felt like the naive young girl Lady Elwood had escorted to Almack's so many years before. At length, she snatched out her azure morning dress, bore it back across the room, and draped it over the footboard of the bed.

At this point in her toilette, Susanna would normally have summoned her abigail, and she glared at the bellpull beside the fireplace. But Polly, to phrase it kindly, had always been rather too interested in her mistress's activities, and Susanna was in no mood to explain Lord Langham's mysterious absence and equally mystifying reappearance. So she dressed unaided and remembered only as she finished that blue was Ned's favorite color.

"Good morning, Lady Langham."

Putnam turned away from the sideboard at the precise instant Susanna reached the breakfast-parlor entry, leading her to suspect—as she often had before—that an extra eye was imbedded in the thick gray hair at the back of his head. The butler bounded to the chair at the head of the table, drew it out, seated Susanna, and scurried back to the sideboard.

"You are up early today," he remarked, pouring coffee from the silver pot into one of the Wedgwood cups. "But we shall have your breakfast ready in a moment."

He looked pointedly at Ward, the new footman, who was carefully arranging the plates and serving utensils on the sideboard. Well, not so carefully, Susanna amended: even as she glanced in his direction, Ward dropped a meat fork on the carpet, plucked it up, wiped it on his sleeve, and replaced it on the sideboard.

"Ward!" Putnam snapped.

The hapless footman started and knocked a spoon to the floor.

"Her ladyship is awaiting her breakfast!" Putnam roared. "Pray go to the kitchen and bring up the food!"

"Yes, sir."

Ward raced out of the breakfast parlor, kicking the spoon in the air as he went, and the butler winced as it bounced off the rear wall.

"I fear Ward is not working out," he said politely, crossing the room again and placing Susanna's coffee cup expertly, *exactly*, at her right hand.

"No, I fear not."

Susanna busily stirred her coffee. Putnam had not wished to engage the young footman in the first place, but she had been charmed by his gap-toothed smile, which inevitably reminded her of Ned's . . . Her own spoon clattered into the cup, and she hastily retrieved it.

"Perhaps . . ."

She had been at the point of suggesting that they assign Ward to some other task, but her voice trailed off. During the few weeks of his employment, Ward had been assigned to every conceivable task already and had demonstrated a remarkably consistent lack of competence. When asked to deliver two messages on the same morning, he had somehow mixed them up; and when appointed to accompany Lady Langham on her errands, he had wandered away while she was browsing in a bookstore. He had dropped Alicia's trunk as he carried it up the staircase (though, fortunately, no damage had been done), and he could not set a sideboard without strewing silverware around the room.

"Perhaps he will have to be discharged," Susanna finished lamely.

"My conclusion precisely."

Putnam nodded his agreement, and, as if to seal his fate, Ward strode back through the entry and tripped on the edge of the rug. Susanna held her breath as he staggered ahead to the sideboard, and drew a sigh of relief when he crashed the heavy tray he bore safely on its surface. He unloaded the tray with a frightful clatter, then rushed out of the room again, stumbling over the little hump he had previously created in the carpet.

"Yes," Putnam said with a sigh of his own, "he will definitely have to be discharged." He marched to the sideboard and returned to the table with a bread plate, which he deposited at Susanna's left. "I shall speak to him, of course. I shouldn't want you to be teasing yourself about the staff in the midst of your many other trials."

Trials? Susanna peered sharply up at him, but he was already speeding back to the sideboard. Nancy maintained that all servants were incorrigible spies, but Susanna had never caught Putnam on the listen for her private conversations.

"Trials?" she echoed aloud. "What trials are those, Putnam?"

"I was referring to your many responsibilities, ma'am." He began once more to cross the room, carrying a basket of bread in one hand and a dish of butter in the other. "Your salons, for one thing, and I couldn't help noticing that Lord Byron didn't come last Thursday."

He had reached the table, and he set the butter dish just beside Susanna's bread plate. "And then, bringing your sister out and all . . ." He stopped and straightened. "Well, if you'll pardon me for saying so, you do look tired, and I hope you'll rest a bit easier tonight."

Putnam was as interested in her activities as Polly was, Susanna reflected wryly, but years of experience had endowed him with vastly more patience. More patience and far more subtlety: his brown eyes were fairly brimming with solicitude. She was momentarily inclined to postpone her announcement of Ned's arrival, but she judged it quite possible that the butler had seen—or sensed the presence of—a stranger in the bedchamber adjoining hers. And if he had not, it would grow no easier to tell him as the hours passed.

"A muffin, ma'am?"

Putnam's question was academic; she always ate a muffin before he served the eggs and meat. He seized the silver tongs in the bread basket, deftly plunged them between the scones and the toast, extracted a steaming bilberry muffin, and lowered it toward her plate.

"Thank you for your concern, Putnam," she muttered. "The fact is that I had a rather . . ." She had started to say "distressing," and she bit her lip. "I had a rather startling experience last night. My husband returned from America."

The tongs sprang open, and the muffin fell to Susanna's plate, bounced off, and rolled along the table, leaving a trail of purplish crumbs in its wake. She had frequently suspected that her servants thought Lord Langham a myth, created for who-knew-what devious purpose; and Putnam's eyes, now wide with astonishment, tended to confirm this theory.

"But that . . . that is wonderful, ma'am!" the butler stammered. Though he had recovered himself sufficiently to speak, he committed the unprecedented sin of capturing the wayward muffin with his bare fingers and replacing it on Susanna's plate. "I daresay you were quite . . . quite surprised."

"Oh, I was very surprised indeed," she concurred grimly. "At any rate, his lordship is occupying the bedchamber next to mine."

"Of course, ma'am."

Putnam's tone was one of expressionless courtesy, but she fancied she detected a twitch at the corners of his mouth. Her cheeks warmed, and she viciously cut the wounded muffin in half.

"And I should appreciate it if you would inform the rest of the staff that he is here," she concluded in a mumble.

"Yes, ma'am!"

The prospect of circulating such a delicious *on-dit* evidently rendered Putnam insensible with ecstasy, for he galloped to the sideboard without a further glance at the crumbs on the tablecloth. He smashed the bread basket down in the middle of the bacon platter and dashed toward the dining room, but duty caught him up just as he reached the threshold.

"He'll be needing a valet then," he said breathlessly, spinning back to face the table. "Lord Langham, I mean. Shall I place an advertisement in the newspapers or inquire round the neighborhood?"

A valet for Ned. Susanna had failed to consider this aspect of their brief, artificial reunion, and she knit her brows. She had always been exceedingly reluctant to dismiss a servant (Nancy judged her much too weak in that respect), and she could scarcely bear the notion of engaging a man with the specific intention of discharging him in a few months' time. As she pondered, Ward panted back into the breakfast parlor with the remainder of the meal, and she idly watched his progress. He traversed the room without incident and unloaded the tray with only an occasional rattle, but even as she heaved another sigh of relief in his behalf, he dropped a serving spoon into the porridge bowl. He gamely retrieved the spoon and—globules of porridge clinging to his shirt cuff and dripping on the carpet—bore it out of the room.

"Well, what is it to be, ma'am?" Putnam's voice was uncharacteristically sharp, and when Susanna transferred her eyes to him, she found him tapping one foot with impatience. "Do you wish me to publish a notice or seek a valet by word of mouth?"

There was a great clatter in the rear corridor, and Susanna surmised that Ward had now dropped the tray. Yes, he would either have to be dismissed or . . . She suddenly perceived an excellent solution to her dilemma.

"We shall appoint Ward to serve as his lordship's valet," she said.

"Ward?" The butler's eyebrows rose to the fringes of his hair. "Begging your pardon, ma'am, but Lord Langham will be most displeased—"

"Lord Langham will abide by my decision," she snapped. "Pray see to it, Putnam."

"Yes, ma'am."

He bowed—albeit with visible doubt—whirled around again, and hurried on into the dining room. In fact, Susanna belatedly noted, he was in such a rush that he had neglected to serve her, and she rose and went to the sideboard herself. She filled a plate with her customary hearty breakfast and carried it back to the table, but every morsel of food she swallowed seemed more tasteless than the last. Her humor was such that she grouchily searched for lumps in the porridge and traces of excess milk in the scrambled eggs, but at length, she owned that her loss of appetite was not attributable to Mrs. Putnam's cooking. She shoved the plate away and sipped at her coffee, which—as if to heap insult upon injury—had grown lukewarm.

"Humph!"

Nancy's inimitable sniff was accompanied by a slight rustle at the breakfast-parlor entry, and Susanna started and glanced up.

"No one answered my ring," Lady Hadleigh reported with another sniff. "But I was certain you'd be awake and would not object if I admitted myself."

Whether Susanna objected or not was clearly immaterial: Nancy bounded across the room, removed her bonnet and gloves, then peered about for a servant to whisk them conveniently away.

"The staff are otherwise occupied," Susanna murmured. "Just set your things down and serve yourself."

"Very well." Lady Hadleigh laid her hat and gloves on the table, scowling with disapproval at the muffin crumbs. "However, if you'll forgive me for saying so, you allow your servants far too much independence." She stalked to the sideboard. "Putnam was *otherwise occupied* the last time I called as well." She poured a cup of coffee. "And today you've been left to fend quite for yourself." She stepped along the sideboard. "Left with no one at all to attend you and . . . And the bread basket is sitting on top of the bacon platter!"

She should have moved the basket, Susanna chided herself, but she was peculiarly lacking in energy this morning. Nancy marched back to the table, and Susanna observed that she, too, had taken her customary breakfast: a single scone. Well, Susanna amended, this was Lady Hadleigh's *initial* breakfast; eventually she would sample the muffins and toast and perhaps have another scone or two. Not all at once, for Nancy was perennially trying to lose weight. She consequently consumed her food bit by tiny bit—a quarter of a muffin here, half a slice of toast there—and lamented, with genuine puzzlement, her failure to grow thinner. How could she remain so strapping when she ate only *one scone* for breakfast?

"But I promised not to interfere," Lady Hadleigh said, sinking into the chair at Susanna's right, "and I shan't utter a further word on the subject." She broke her scone in two and gulped down one of the halves. "Except to warn you that if you do not take matters in hand, your household will shortly be in total disarray."

She finished the scone and glowered at the sideboard. "If it is not already," she added darkly. "However, as I indicated, I have no wish to interfere in your affairs. I merely wanted to know the outcome of your conversation with Percy last evening."

Was it only last evening? Susanna marveled. So much

had happened in the ensuing hours that it seemed she had spoken with Colonel Fordyce weeks before.

"Did he understand that your annulment must be delayed till Alicia is married?" Nancy pressed.

"Yes," Susanna muttered.

"And did he agree to conduct himself discreetly in the interim?"

"Oh, yes. Yes, he even suggested we avoid any private meetings so long as Alicia and Lady Calthrop are in town."

"Did I not tell you?" Lady Hadleigh said triumphantly. "Did I not say you could rely on Percy's complete cooperation? Yes"—she answered her own rhetorical questions—"I assured you everything would work out, and it has, has it not?"

Susanna peered studiedly into her coffee cup. She was once more tempted to postpone the inevitable, to agree that everything had indeed worked out and send Nancy on her way. But the servants of the *ton* maintained a notoriously efficient grapevine, and Susanna counted it likely that word of Lord Langham's arrival would reach Bruton Street well before Lady Hadleigh herself. And Nancy would be justifiably wounded if she were left to learn the news from her butler or her abigail . . . Susanna looked up and found Lady Hadleigh gazing longingly at the bread basket on the sideboard.

"Everything did not quite work out," she said. "Immediately after Percy left, Ned rang the doorbell."

"Ned." Nancy's eyes flickered idly away from the sideboard, started to drift back, then bulged with shocked enlightenment. "*Ned?*" she gasped, her mouth falling open. "*Your husband?*"

"Yes, my husband," Susanna confirmed dryly. "As I said, he just . . . just rang the bell—"

"But that is marvelous!"

Nancy's words were a paraphrase of Putnam's, and Susanna dismally wondered how many times she would be compelled to hear the same empty sentiment in the months to come.

"Not marvelous for Percy, of course," Lady Hadleigh went on, "but I shall make it a point to introduce him to all the eligible women I know. In the circumstances, he'll soon accept his loss . . ."

She stopped, and her green eyes narrowed. "If you'll forgive me for saying so"—this was one of Nancy's favorite phrases—"you do not appear particularly happy about it. About Ned's return, that is. Not at all like a woman who has recently enjoyed a . . ." She paused again. "Shall we say a *warm reunion* with the man she loves?"

The provocative arch of Lady Hadleigh's brows rendered her meaning unmistakably clear, and Susanna strove to quell another blush.

"No, there was no . . . no warm reunion." Her voice had once more degenerated to a mumble. "Ned reached the house at an extremely awkward moment . . ." She related the sequence of events, Nancy clucking with dismay at all the appropriate points in the story.

"In the end, he consented to affect a reconciliation until Alicia is wed," Susanna concluded. "We shall then seek an annulment or a divorce, and I shall marry Percy." She attempted to summon a bright smile, but her mouth was inexplicably quivering.

"And there is no hope of a true reconciliation?" Lady Hadleigh asked.

"None," Susanna said firmly.

"You no longer love him?"

Susanna felt a prickle of annoyance. Love Ned? Had Nancy not been listening? "How could I love him?" she demanded aloud. "His behavior was wholly thoroughly odious."

She was interrupted by a tap of footfalls in the dining room, and as she turned her head in that direction, Ned loomed up in the breakfast-parlor entry. His shirt-points and neckcloth had not survived the night, she observed—the former were wilting over the collar of his waistcoat, the latter spilling limply down the front of his shirt—and there was a stubble of blond beard on his cheeks and chin and above his upper lip. But he was prodigious well-looking nonetheless, infinitely handsomer than the immaculate aristocrats who attended her salons; and, perversely, his good appearance fueled Susanna's irritation.

"You are up early," she snapped. In the months they had lived together, Ned had rarely bestirred himself before noon.

"To the contrary, I am up quite late. I rose at dawn in Louisiana, and my body does not yet realize that dawn in England presently comes in the middle of the night. I woke at first light and fell back to sleep, but my valet kindly knocked me up to inquire whether I needed his services. A most conscientious lad." He sketched a sardonic smile. "Warren, is it? Warfield? He was chattering so that I didn't catch his name."

"Ward," Susanna muttered.

"Ward. At any rate, I desired him to press my neckcloth, but as he seemed utterly baffled by such an unusual request, I elected to let it pass."

He flashed another caustic grin, then shifted his eyes across the table. "Good morning," he said politely. "In the remote event you have not been informed of my identity, I am the Earl of Langham."

"And I am the Countess of Hadleigh," Nancy cooed.

Susanna had altogether forgotten Lady Hadleigh, and when she spun her head again, she saw—to her further keen annoyance—that Nancy was regarding the earl with undisguised admiration.

"And I am delighted to meet you at last," her ladyship continued in the same silky tone. "I am Susanna's closest friend, and she has mentioned you often during the course of our acquaintance."

"A singular honor." The earl strode around the foot of the table. "To be Susanna's closest friend, I mean. Inasmuch as she formed so many *close friendships* in my absence."

"What a lovely compliment," Nancy gushed.

Evidently she had failed to register Ned's sarcasm, and Susanna cast her an incredulous scowl. But her effort was wasted, for Lady Hadleigh's eyes were following the earl as he proceeded to the sideboard.

"If it would not pose too much trouble"—Nancy twisted round in her chair—"could you bring me half a muffin? Only a half, Lord Langham; I generally have just a single scone for breakfast."

She punctuated this revelation with a coy giggle, and Susanna shot her another quelling, gratuitous glare.

At length, Ned turned away from the sideboard, crossed the room, gallantly set exactly half a muffin on Lady Hadleigh's plate, stepped behind Susanna, and took the place at her left. His own plate was quite heaped with food—so crowded that the kidney was well in the way of slipping over the edge—and she watched with ever-mounting vexation as he began to eat. He employed all the restraint of a starving wolf, she noted furiously; their disastrous reunion had not diminished *his* appetite a whit.

"You must tell me about Louisiana, Lord Langham," Nancy chirped. She had finished the muffin, but even as she pushed her plate away, a stray bilberry rolled from the rim to the middle. Before this last juicy morsel could escape, she snatched it up and popped it into her mouth. "I daresay it is a fascinating place."

"It would be more accurate to say that the United States is a fascinating country." Ned choked down a rasher of bacon. "A very large country to begin with, and a substantial portion of the land remains unsettled. My journey from Savannah to New Orleans required almost a month, much of it through virtual wilderness. So you can imagine my joy when I reached New Orleans and found a thriving, sophisticated city—"

"I doubt Nancy wished to know every detail of your life these three years past," Susanna interjected sharply.

"No? Then I shan't bore *Nancy* any further." He returned his attention to his plate, but it had been picked nearly bare by now, and a final enormous forkful served to clean it altogether. "And I must retrieve my luggage in any case." He drained his coffee and replaced the cup in the saucer.

"You can't carry your bags all the way from Charles Street." Susanna was mumbling again, but she attributed this to the circumstance that her lips were fairly paralyzed with aggravation. "I shall order out the carriage."

"I shouldn't *dream* of putting you to such inconvenience. No, I shall walk to Dickie's and prevail on him to drive me back. He'll be eager to show off his new curricle; he could talk of little else last night. But I don't want to bore you on that head either." He tossed his napkin on the table and rose. "It was a pleasure to make your acquaintance, Lady Hadleigh. I hope to encounter you again in the near future."

"And so you will," Nancy said brightly. "At Susanna's soiree tomorrow evening."

Susanna opened her mouth to protest, but the words died in her throat. Of course Ned would have to attend her soiree; they could hardly create the impression of a happy marriage if he was banned from his wife's celebrated salons. She closed her mouth and swallowed another surge of exasperation.

"Sooner than my *fondest* hope." Ned's tone was so cloying that Susanna inspected his lips for telltale traces of sugar. "Until tomorrow evening then. Good day, Lady Hadleigh. Susanna."

He swept a deep bow, straightened, and at that moment, Alicia hurtled into the breakfast parlor and literally leapt upon his back.

"Ned!" she squealed. "Putnam told Polly you'd come back, and Polly told me, but I scarcely dared believe it!"

Alicia—who was far from being light in the first place —had attacked the earl without warning, and Susanna watched with alarm as he fought to regain his balance. Not alarm on Ned's account: she would not have spared a moment's regret had he fallen and broken several critical bones. But she was genuinely fond of her sister, and she drew a sigh of relief when Ned found his footing, ducked out of Alicia's embrace, and whirled around.

"Alicia, my dear girl! Though you're not a girl any longer, are you? All grown up and shortly to be wed ... But Susanna did not advise me how very handsome you've become! It's fortunate for Hugh that he won your heart before you could beguile every buck in Britain."

"Oh, Ned." Alicia's giggle was remarkably similar to Lady Hadleigh's. "You're the one who's handsomer. The climate of Louisiana must be most agreeable."

"In truth, the climate is Louisiana's *least* agreeable feature. The weather is far too warm for an Englishman, but one grows accustomed to it ..."

He rattled on—Alicia gazing raptly up at him, Nancy smiling across the table—and Susanna's vision began to blur with rage. An uninformed witness to the scene might well infer that Ned had returned from a brief holiday excursion. A hunting trip to Scotland perhaps: *Did you encounter much rain, Lord Langham? Did you bag your share of game?* The observer would never guess that the earl had abandoned his wife for years on end ...

"You have not yet greeted our guest, Alicia," she interposed shrilly. "You do remember Lady Hadleigh, I trust? You were introduced when you and Papa came to town last fall."

"Umm?" Alicia absently transferred her eyes to Nancy. "Ah, yes, Lady Hadleigh. I'm pleased to see you again."

"Sit down and have your breakfast now," Susanna said. "Ned was just leaving," she added pointedly as Alicia's eyes stole back toward the earl.

"So was I!" Alicia clapped her hands, and Susanna belatedly noticed that she was wearing gloves and a small Parisian bonnet. "Lady Calthrop invited me to breakfast with them in Berkeley Street. Perhaps we could walk together, Ned, if you're going in the same direction."

"Indeed I am, and I shall escort you to Lady Calthrop's before I proceed to Dickie's."

Susanna bit back another protest. Alicia had always

adored her brother-in-law, and that circumstance—however irritating—would no doubt reinforce the myth of Ned and Susanna's blissful reconciliation.

"Very well," she agreed grudgingly. "But don't go in to speak to them, Ned. To the Dickinsons, I mean. Let Alicia inform them of your . . . your dramatic resurrection."

"As you will." He inclined his head so pleasantly that the fictional observer would altogether miss the ironic quirk of his brows. "My very last wish is to embarrass you in any way."

He offered Alicia his arm with great mock gravity—the witness would also fail to detect that the mockery was real—but Alicia hesitated.

"If you would not mind," she said, looking directly at Susanna for the first time, "I should like to invite Hugh to your salon."

"No, I shouldn't mind." In fact, Hugh could serve as Alicia's supper partner. "However, I fear Lady Calthrop does not approve of my soirees. She made it clear that I was not to expose Hugh to Byron and his kind."

"But how could she object to Tom Moore?" Nancy said. "He entertains at all the best parties."

This was true; the engaging young Irishman was asked to sing his original compositions in London's finest drawing rooms. His social prominence was primarily due to his friendship with Lord Byron, but Susanna judged it possible—indeed, likely—that Lady Calthrop was unaware of the connection.

"Very well," she repeated. "You may invite Hugh to come tomorrow evening."

"Then perhaps I might invite a friend as well."

His phraseology notwithstanding, Ned's words were a statement rather than a request, and Susanna inwardly bristled. She had forgotten that her wayward husband would be attending the salon. Hugh now represented an extra man, and if Viscount Buckley came, she would have *two* extra men. But she fancied Alicia would count it most suspicious if she declined to grant such a modest favor, and she reluctantly bobbed her own head.

"Yes," she muttered. "Yes, that will be all right."

"Then I shall once more bid you good day. Are you ready, Alicia?"

"Oh, yes."

She took the earl's arm, and even as they stepped into the dining room, he resumed his interrupted discourse.

"I was mentioning that in addition to the oppressive heat, Louisiana is infested by mosquitoes . . ."

Louisiana again. Susanna was monstrous tired of hearing about it, and she determinedly closed her ears until the slam of the front door cut off Ned's voice.

"Well!" Nancy had a unique ability to inject a whole world of meaning into a single syllable. "I must own myself surprised. I believe Alicia was right to say that your husband has grown handsomer over the years. He's certainly handsomer than his portrait, is he not? And I found him quite charming."

"So I collected," Susanna snapped, "and I am equally surprised by your reaction."

She paused, waiting for Lady Hadleigh to display some small sign of remorse, but Nancy was still gazing in Ned's wake.

"Surprised and distressed," Susanna continued. "I can understand why he was able to deceive Alicia; she's young and impressionable, and she's worshiped Ned from the moment they met. But you should know better. I told you how he behaved last night."

"Perhaps that is understandable as well. He did see you with Percy."

"You sound as though you are taking his part," Susanna said stiffly.

"I am taking no one's part." Lady Hadleigh looked away from the entry at last. "I merely wonder whether you acted prematurely. By concluding within the space of a few minutes that your marriage could not be salvaged."

"That bears the palm, Nancy! You were counseling me not a week ago to have my marriage dissolved and wed Percy."

"So I was." Lady Hadleigh nodded. "But that was before—"

"Before you met Ned and succumbed to his wiles. As I did when I first met him. I assure you he wasn't half so charming last evening . . ." Susanna had begun to tremble with anger, and she clenched her hands to stop their shaking. "But I shan't argue the matter any longer; my mind is made up. I shall endure this absurd reunion as long as I must, and then I shall marry Percy. And if you elect not to support my decision—"

"Of course I shall support you!" Nancy soothingly patted Susanna's knotted hands. "If you still wish to wed Percy, I shall assist you as much as I can." She frowned. "I only hope he will not be so intimidated as to abandon his suit."

"Intimidated?" Susanna echoed. "Why should Percy be intimidated?"

"My dear Susanna." Lady Hadleigh shook her head. "Put your prejudices aside a moment and try to view the situation through Percy's eyes. Ned is marvelously well-looking, a dashing adventurer . . ." She stopped, apparently registering Susanna's latest glower. "And he is, above all, your legal husband. Even should you succeed in persuading Percy that the reconciliation is temporary, he will judge himself on very precarious ground."

"Not when I explain the . . . the conditions of the reconciliation." Susanna's face flamed with embarrassment at the prospect. "That it is a reunion in name alone, I mean."

"That might work," Nancy conceded. "If you speak to Percy without delay. You must inform him of Ned's return before he learns the news from one of his servants." She flung her napkin on the table and sprang to her feet. "My carriage is outside; I am on my way to meet Lord Illingworth in Hampstead. Fetch a hat and gloves, and I shall drop you at Percy's en route."

"No!" Susanna screeched.

"You needn't raise your voice." Lady Hadleigh indignantly snatched her own hat off the table. "I was not interfering; I was merely attempting to be of help."

"I am sorry," Susanna said contritely. "Percy should certainly be advised of Ned's arrival, but . . ."

But she was too tired, too overwrought, to undertake such a difficult conversation with no prior planning. She stared at her hands, still clenched on the tablecloth, and conceived a wonderful idea. A solution to her problem, a sop to Nancy's wounded vanity . . . She looked eagerly up.

"But you could be of considerable help if you would speak to Percy in my behalf."

"Speak to him about what?" Lady Hadleigh had tied her bonnet ribbons, and she irritably retrieved her gloves. "I promised to aid you, but my assistance has its limits. Do not expect me to tell Percy that you have banished your husband from your bed."

"No, I shouldn't expect that." Susanna detected the onset of another flush, and she unclasped her hands and discreetly fanned her face. "Just stop at Percy's, tell him Ned has come back, and assure him that nothing has changed between us. Between Percy and me, that is. Add that I shall explain the details when I see him tomorrow night."

"Very well."

Nancy's expression softened a bit, and as if to reward herself for her nobility, she stepped to the sideboard. She tore a slice of toast in quarters, devoured three of the resulting pieces, then turned around.

"I shall assist you as much as I can," she repeated, brushing a few stray crumbs from her mouth. "However, as your dearest friend, I should hold myself remiss did I not warn you that you are embarking on an excessively difficult course. You will be hard pressed to keep Percy's suit alive while simultaneously convincing the rest of the world that you and Ned are happily married."

She licked a final crumb from her lower lip, swallowed it, sailed out of the breakfast parlor, but her warning echoed ominously behind her. Warning or prediction? Susanna wondered as the front door slammed again. She could not but fear that her and Ned's charade—however brief—would prove excessively difficult indeed.

Chapter 6

SUSANNA'S WAS NOT the first or only salon in London, and—rather immodestly, she owned—she attributed her prodigious success to the fact that she personally planned and supervised every detail of her soirees. She had devised an exacting schedule to ensure that nothing was overlooked, and on the following evening, in accordance with this schedule, she finished her toilette at precisely twenty-five past seven. The schedule allowed five minutes for Polly to make any final adjustments to her mistress's clothes, hair, et cetera, but tonight the abigail had been dismissed early to help Alicia dress.

Early but not a moment too soon, Susanna thought grouchily, for she could not have borne another second of Polly's chatter. Like a hundred—a thousand—women before her, Polly had fallen under Ned's spell, and she could talk of nothing else. She hadn't really got a proper look at the earl until this afternoon, and wasn't he just the *handsomest* man! So tall and lean and brown, and didn't Lady Langham love the way the sun had streaked his hair? And he was so *kind*! He had smiled at Polly and inquired her name and asked where she was from.

"From Herefordshire, I says, and he wants to know all about it. Like it was some grand, mysterious place, when you and I both know he's traveled halfway round the world."

That was another thing, the abigail continued, warming to her theme: his lordship was so *exciting*! Polly hadn't heard his adventures firsthand, of course, but Ward had repeated several tales that left the rest of the staff breathless with awe . . .

Susanna scowled into the cheval glass, then hastily cleared her face so as to check her appearance. Her cheeks seemed a trifle overbright, and she snatched a handkerchief from the dressing table to remove the excess rouge. But by the time she returned her eyes to the mirror, the color had begun to fade, and she realized she had merely been flushed with irritation. She studied her evening dress inch by inch—from the white crepe corsage to the black velvet vandykes around the bottom of the skirt—and judged everything to be in order. Well, almost everything; she picked a speck of lint from the white satin rouleau above the vandykes and smoothed a tiny wrinkle from the black crepe skirt. Yes, that was better. She pulled on her gloves and, as the mantel clock chimed half past seven, sped into the corridor.

The initial stop on Susanna's tour of the house was the drawing room, where it required only a glance to confirm that the sofas and chairs had been arranged in a rough circle. Her recollection was that Mr. Moore preferred to stand while he sang, but in the event she was mistaken, an armchair had been situated in the middle of the circle. She transferred her attention to the Chippendale side table beneath the window and found, per her standing instructions, that two trays of champagne glasses sat atop it, waiting to be filled.

There was really no need to inspect the music room and morning parlor across from the saloon, for the supper tables in both were laid by midafternoon, and Susanna herself set out the place cards just before she dressed. However, she always gave the rooms a final cursory look to be sure the floral centerpieces on the tables hadn't wilted since her previous visit. As the flowers tonight appeared in the very bloom of health, she hurried to the ground floor and down the rear stairs to the kitchen.

Susanna's schedule included a full ten minutes to deal with Mrs. Putnam, and it was a rare evening indeed when a single one of these minutes went unused. Like her husband, Mrs. Putnam seemed to have an eye in the back of her head; and whether she was working at the range or the oven, the dresser or the hot plate, she would spin around and embark upon her tirade the instant Susanna crossed the threshold. She had warned Lady Langham time and time again that she could not prepare a meal for two dozen people, the cook would begin with a martyred sigh. Not without assistance, and the scullery maids were hardly that; to the contrary, they tended to do more harm than good. She would punctuate this declaration with withering glares at Cassie and Connie, who tolerated her endless abuse because Susanna paid them twice the wages of any other scullery maid in Britain.

At any rate, Mrs. Putnam would continue, Lady Langham had elected to ignore her repeated warnings; and tonight, at last, her worst fears were coming to pass. Yes, tonight the supper was certain to be an unqualified disaster. The (Mrs. Putnam would name one of the specific dishes to be served) was (she would describe in detail the particular flaw she had detected). Susanna would listen to the cook's lament for approximately five minutes and then, in her most soothing voice, tender an optimistic interjection.

"Well, let us see. Maybe the" (roast beef/asparagus/ blancmange) "is not" (overdone/tough/watery) "after all." She would study or sample the suspect item and affect an expression of astonished relief. "You are far too critical of your efforts, Mrs. Putnam," she would chide gently. "I judge it quite satisfactory, and I am confident my guests will agree. But I do appreciate your concern."

With a smile designed to illustrate this heartfelt appreciation, Susanna would flee back up the stairs, but she was never quick enough to escape the cook's Revised Warning. They had only managed to postpone the inevitable, Mrs. Putnam would shriek, her words like the bark of a small but vicious dog nipping at Susanna's heels. They had been fortunate this evening, but Lady Langham could not indefinitely rely on good luck to compensate for her lack of a proper staff. Sooner or later—probably next week—the supper would be wholly unfit for human consumption . . .

Susanna stepped into the dining room, shaking her head with exasperation. Of all the servants she had ever employed, Mrs. Putnam was the only one she could have discharged without a twinge of regret. But if she dismissed the querulous cook, her husband would leave as well, and that would be a disaster indeed. She peered at the table and saw, as she had anticipated, that it was perfectly arranged: her mother's Sevres plates stacked at the head and an assortment of silver dishes and platters arrayed along either side. Yes, Putnam was indispensable, and—like the long-suffering scullery maids—Susanna must simply bear his difficult wife as best she could.

The hands of the long-case clock read seven minutes till eight as Susanna crossed the vestibule, and she had no doubt the first guests would arrive promptly at eight o'clock. In the beginning, grateful that anyone would condescend to attend her "little parties," she had instructed Putnam to admit all latecomers, however tardy they might be. She had maintained this policy until the memorable evening when Madame Catalani—interrupted in mid-aria by the noisy entrance of Scrope Davies, who was considerably the worse for drink—flew into a tantrum of truly historic proportions. Unable to launch a direct attack on Mr. Davies, who was protected by a solid line of furniture, the temperamental prima donna vented her wrath by seizing three champagne glasses from the fingers of three startled guests and hurling them, one by one, at the intruder's head. Whether fortunately or un-, these projectiles missed their target and crashed into the pier mirror behind Mr. Davies's left shoulder, reducing the glasses and the mirror as well to a heap of sparkling fragments.

Though Susanna thought Madame Catalani's reaction a trifle extreme, she recognized that the fiery soprano had raised a valid point. Lady Langham's salons were rapidly becoming the talk of London: those not yet privileged to attend were beginning to fish, none too subtly, for an invitation. So why should she continue to accommodate rude guests who fancied they could burst into her drawing room whenever they pleased? The doors of Almack's did not remain open all night.

When Susanna wrote the invitations to her next soiree, she added that, in deference to her guest of honor, no one would be admitted after eight-fifteen, and she had made no exception in the ensuing years. Indeed, the Duke of Clarence had once appeared at half past eight and been politely turned away. Nancy had sharply questioned the wisdom of offending the Regent's own brother, but his highness had never been late again.

Assured that her guests would be seated by eight-fifteen, Susanna was able to conduct her salons with nearly the same precision she employed in their planning. Between eight-fifteen and nine, the guest of honor entertained the rest of the party—a poet would recite his poems, an artist would demonstrate his technique, a political figure would deliver an address on a topic of current interest. Susanna had occasionally toyed with the notion of featuring two guests on the same evening: an actor or actress could present a reading, for example; and Mr. Hazlitt, the drama critic for the *Morning Chronicle*, could comment on the performance. But one honored guest was trouble enough, she would decide, remembering Madame Catalani, and it seemed foolish to alter the formula which had heretofore proved so successful.

The formal entertainment was followed by a discussion period, which Susanna strove to make as lively as possible. If necessary, she would initiate the discussion herself, and she always prepared a particularly provocative question to pose should her intervention be required. Normally, however, her guests—their tongues loosened by a bottomless supply of champagne—had ample inquiries and remarks of their own; and the conversation, eventually ranging far afield of the original subject, would become very lively indeed.

Normally, in fact, Susanna was hard pressed to

restore order and announce, at half past ten, that supper was served. She realized that many of her guests would be content to drink and argue into the small hours of the morning, but they could do that at any rout in town; and she believed it critically important to maintain a refined, cultured atmosphere. So she insisted that everyone go to the dining room "while the food is still hot," fill a plate, and repair to his or her assigned table.

Susanna stepped into the library, and for the first time during the course of her inspection, her eyes narrowed with disapproval. She generally placed two men and two women at each of the supper tables, but the unwelcome intrusion of Ned and Viscount Buckley had destroyed her pattern. After carefully deliberating the alternatives, she had instructed that one of the tables in the library be set for six, and it appeared most uncomfortably crowded. Nor was she entirely pleased with the seating arrangement. In accordance with her custom, she had put herself at the head of the table and situated the guest of honor, Mr. Moore, at her right. Then, in an effort to minimize the embarrassment of Lord Buckley's presence, she had placed him at her left and cast about for the proper person to seat beside him —a person who would not begin to nod after five minutes of exposure to his drivel.

At length, she selected Lady Rowe, who was even more sapskulled than the viscount, and put her ladyship's unfortunate husband, Sir Cecil, at the foot of the table. That left but one chair to be filled, and judging that it would be least disruptive to place both extra men at her own table, Susanna assigned it to General Mumford. But the retired general was rather cantankerous, she now recalled, and likely to lose his patience when Lord Buckley and Lady Rowe displayed their excessively limited wit.

So perhaps she should switch Lady Hadleigh with Lady Rowe. Nancy could charm a stone, and by the end of the evening, she would have General Mumford fairly eating from her hand. And she would probably get on with Lord Buckley as well. His intellectual deficiencies notwithstanding, the viscount was prodigious attractive, and Nancy was prepared to make almost any allowance for a sufficiently handsome man. As demonstrated by her recent response to Ned; Susanna scowled at the memory. Furthermore, Sir Cecil would no doubt be delighted by the opportunity to escape his wife for an hour or two—

"May I be of any assistance?"

Ned's words suggested that he had somehow divined her thoughts, and Susanna started and whirled around. The earl was lounging in the library doorway, one broad shoulder propped against the jamb.

"No, I fancy not. I observed in passing that everything appears in readiness for your guests. Including yourself, if I may say so." He drew himself up, and his silver eyes swept appraisingly from the crown of her white satin toque to the toes of her black kid slippers. "Yes, you look exceedingly well this evening."

"Thank you," she murmured. "You are also looking very well."

She had returned his compliment from force of habit; it was just the sort of empty repartee she was accustomed to exchanging with her guests. But he did look very well, she owned, conducting a discreet appraisal of her own: his white pantaloons and waistcoat and neckcloth contrasted dramatically with his sunburned skin, and the border of the waistcoat exactly matched his sapphire coat. The coat itself was longer and fuller than those currently worn in England . . . She sensed that he was watching her, and she raised her own eyes and essayed a cool smile.

"Though I fear the cut of your clothes will cause quite a stir. Since Napoleon's escape from Elba, there is scant tolerance for anything French. I hope your patriotism won't be called into question."

"Patriotism." Ned wryly shook his head. "I learned a bit about that when I was in Louisiana. I never could determine whom the native Creoles hated more—the Americans or the British. They were forced to side with America, of course: Louisiana had become a state, the

United States was at war with England, and England was at war with France. So I—"

"Never mind," Susanna interrupted testily. Was no subject too remote to inspire one of his interminable lectures about Louisiana? "You might, in fact, be of some assistance. I was pondering whether to place Nancy next to—"

She herself was interrupted by the peal of the doorbell, and she patted the curls below her toque and hurried into the entry hall. Another component of her success, or so she believed, was her habit of personally greeting her guests before Putnam or Blake—the first footman—escorted them to the saloon. She swiftly checked her gown again, assumed her brightest smile, threw the door open, and felt her jaws sag with shock.

Susanna had met Lady Thornton only once, and her confusion was such that she could not immediately recollect the occasion. She was certain it had been prior to her ladyship's marriage—she had been introduced as Miss Murray—but she had changed very little in the intervening years. She must be eight and twenty, Susanna calculated, but she was short and excessively slight, and her diminutive stature made her appear far younger than her age. Like Susanna, she was clad in a gown of black and white, and Susanna was inexplicably pleased to observe that this combination of colors did not suit Lady Thornton's pale brown hair and brown-gold eyes.

"Ned!" her ladyship said warmly.

Susanna had not detected the earl's approach, and she started again when she perceived that he was standing beside her.

"And Lady Langham," the viscountess continued, shifting her amber eyes to Susanna. "You can imagine how thrilled I was to be invited to one of your famous salons. I trust I did not arrive too early?" She peered anxiously at the foyer clock, which, as if on cue, began to chime the hour.

"No," Susanna muttered. She clenched her hands and became dismally aware that her palms were damp.

"No, you are precisely on time. Putnam will show you to the drawing room."

She nodded peremptorily at the butler—a haughty gesture she had never before employed with him or any other servant—but he did not notice her ill humor. Or was skilled enough to *pretend* not to notice: with a deep bow, he ushered Lady Thornton across the vestibule. They mounted the stairs, and when they had disappeared around the landing, Susanna whirled furiously on Ned.

"How dare you?" she hissed. Blake was stationed at the dining-room archway, awaiting the arrival of the next party; and with a cautious glance in his direction, she lowered her voice still further. "You asked if you could invite Viscount Buckley to my soiree—"

"I asked if I could invite a *friend*," he corrected. "Dickie advised me of Julia's situation on the night of my arrival, and I fanced she would be delighted to attend such a prestigious event."

"*She* would be delighted?" Susanna snapped. "What of *my* feelings?"

"An interesting question." Ned raised his pale brows. "I am at a loss to comprehend why you find her presence so distressing."

Susanna was equally puzzled on this head, and she snatched at the first explanation that came to mind. "I am distressed because Lady Thornton has overset my seating arrangment," she said stiffly. "I put Viscount Buckley at my left, or so I thought—"

"Then pray do not tease yourself about it a moment longer." Ned was whispering as well, but his words were edged with frost. "Julia and I shall dine elsewhere—"

"Do not be absurd!"

Susanna's voice had risen, and Blake—lacking Putnam's vast experience—emitted a nervous cough.

"Do not be absurd," she repeated, her voice sinking once more to a hiss. "It wouldn't do at all for you and Lady Thornton to leave." She had neglected to close the front door, and she saw General Mumford's distinctive barouche drawing to a halt in the street.

"Just go upstairs," she croaked. "Go to the saloon and entertain Lady Thornton until the rest of the guests arrive."

"As you will."

He swept a bow nearly as deep as Putnam's, and the tap of his footfalls had faded away by the time General Mumford reached the door.

As Susanna had expected, her guests were punctual to a fault—appearing in such rapid succession that Putnam and Blake could scarcely keep pace. But keep pace they did, and by ten past eight, everyone had been escorted to the drawing room. Everyone except Nancy and Percy, and Susanna frowned at the clock. Lady Hadleigh normally took the colonel up in her carriage (he could not yet afford an equipage of his own), and they were generally among the first to arrive. She gazed back at the door and saw, to her relief, that Nancy was bounding up the front steps.

"Sorry to be late," Lady Hadleigh panted.

Her exertions had wreaked considerable havoc on her clothes, and she ground to a halt and jerked up the emerald satin bodice of her gown, which had fallen perilously close to the point of indecency. Susanna peered past her and knit her brows again.

"Where is Percy?" she demanded.

"That is *why* I am late." Nancy began to adjust her headdress, which had slipped well over her left ear. "When I got to Percy's, he informed me he had decided not to come. He had debated the matter all day, he said, and concluded it would be most awkward if he were compelled to meet your husband in such public circumstances."

Her left earring had snagged in her toque, and with a wince, she tugged it free. "I tried to persuade him to change his mind, but he was adamant. He insisted he must speak with you before he meets Lord Langham, and he plans to call at ten tomorrow morning."

Susanna drew another small sigh of relief. It would, indeed, be best for her and Percy to speak privately before he was introduced to Ned, and the colonel's absence would additionally enable her to balance the seating arrangement. Putnam had repaired to the saloon to pour the champagne, but as soon as Mr. Moore's performance was underway, she would instruct the butler to put General Mumford in Percy's place. She could shift the cards at her own table while the guests were serving themselves to supper . . . The clock chimed a quarter past the hour, and she hastily closed the front door and beckoned Lady Hadleigh up the marble staircase.

The conversation in the drawing room had already assumed the proportions of a low roar, and Susanna paused at the threshold to survey the scene with satisfaction. Though none of her salons could be termed a failure, some were inevitably more successful than others, and this soiree promised to be particularly amusing. Nancy took the vacant chair beside Sir Cecil Rowe, and Susanna stepped forward, cleared her throat, and announced that it gave her great pleasure to present Mr. Tom Moore.

"You are very kind, Lady Langham." The young Irishman flashed his engaging grin. "However, I could not but overhear your husband mention that he has just returned from North America. I daresay the rest of your guests would be as fascinated as I if he would consent to relate a few of his adventures."

"The rest of my guests came to hear you sing, Mr. Moore," Susanna said sharply.

"They have heard me sing before, and I fear I have not improved."

His remark elicited an appreciative titter of laughter, and Susanna managed a tight smile.

"Since I am something of a foreigner myself," Mr. Moore went on, "I am especially curious to know how Lord Langham was able to get on in a nation at war with his own." He transferred his attention to the earl. "Did the Americans impose no restrictions on British citizens?"

"They did," Ned replied, "but I was not known to be a British citizen. Throughout my residence in Louisiana, I represented myself as an American."

"A clever ploy." Mr. Moore sketched another grin. "I wish I had thought to pose as an Englishman when I came over from Dublin. Though I fancy my accent would have betrayed me in an instant."

"I must admit that I had the advantage in that respect." Ned, clearly beginning to enjoy himself, thrust his long legs forward and laced his fingers over his ribs. "The majority of Louisiana's natives speak English as a foreign tongue, and they can't determine whether a man comes from Newcastle or New York. Or even from Dublin."

There was another burst of laughter, and Susanna forced another artificial smile.

"At any rate, by the time I reached New Orleans, there were rumors of impending warfare between the United States and England. I consequently judged it wisest to claim that I was a Virginian by birth and had come to seek my fortune in America's newest state."

"You may have judged it wise," General Mumford snapped, "but I am inclined to judge it the act of a traitor. Did you suffer no qualms of conscience when the fortunes of war turned against us? When there was a major battle at your very doorstep? I was well acquainted with General Packenham, who lost his life in the course of that engagement."

"I cannot suppose that my disguise in any way affected the outcome of the battle," Ned responded dryly. "I am not a soldier, sir. Had I been able to locate General Packenham so as to volunteer my services, I suspect he would have suggested that I could better aid the British cause by fighting on the American side."

The crowd roared with mirth at the earl's great wit—even General Mumford's lips twitched a bit around the edges—and Susanna ground her teeth.

"And General Jackson might well have taken me on," Ned continued, "for his army was little more than a rabble. You are no doubt aware that *his* volunteers included a band of pirates."

"Who," General Mumford growled, "unfortunately acquitted themselves quite admirably."

"Pirates!" Lady Thornton shivered with delicious horror and sympathetically patted the earl's sleeve. "It was excessively brave of you to settle in such an uncivilized place."

She shuddered again, and Susanna noted that she was astonishingly buxom for a woman of her size. One more quiver was likely to spill her generous bosom from the plunging corsage of her gown.

"In point of fact, New Orleans is far more civilized than the majority of American cities," Ned said. "The pirates kept to their colony in the swamp and posed no danger to the local inhabitants. Indeed, at the risk of disappointing you, I am obliged to confess that I never met Monsieur Lafitte or any of his men."

"That was immensely interesting," Susanna said shrilly. "And now my dear husband has recounted his adventures, perhaps we can proceed with the scheduled entertainment—"

"Which is not to imply that New Orleans is like a *European* city," the earl went on. "I trust you can conceive my reaction the first time I visited the central market and encountered dozens of Indians."

There was a universal gasp of shock, and several of the female guests began to fan themselves.

"Yes, that was exactly my reaction." Ned nodded, and the shock dissolved in another round of chuckles. "However, I soon learned that the Indians are quite harmless. As are the blacks, who far outnumber the Indians. Though many of the blacks do practice a rather alarming form of religion."

"They are noncomformists, you mean?" Lady Rowe said.

Mr. Moore choked on his champagne, but the earl somehow succeeded in keeping his countenance.

"No, the religion I refer to—known as voodoo— more nearly resembles witchcraft. The adherents of voodoo profess to cast spells by the use of various charms, which they call gris-gris. The charms may be good or evil, but the Creoles tend to remember only the evil ones. They all claim to have known someone who was struck dead shortly after finding a gris-gris under his pillow."

"How ridiculous!" General Mumford snorted. "Surely *you* do not subscribe to such nonsense."

"I maintain an open mind, sir," Ned said solemnly. "As you can see for yourself, I was not personally struck dead, but neither was I cursed with a gris-gris."

"That was very interesting indeed," Susanna screeched, raising her voice above still another ripple of laughter. "And now I fancy we are all ready to hear Mr. Moore . . ."

Her words were drowned in a flurry of questions about the fatal voodoo curses, and she closed her mouth and bit her lip with frustration. She had never lost control of any of her previous salons (she had even been able to effect an uneasy truce between Madame Catalani and Mr. Davies), but she sensed that further protest would be futile. Useless and embarrassing as well, and she sank into the empty chair in front of the entry and pretended to listen to the earl's discourse. In fact, she did catch portions of his commentary—remarks concerning the peculiar architecture of New Orleans and its eerie aboveground cemeteries—but at length, her eyes drifted to the portrait above the mantel. Ned had mentioned that one of the most dreaded voodoo spells utilized a small, crude likeness of the victim, which was subjected to all manner of frightful punishment; and she wondered if one could simply *wish* harm on the painted image of one's enemy. She was still attempting to strike Ned dumb when Putnam came to remind her that it was time to summon the guests to supper.

Susanna was reasonably confident that nothing else could go amiss, but when she reached the library, she remembered that she had failed to rearrange the seating. Percy's place in the music room was empty, and, worse yet, Susanna would be compelled to sit beside Lady Thornton, whom Ned had evidently directed to Viscount Buckley's chair. But it was too late to rectify the situation, and she slipped into her own chair and smiled apologetically at Mr. Moore.

"I regret that the evening went so badly," she whispered. "I am sure you would not have invited my husband to speak had you known he would rattle on and on, boring everyone to the point of tears—"

"Boring?" Mr. Moore interposed. Apparently he perceived no need to whisper, for his rich, deep baritone brought the rest of the table to silence. "To the contrary, I found Lord Langham's narrative most enlightening."

"And highly entertaining," General Mumford added. "His scruples are a trifle loose to suit my taste, but he's a damned amusing fellow."

"Let us not criticize his scruples too harshly," Mr. Moore chided. "He was in a monstrous difficult position . . ."

They chattered on in this vein until it began to sound as though the Earl of Langham might well be a candidate for sainthood. At one juncture, Susanna stole a glance at Lady Thornton, wondering if the woman Ned had jilted was as vexed by the conversation as Susanna herself. Apparently not; her ladyship's face was wreathed in a happy smile, and she was bobbing her head—and her ample bosom—in agreement.

At last, the long-case clock chimed midnight, and Susanna flung her napkin on the table and leapt to her feet. Though her soirees were officially scheduled to end at twelve, she always permitted the discussion to continue another hour or so, but she could not bear to hear a further word about her fascinating husband and his remarkable adventures. She sped into the vestibule, looking Putnam a pointed signal; and as her startled guests rose to follow in her wake, the butler raced up the stairs. By the time Susanna had showed her supper companions out, the remaining guests were descending the staircase, Ned in the lead. He was still talking, she observed, casting a few final witticisms over his shoulder . . . He strode across the foyer and stopped on the opposite side of the door, from which post he proceeded to bid his numerous new friends a cheerful goodnight.

"Well!" he said as Susanna slammed the door closed. "I must own myself impressed. Your salons quite deserve their splendid reputation."

"This was not in the least typical of my salons," Susanna choked. She was literally trembling with rage, shaking so violently that she was hard put to turn around. "My salons *repute* to feature the most talented people in England, who consent to appear because they can be assured of an influential and attentive audience. They *did* consent to appear, I should have said. When word of Mr. Moore's shameful treatment gets about, I doubt I shall be able to engage a Gypsy fortune-teller."

"Shameful treatment?" Ned echoed. "It was Mr. Moore who proposed I speak in the first place."

"Little guessing you would never yield the floor," Susanna snapped.

"Had he demonstrated any desire to reclaim the floor, I should have yielded to him at once. As it was, he seemed as eager as everyone else to learn about Louisiana—"

"Louisiana!"

Susanna's voice rose to a furious shriek, and Putnam, who had just reached the landing, spun about and scurried back out of sight.

"I am sick to death of Louisiana!" She no longer cared whether Putnam or any of the other servants might be on the listen. "You have talked of nothing else since the moment of your return. Indeed, I wonder—since you found it so enthralling—why you troubled yourself to return at all."

"A most perceptive observation," the earl said frigidly. "I am beginning to wonder precisely the same thing."

He executed a mocking bow, whirled around, and stalked up the staircase, and Susanna passionately wished he *had* been felled by a voodoo curse.

Chapter 7

COLONEL FORDYCE'S long years of military service had rendered him punctual in the extreme, and Susanna had no doubt he would appear promptly at ten the following morning. As she normally woke at half past eight, she calculated she would have ample time to dress and breakfast before he arrived; and when the mantel clock chimed twice, she rose, walked leisurely to the wardrobe, and extracted her lavender morning dress. She laid the gown over the footboard, sauntered toward the bell-pull beside the fireplace, and observed—to her horror—that the hands of the clock had crept beyond half past *nine*. Which was not really surprising in view of the fact that her life had been far from "normal" since Ned's disastrous return.

Susanna scowled at the connecting door, then realized she was wasting precious seconds. Percy had no patience for tardiness, and he was unlikely to accept the explanation that her husband had indirectly caused her to oversleep. Well, perhaps he would *accept* it, but such an excuse invited the most awful misinterpretation . . .

Susanna flushed and glanced again at the bellpull, but she fancied it would be faster—and infinitely more peaceful—to dress without Polly's assistance. She stripped off her nightgown, hastily donned her clothes and brushed her hair, and reached the vestibule just as Putnam was admitting Percy at the front door.

"I shall see if Lady Langham is awake," the butler was saying. "The salon last evening was a most exciting one. It's a pity you were compelled to miss it, sir. Lord

Langham quite captivated the party with his tales of Louisiana—"

"Thank you, Putnam," Susanna interposed sharply, stepping on across the foyer. "Colonel Fordyce and I shall speak in the library. Pray be certain we are not disturbed."

"Yes, ma'am."

The butler closed the door and trotted away, and Susanna led Percy silently to the library. As had happened on the occasion of their previous conversation, she suddenly found herself at a loss for words, and she could hardly offer him a glass of brandy at this early hour. She eyed the bellpull, wondering if she should summon Putnam back and desire him to serve them coffee. Coffee would be a welcome diversion and might, additionally, clear her mind—

"If my visit is inconvenient," Percy said stiffly, "I shall leave at once."

"No!" Susanna spun around. "No, please . . . please sit down."

"Very well, but I shan't stay long." As if to prove his intentions, the colonel perched on the edge of a shield-back chair and set his beaver hat on his knees. "I remember my promise not to call until your sister's situation was resolved. However, I trust you will agree that the circumstances have changed since then."

"Oh, yes!" Susanna herself was too nervous to sit, and she beamed reassuringly down at him. "Yes, we needed to speak in private, and we shouldn't have had a moment alone at my soiree. It was quite . . . quite hectic."

"And quite exciting." Percy sketched a bleak smile.

"Putnam is inclined to exaggerate," Susanna said soothingly. "He takes great personal pride in my salons."

"Then he will be immensely proud to learn that your latest salon is the *on-dit* of London," Percy snapped. "I heard of the proceedings from my valet long before I talked with Putnam, and I collect that half the town is busily casting voodoo spells. Indeed, Turner—my valet

—is hoping to lay a curse on Lord Whitworth's first footman. Who, as I understand it, is Turner's rival for the affections of Lady Rowe's abigail."

Susanna could not repress an hysterical giggle. "It will not work," she sputtered, recalling her fruitless glares at Ned's portrait.

"I beg your pardon?" The colonel peered sharply up at her.

"I mean that Turner and everyone else are being prodigious foolish," she amended, quelling her mirth. "Naturally, there was some interest in Ned's outlandish stories—"

"More than some." Percy's vexation had evaporated, and he gazed despondently at his hat. "Putnam was right to say that your guests were captivated by Lord Langham's adventures."

And Nancy had been right as well, Susanna perceived grimly—all too accurate in her prediction that Percy would be intimidated by the dashing earl. Intimidated already, before they'd even met.

"No more captivated than they were when you first related *your* adventures," she said. She was shading the truth considerably: though Percy's military experiences were genuinely interesting, he lacked Ned's glib tongue and droll wit. But the colonel was desperately in need of encouragement, and she forged ahead.

"Yes, my guests were fairly spellbound when you described your many campaigns. Now, of course, the novelty has worn off, and they no longer wish to hear your reminiscences. And Ned will soon suffer the same fate. Indeed, I daresay he exhausted his store of adventures last night."

"Umm." Percy began to toy with his hat, his right hand drawing the brim slowly between the gloved fingers of his left.

"Which is neither here nor there," Susanna continued briskly, gaining confidence, "because *I* didn't want to hear his adventures in the first place. Ned would have no tales to tell had he not abandoned me for three and a half years, and I shall never forgive him for that.

Were it not for Alicia, I should have insisted we separate at once. As it is, I regret that we must pretend to be reconciled even temporarily."

"You regret so at present." Percy glanced up again, and Susanna observed that his cheeks were distinctly pink. "However, though I have not been wed myself, I can well conceive that the . . . ah . . . familiarity occasioned by the married state might serve to change your mind."

Susanna felt a rush of blood into her own cheeks. She had hoped until this moment that Percy would have read between the lines of Nancy's report, but obviously he had not.

"Evidently . . ." Her throat was clogged, and she paused to clear it. "Evidently you failed to understand that Ned's and my reconciliation is a pretext *in every respect*."

Percy knit his brows, looking quite blank, and Susanna's embarrassment was tempered by a flicker of impatience. Must she paint a picture?

"In short"—she spoke around another cough—"Ned and I are not . . . not living as man and wife."

"I see." Percy signaled his belated comprehension by turning positively scarlet. "But I fancy that could change as well. Alicia will not be wed for some months."

"Were Alicia not to be wed for some *years*, I should still refuse to . . ."

Susanna's voice trailed off. The conversation had long since exceeded the bounds of propriety and was fast beginning to border on lewd. She cast about for a delicate way to put the colonel's fears to rest and, miraculously, found one.

"Not that he would ask." This was far from being delicate, and she hastily took another tack. "I meant to say that Ned is no more eager to perpetuate our marriage than I am. He has already renewed his acquaintance with Lady Thornton."

"Lady Thornton?" Percy shook his head.

"Formerly Miss Murray," Susanna prompted. "The woman Ned was . . ."

But she had never told the colonel about Miss Murray, she recalled as he continued to shake his head. In fact, she had not explained any of the circumstances surrounding her and Ned's whirlwind courtship, and she proceeded to deliver a somewhat edited account of Papa's machinations.

"At any rate, Lady Thornton is now a widow," she concluded. "And as I indicated, Ned wasted no time in seeking her out. He even went so far as to invite her to my salon last night."

"I see," Percy repeated. "Yes, that does put matters in a different light. I infer that your husband intends to wed Lady Thornton once your own union has been dissolved?"

Wed? The thought had not occurred to Susanna, and it came like a fist slamming unexpectedly into her stomach. "I . . . I fancy so," she stammered aloud. She could scarcely find the breath to speak.

"Then I daresay we are all in hopes that nothing will happen to thwart our plans," Percy said. "You and Lord Langham, myself and Lady Thornton . . ." He stopped, and his blue eyes briefly narrowed. "Yes, it is in all our interests to strive for a satisfactory resolution of our dilemma—"

"Ah, here you are, Susanna."

Susanna had not detected the earl's approach, and she collected Percy hadn't either, for he leapt to his feet so abruptly that his hat tumbled to the carpet and rolled halfway to the library door.

"Oh, dear," Ned clucked. "Pray do forgive me. I was not aware you had a guest."

He rushed forward, retrieved the hat, and beat it energetically against his leg, apparently attempting to dislodge any particles of dust it might have gathered during its journey across the rug. He was clad in the same white pantaloons he had worn the night before, Susanna noted; but his coat was the color of smoke, and his waistcoat was edged in brilliant crimson. And he clearly planned to go out: his own beaver hat was tucked beneath his unoccupied arm.

"This is Colonel Fordyce," Susanna said shrilly.

"I apologize to you as well, sir." The earl, his ministrations completed, proceeded across the room. "I do not believe your hat sustained any permanent damage, but if it did, I shall make restitution. It was prodigious careless of me to burst in unannounced." He tendered the hat and, with it, a lopsided smile of remorse.

"This is most awkward, Lord Langham," Percy choked, snatching the hat from Ned's outstretched fingers.

"I am sorry you feel so, colonel. I meant no offense when I offered to pay for your hat."

"I was not referring to my hat." Percy's blush had never altogether faded, and it now deepened to a crimson hue remarkably similar to the trim of the earl's waistcoat. "I was referring to . . . to . . ." He stopped again and waved among the three of them, his gesture vaguely suggesting a triangle.

"But that is not in the least awkward!" Ned protested jovially. "Susanna and I have discussed the situation at length, and I have pledged my complete cooperation."

"Yes, but—"

"And we are all civilized people, are we not?" The earl flew on. "Naturally, I should hope—for Alicia's sake if for no other reason—that we can conduct ourselves discreetly during the months ahead. But that should not be difficult, should it, colonel? You and Susanna have been veritable paragons of discretion in the past."

"We have certainly *tried*," Percy agreed.

"Then let us say no more about it. I was at the point of going out, but I should be delighted to offer you a cup of coffee."

"No, thank you." Percy clapped on his hat, and Susanna observed that the brim was dented in half a dozen places. "No, I was also at the point of leaving. I have an appointment with my uncle's solicitor. Mr. Ransom stressed that it is imperative to put Uncle Charles's affairs in order without delay."

"That sounds rather ominous." Ned sorrowfully lowered his eyes. "My good friend Viscount Buckley mentioned that Lord Grafton is seriously ill."

"Very seriously ill and declining rapidly, I surmise." Percy sighed and adjusted his hat, frowning a bit as his fingers detected the dents. "But I shall learn his precise condition when I speak with Mr. Ransom. Good day, Lord Langham. Susanna. I shall let myself out." He bowed, marched to the library entry, executed a perfect right-face turn, and marched on into the vestibule.

"What a genial fellow," the earl said approvingly as the front door clicked shut. "And how fortunate that he stands to become a viscount before you marry. I attach no importance to titles myself, but I fancy Simon would much prefer to welcome another peer into the family."

"How dare you?" Susanna hissed.

"I seem to recollect you using those precise words last evening. And I am once more at a loss to comprehend what I have done to overset you. I attempted to be pleasant to Colonel Fordyce—"

"Pleasant?" Susanna screeched. "Yes, you were enormously pleasant. You were discussing me with Percy as though I were a . . . a head of livestock to be traded."

"I cannot conceive how you arrived at such an absurd interpretation." Ned shook his head, the very picture of bewilderment. "I merely wanted Colonel Fordyce to understand that I have accepted the inevitable. The two of you are determined to wed, and I shan't make a cake of myself by casting petty obstacles in your way."

"Particularly inasmuch as you have no desire to do so," Susanna snapped. "It did not occur to me till Percy mentioned it, but I now see quite clearly what you're at. You are contemplating a wedding of your own, are you not?"

"I beg your pardon?"

"Spare me your innocence, Ned! It cannot have

escaped your attention that Lady Thornton is one of the most eligible women in Britain. Not so rich as Papa, of course, but her wealth is sufficient to support the both of you in splendid fashion."

She was distantly pleased to note the spots of color high on his cheekbones—slashes of rose which turned his sunburned skin to copper. "Indeed," she added, "I daresay you and Lady Thornton will be married before Percy and myself."

"Are you proposing we make a contest of it?" he said coolly.

"I am proposing that you cease to cloak your personal wishes in noble concern for *my* well-being—"

The doorbell pealed, and Susanna tilted one ear toward the foyer, awaiting the tap of Putnam's footfalls. But she had instructed him not to disturb her, she recalled, and he had no doubt repaired to some distant corner of the house. She stood in silence, hoping the visitor would give up and depart, but the bell continued to ring. It could only be Nancy, she decided; Lady Hadleigh would be wild to hear the outcome of her conversation with Percy. And Nancy would *never* give up. The bell emitted yet another strident summons, and Susanna hurried into the entry hall and irritably threw the door open.

"Well!" Lady Calthrop sniffed. "I was beginning to suppose I should be left on your doorstep all day. Though I realize it's a trifle early to be calling." This realization notwithstanding, she sailed over the threshold. "However, I could no longer contain my impatience to greet . . . Lord Langham!"

Her eyes lit up, and when Susanna turned around, she saw the earl peering curiously out the library doorway. Lady Calthrop bounded across the vestibule, treading most painfully on the toes of Susanna's lavender slippers, and seized Ned's right hand in both of hers.

"Lord Langham," she repeated. "I am delighted to see you again. As I indicated, I have been eager to welcome you back, but I judged it best to afford you and Susanna an interval of privacy. Permit me to say now that I was greatly relieved to learn of your safe return."

"Thank you. I am delighted to see you again as well."

Ned flashed his crooked, winsome grin, but his own eyes darted to Susanna. It was obvious he hadn't the slightest notion whom he was addressing, and Susanna was sorely inclined to let him stew in his own gravy. But it wouldn't do to offend Lady Calthrop; their whole ludicrous charade had been designed for her ladyship's exclusive benefit.

"How good of you to remember my husband, *Lady Calthrop*," she said. "Your memory is particularly remarkable in view of the fact that you encountered him *only once*, on the occasion of *our wedding*."

"Lady Calthrop?" Ned gasped. "No wonder I was confused! I well recollect our meeting, but I do believe you look much younger now than you did then."

"Oh, Lord Langham." Her ladyship giggled.

"At any rate," the earl continued smoothly, "I deeply appreciate your interest in my welfare."

"Umm." Lady Calthrop's smile faded, and she released his hand. "I am compelled to own that my interest was somewhat selfish. As I am sure you are aware, there may soon be a connection between our two families."

"I am indeed aware of that, and I could not be happier. I had the pleasure of supping at Hugh's table last evening, and I found him a most delightful young man. He much resembles you, if I may say so."

"Oh, Lord Langham." Her ladyship giggled again, sobered again. "I judge Alicia a delightful young woman as well, but pray remember that they are not yet engaged. I must be certain . . ."

She stopped and gnawed her lip a moment. "Well, let me be frank. I was relieved by your return because it resolves a potentially grave problem. As I told Susanna earlier in the week, I was quite distressed by her peculiar marital situation."

"And I quite understand your distress," Ned said

soothingly. "You would naturally be reluctant to approve a connection which might in any way tarnish your impeccable reputation. I trust Hugh explained that I was trapped in America by circumstances beyond my control."

"So he did." Lady Calthrop nodded, her multiple chins spilling over the high collar of her spencer. "In fact, he could talk of nothing else at breakfast. Nothing but your adventures in Louisiana, that is. Were it not for his familial responsibilities, I fancy he would embark on the next ship."

"I am glad he enjoyed the evening," Ned said. "It's a pity you weren't present, Lady Calthrop."

"I?" She shook her head. "No, Lord Langham, I do not choose to associate with such people. As I have advised Susanna in the past, I have no tolerance for the immorality of Byron and his kind."

"Nor do I." The earl indignantly squared his shoulders. "But Mr. Moore is hardly a Byron. Indeed, I daresay you would find the majority of Susanna's guests entirely unobjectionable. Who will be appearing next week, Susanna?"

"Edmund Kean."

"Edmund Kean!" Lady Calthrop clapped her hands. "Walter and I saw him last Friday at Drury Lane!"

Susanna had heretofore listened to the conversation with a perverse mix of emotions: relief that Ned had made such a favorable impression on Lady Calthrop; annoyance that her ladyship had so readily succumbed to his saccharine charm. Now she perceived, with a wrench of dismay, that the discussion was drifting in a most precarious direction. She cast the earl a quelling look, but he was beaming down at Lady Calthrop.

"You see?" he said triumphantly. "The finest actor in Britain. Certainly not a person one need hesitate to associate with."

"You are right, Lord Langham. Yes, I fear I have done dear Susanna a terrible injustice. Walter and I shall be pleased to come next Thursday and meet Mr. Kean."

Susanna's mouth fell open, but she managed to snap it shut again as Lady Calthrop whirled around.

"I shall go tell Walter at once," her ladyship said, speeding back across the foyer. "Lest he make alternate plans without consulting me."

This was such an unlikely possibility that had she not been so distraught, Susanna would have laughed. Lady Calthrop reached the door, then turned once more to Ned.

"Permit me to reiterate, Lord Langham, that I am enormously comforted by your return. Indeed, though I am not yet prepared to make a firm commitment, I am growing increasingly confident that the union between our families will proceed without a hitch."

"I do hope so, Lady Calthrop."

Ned executed a splendid bow, and with a final girlish giggle, Lady Calthrop transferred her attention to Susanna.

"Speaking of hitches," she said, "I trust you have encountered none in the preparations for Alicia's ball?"

"No," Susanna mumbled. Her teeth were clenched so tightly that she could barely force the words between them. "The printer promised to complete the invitations by this afternoon—"

"I shall leave the details to you, dear. I am sure you have the situation well in hand."

Her ladyship sailed back out the door, slamming it closed behind her, and Susanna sagged against it.

"How dare you?" she whispered.

"There you go again." Ned heaved a despairing sigh. "What the devil have I done now? I made every effort to ingratiate myself with Lady Calthrop."

"*Every* effort," Susanna agreed bitterly. "Especially when you took the liberty of inviting her to my salon."

"I do not recall inviting Lady Calthrop to your salon. My recollection is that she invited herself."

"After your considerable encouragement to do so."

"I didn't intend to encourage her either. I was merely trying to modify her poor opinion of your friends—"

"I am tired of arguing with you, Ned." She truly was;

she could scarcely draw herself erect. "Whatever the circumstances of Lady Calthrop's invitation, it could not have come at a worse time. Mr. Kean is not at all as he appears on the stage. He's far too fond of drink, and if he's foxed—which he usually is—he may behave very badly . . ."

She was inexplicably close to tears, and she bit her lip and gazed down at her shoes. She was not in the least cheered to discover that Lady Calthrop had deposited a great black smudge on the toe of her left slipper.

"Do not tease yourself about it, Susanna," Ned said gently.

She assumed he was referring to her damaged shoe, but when she looked up, she found his silver eyes on her face. It had been just this way the night he decided to go to America, she remembered. They had stood on opposite sides of their bedchamber—she at the point of tears, the earl sketching a lopsided smile. In fact, he had used exactly the same words: *Do not tease yourself about it, Susanna*. He had then crossed the room and taken her in his arms . . . Ned strode forward, and her heart crashed against her ribs.

"No, you needn't worry about Mr. Kean's behavior. Lady Calthrop will be so thrilled to meet him that she will fail to notice if he strips himself naked and dances on the ceiling."

He grinned and casually patted her shoulder, and Susanna could not quell a crushing sense of disappointment.

"Now, if you will excuse me, I really must be off." Ned donned his hat, opened the door, stepped outside, turned back round. "I daresay Julia will be equally thrilled to make Mr. Kean's acquaintance."

"Julia?" Susanna echoed sharply. "You think to invite Lady Thornton to my salon as well?"

"Do you object?" he countered. "I have pledged not to raise any obstacles between you and Colonel Fordyce, and I fancy I am entitled to the same consideration. And bound by the same restrictions, of course; I shall also conduct myself with perfect discretion. Surely that is a fair bargain."

"Yes," Susanna muttered.

Indeed, the bargain he proposed was to her distinct advantage: if Percy entertained any lingering doubts of her fidelity, Lady Thornton's presence would serve to allay them. She wondered why her victory seemed so very hollow.

"I was only concerned about the seating arrangement," she said stiffly. "Until I remembered that I've nearly a week to devise a suitable plan."

"Were you to solicit my advice, I should counsel you to seat Lady Calthrop next to Mr. Kean. But I daresay your plan will be infinitely more imaginative. Be that as it may, I shall leave you to your scheming." He patted her shoulder again and hurried down the steps.

"Do not forget that we are to attend Lord Whitworth's ball this evening," Susanna called after him.

But he did not hear her; he was already walking briskly toward Duke Street. Susanna closed the door and fled up the staircase, the maddening prickle of tears still behind her eyelids.

Chapter 8

AS THE PRINTER had promised, the assembly invitations were ready Friday afternoon, and Susanna addressed them on Saturday and Sunday. Early Monday morning, she dispatched Blake to deliver them, and several responses arrived before the footman had even completed his rounds. By Wednesday morning, the writing table in Susanna's bedchamber was fairly heaped with heavy, embossed envelopes; and after breakfast—the invitation list beside her, the inkstand freshly filled—she sat down at the desk and started to open them.

The first four envelopes contained acceptances, she was pleased to note, placing a neat check next to each of the names. The fifth, from Lady Ramsey, conveyed deep regrets that she and Sir Samuel would be unable to attend: as luck would have it, their newest grandchild was to be christened that week, and they were traveling to Cumberland for the festivities. Susanna crossed the Ramseys from her list and plucked up the next envelope, but as she unsealed it, her mind began to wander.

During the Season of their courtship, Ned had expressed considerable disdain for the annual gathering of the *ton* in London. It was little more than an excuse for the peers of the realm to meet and exchange juicy *on-dits*, he claimed. And, of course, for the eligible young women of the peerage to ensnare a suitable husband. (In the circumstances, he had glossed rather lightly over the latter point.) At any rate, the earl declared, he would not care a whit if he were never to go to another ball or rout or endless, boring dinner party.

Evidently, Susanna thought grouchily, his years

abroad had served to modify his opinion, for he appeared to have had a perfectly marvelous time during the preceding five days. But how could he *not* have had a splendid time? He was the center of attention wherever he went, the proverbial toast of the town.

Susanna's assurance to Percy had been an honest one: she had sincerely believed that the jaded British aristocracy would soon tire of listening to Lord Langham's adventures. Indeed, she still did believe it, but "soon" was not proving nearly so rapid as she'd calculated. Ned had related his experiences only to the small company at her salon; the rest of London had heard them secondhand. And those of the rest who were present at Lord Whitworth's ball immediately swarmed around the earl and demanded clarification of this or that aspect of his tales.

Was it true that the principal public building in New Orleans was constructed on pillars? Yes. And that the dead were interred above the ground? Yes. And that the president of Louisiana had died as the result of a voodoo curse?

"Louisiana does not have a president," Ned replied kindly. "At the time of my departure, the governor was alive and well."

This remark led to a discussion of America's peculiar political system, but Susanna caught only the occasional word. Her cheekbones literally ached, and she feared that if the earl went on much longer, her facial muscles would be frozen in a permanent, vacuous smile. To her relief, he shortly announced that he was hungry and—his adoring audience trailing in his wake—strode toward the refreshment parlor. Susanna relaxed her face, gingerly felt it, and decided that no irreparable damage had been done.

"Your husband is charming, Lady Langham."

Susanna whirled around and met Lord Whitworth's owlish, bespectacled eyes.

"And immensely interesting," his lordship continued. "Does he have any literary talent? If so, I fancy he could write poems even more compelling than Byron's."

"No," Susanna snapped. "No, he has no such talent."

"What a pity." Lord Whitworth shook his head, bowed, and moved on to the adjacent knot of guests.

Saturday evening provided some respite inasmuch as Ned was unable to hold court during the opera performance at the King's Theatre. Afterward, however, he and Susanna were invited to sup at Madame Catalani's, where the earl was asked to compare London opera to that of New Orleans.

"There really is no comparison," he said. "The productions in New Orleans are generally performed by companies imported from France." Madame made a moue of disdain. "And naturally, they have no artists of *your* caliber, Madame Catalani."

The prima donna beamed and commanded one of her footmen to refill Lord Langham's glass. "Your husband is charming," she whispered as the earl began to describe the occasional English plays performed in New Orleans.

"Thank you," Susanna muttered. Her cheeks were starting to ache again.

Sunday offered no relief whatever because Lady Calthrop had summoned her prospective in-laws to dine in Berkeley Street and meet "our family." To Susanna's utter lack of surprise, "our" family consisted of her ladyship's two sistes, who were as plump and prim as Lady Calthrop herself; and their husbands, who appeared to be at least as henpecked as the long-suffering viscount. How the sisters had got so large Susanna could not conceive, for they stopped eating every thirty seconds or so to correct the disgusting habits of their mates.

"Pray do not slurp your soup, Walter!" "Will you please remove your elbow from the table, Henry!" "You have had quite enough wine already, Alfred!"

Between admonishments, Lady Calthrop coaxed the earl to repeat his remarkable stories of Louisiana, and despite the frequent interruptions, he scarcely missed a syllable. Fortunately, Susanna was not required to smile—the sisters were watching their husbands, and the husbands were warily watching the sisters—and she concentrated on cutting her chicken into tiny pieces and distributing the pieces artfully round her plate.

At last, the interminable meal was over, and the sisters escorted their guests to the vestibule, leaving the husbands to contemplate their many sins. Lady Calthrop shrieked for her butler to retrieve Lord Langham's hat, and as he did so, Mrs. Adcock—the youngest sister—gripped Susanna's hand.

"How lucky you are." She sighed with envy. "*Your* husband is charming."

"So I have been told."

Susanna snatched her hand away and stalked out the front door, assuring herself that Monday evening would be different. She and Ned had been invited to dine at the home of Viscount Castlereagh, the foreign secretary, and she was confident that neither he nor his sophisticated guests would be interested in voodoo curses and similar nonsense. She was correct on this head: the reality proved far worse.

"I am given to understand that you have been regaling the town with tales of black magic, Langham," Lord Castlereagh said sternly. "You will find that none of us here wishes to discuss such fanciful matters."

The soup had just been served, and Susanna happily raised a spoonful to her mouth.

"No," the viscount went on, "our concerns are considerably more serious." He nodded round the group at table, which included the other members of the cabinet. "We should like to know your opinion of conditions in the United States."

Susanna choked on her mulligatawny, and Lord Sidmouth pounded her solicitously on the back. "My husband is hardly an authority on American affairs, Lord Castlereagh," she sputtered when her coughing subsided.

"Perhaps not, but he is the best authority we have at the moment." The viscount sketched a wintry smile. "So if it would not pose too great an imposition"—he returned his eyes to Ned—"we are eager to hear your views."

The earl, needing no further urging to expound these views, launched into still another lecture on life in Louisiana. Well, it wasn't exactly a lecture, Susanna conceded, for the company interposed dozens of questions. The conversation grew so lively that Lady Castlereagh did not escort the women to the saloon until dessert had been finished nearly an hour, and even then she left the dining room with visible reluctance.

"I should like to have stayed for the rest of your husband's commentary," she said, handing Susanna a cup of tea. "His experiences are fascinating, are they not?"

"Yes," Susanna mumbled.

"And he is so very charming," her ladyship added.

Susanna's hands began to tremble, and she hastily set her cup and saucer on the sofa table.

Vexed as she was, Susanna took some dim comfort in the knowledge that the worst was over. Ned had related his "fascinating" tales to virtually everyone in London by now, and she fancied he would be quite ignored at Lady Escott's assembly Tuesday evening. With this delightful prospect in mind, she elected to wear her elegant new blue net gown, but she was once more doomed to disappointment.

"Lord Langham!" Lady Escott bounded forward to greet them. "I'm so pleased you could find room in your busy schedule to attend my ball."

His schedule? Susanna's jaws sagged with disbelief. She had accepted the invitation weeks ago, long before the earl's return.

"Yes," Lady Escott continued, "I daresay you are very busy indeed now you've been engaged as a consultant to the government. I do not care for politics myself, but Robert and the other gentlemen are most anxious to learn what occurred at Lord Castlereagh's."

She waved Lord Escott a signal, and within the space of a few minutes, Ned was once more surrounded by a flock of admirers. The congregation much resembled a meeting of the House of Lords, Susanna observed irritably, and she fancied the earl could save a great deal of time and trouble if he introduced their bill of divorcement at once.

"You must be excessively proud of your husband," Lady Escott gushed. "Robert and I were remarking as we dressed that he has been back in England only a week. It is astonishing that he has already gained such wide attention."

"Yes, it is," Susanna agreed grimly.

"And even more astonishing that his head has not been swelled by his fame," her ladyship said. "Most men would grow impossibly conceited in the circumstances, but Lord Langham remains as charming as he was at the outset."

Charming, charming, charming. Susanna yanked the folded message from the envelope in her hand. If she was compelled to hear once more how charming her husband was—

"Good morning, Susanna," Ned said cheerfully.

She spun her head and found the earl at her bedchamber door. The door on the corridor; he never used the one between their bedrooms. For some reason, this recollection fueled her annoyance.

"Putnam advised me that you were reviewing the responses for Alicia's come-out." He glanced at the writing table. "It appears we shall have a large crowd."

"I don't yet know," Susanna snapped. "I was just starting to open them."

"Then I shall leave you to it. I am bound for Guthrie's, and after that, I have several other errands to attend. I shall probably be from home the rest of the day, but I'll return in ample time to dress for Almack's."

He hurried away, and Susanna smashed the unread note between her fingers and her palm. As much as—perhaps more than—the constant references to Ned's charm, she had come to hate his daily report that he would be "from home." Or "going out" or "occupied"; he, at least, varied his wording. His wording and his excuses: he had offered quite an imaginative assortment of explanations for his absences. These explanations ranged from the frivolous (a visit to White's to play macao) to the familial (a call on his maiden grandaunt in Welbeck Street) to the financial (a conference with his man of business, who had managed the pathetic remnants of the Sutton estate while the earl was abroad). Now it was an appointment with his tailor and mysterious "other errands." Susanna could only surmise that he created such fictions for the benefit of Alicia and the staff; there was no doubt in *her* mind that he spent every day with Lady Thornton.

Susanna smoothed the crumpled wad of paper in her hand and discovered, with a stab of remorse, that it was Percy's response. She had caught a brief glimpse of the colonel at Lord Whitworth's assembly, but she could not remember whether he had been at Lady Escott's or not. In fact, she had been so distracted by Ned's antics that she had almost forgotten Percy altogether, and she contritely resolved to make amends at her salon tomorrow evening.

At any rate, Colonel Fordyce had accepted his invitation to Alicia's ball, and Susanna put a check beside his name and drew the next response from the top of the stack. But it was not a response, she saw, recognizing the bold script on the envelope; a letter from Papa had somehow got mixed among the replies. She felt another prickle of guilt. She had written her father late the preceding week, and though she hadn't exactly *lied*, neither had she elected to disclose the full truth. She had simply informed Papa of the earl's return and left him to draw his own conclusion.

The conclusion he had reached was the obvious one, of course: he was delighted that Susanna's marital situation had been "happily" resolved and there need be no further talk of an annulment. Susanna stopped reading and attempted to visualize his reaction when he learned that—immeasurably worse than an annulment—there was to be a divorce. The picture was so awful that she hastily returned her attention to the letter.

He was most eager to hear his son-in-law's adventures, Papa continued; in fact, he had briefly considered coming to town for Alicia's debut after all. Susanna shuddered. But he had resisted the temptation, Papa finished, and would look forward to seeing Ned at Lady Calthrop's house party.

The house party. Good God. Susanna had forgotten it as well, and she emitted a little whimper of dismay. Whatever his faults, Simon Randall was the shrewdest man alive, and he would perceive at once that she and Ned were far from being "happily" reunited.

But Papa's opinion didn't signify, she reminded herself, swallowing her panic. The only opinion that mattered was that of Lady Calthrop, and she had been successfully deceived already. Indeed, her ladyship had indicated that Hugh's engagement to Alicia was all but official—the announcement a mere formality—and unless something went very badly amiss, she was unlikely to change her mind.

And what could go amiss? Papa certainly wouldn't share his suspicions with Lady Calthrop, and Ned had promised to conduct himself with perfect discretion. Susanna tossed the letter into the wastepaper basket beside the desk and picked up the next envelope.

Chapter 9

AFTER THREE YEARS of experience, Susanna could swiftly judge whether one of her salons would be more or less successful than the average. Thus it was that by a quarter to nine the following evening, she perceived that this soiree was well in the way of becoming a disaster.

She had told Ned that Edmund Kean was not at all as he appeared on the stage, but she had forgotten how very different he was. Divested of costume and makeup, he was, to begin with, a singularly unattractive man: excessively slight in stature and cursed with an overlarge nose and a wild mop of dark hair. In the second place, as Susanna had feared, he was thoroughly jug-bitten. He literally staggered through the front door and stumbled over every riser as he lurched up the staircase. At one perilous point, he lost his balance and began to stumble *backward*, but Putnam seized his sleeve in time to prevent a possibly fatal fall. Susanna hoped—had even obliquely suggested—that he would cease drinking till his performance was finished; but, electing to ignore this suggestion, Mr. Kean paused at frequent intervals to gulp down an entire fresh glass of champagne.

His performance; that was another thing. Susanna had proposed that he entertain the group with a reprise of his most notable roles—Shylock, Richard III, Iago—but Mr. Kean had other ideas. Though he did deliver a few passages of Shakespeare, he devoted by far the bulk of his performance to a repetition of the bawdy jokes currently popular at the taverns he haunted. Lady Calthrop was but the first of the female guests to turn scarlet with horror; within half an hour, even Nancy was blushing.

Susanna heard the distant chime of the foyer clock and leapt to her feet. "That was a very . . . very unusual presentation, Mr. Kean," she said shrilly. "However, it is nine o'clock, and I daresay my guests are as eager as I to engage you in discussion."

She glanced around, but the women were frantically fanning their flushed faces, and the men were still chuckling their appreciation of the actor's last scandalous joke. She recollected the emergency question she had prepared and assumed her brightest smile. "I, for one, should like to know which of your many roles you prefer."

Mr. Kean nodded and downed another glass of champagne, but when he started to talk again, it was not about his roles. No, he wished to discuss the various *secret societies* in which he was involved. Apparently these organizations were so secret that he could not divulge their names, but he readily disclosed their purpose, which was the "damnation of all lords and gentlemen." Not surprisingly, the lords and gentlemen present were considerably distressed by his views, and the room was soon abuzz with furious argument. Susanna counted it quite likely that if the altercation continued till half past ten, it would become physical as well as verbal; and when she was certain all eyes were on Mr. Kean, she slipped into the corridor, raced to the kitchen, and begged Mrs. Putnam to serve the supper as quickly as possible.

"That will present no problem," the cook sniffed. "As I told you earlier, the butcher had only the most wretched pieces of meat to offer, and they are already charred to a cinder." She grimly indicated two delectable-looking filets of beef on the dresser. "And the French beans are so very tough that I fancy no amount of cooking would suffice to make them edible." She glared at the raw beans and then, for good measure, at Cassie and Connie, as though the scullery maids had personally cultivated and harvested this sorry excuse for a vegetable.

"Well, just do the best you can, Mrs. Putnam,"

Susanna said, somehow summoning forth her most soothing voice. "I realize I am asking a great deal, but you are, after all, the finest cook in London."

Mrs. Putnam grudgingly agreed that she did, indeed, possess superior culinary skills—skills which had saved Lady Langham from humiliation on innumerable occasions in the past; and that supper, "such as it is," could be served in half an hour. With this dubious promise ringing in her ears, Susanna sped back up the rear steps and into the library.

In accordance with Ned's counsel, she had seated Lord and Lady Calthrop with herself and Mr. Kean, but it was now clear that this arrangement wouldn't do at all. The earl's assurances to the contrary, Lady Calthrop had taken full and dismal note of Mr. Kean's shocking behavior; and if she found herself situated next to him at supper, she might well stalk indignantly out of the house. Susanna scurried round the room, reviewing the place cards, but glimpsed no perfect solution to her dilemma. No solution except a total revision of the seating plan, and she would surely be detected if she attempted to smuggle place cards back and forth between the library and the first floor. She eventually decided, as she had advised Mrs. Putnam, simply to do the best she could; and she switched Lord and Lady Calthrop with Percy and Nancy, whom she had put at the table adjacent to her own.

At twenty-five past nine, Blake deposited the last bowl of beans on the dining-room table, and Susanna galloped back to the saloon. She was not a moment too soon, she observed: Lord Whitworth—who, despite his owlish appearance, was famous for his quick temper—was on his feet and advancing in a highly threatening manner toward Mr. Kean. Shouting to make herself heard above the din, Susanna announced that supper was served, and her guests welcomed this news with such enthusiasm that she was nearly trampled in the ensuing rush to the hall. Mr. Kean, evidently unaware that his audience had vanished, continued to declaim his radical notions to the circle of abandoned chairs, and

Susanna was briefly tempted to leave him alone in the drawing room for the remainder of the evening. At length, however, when she calculated that the rest of the guests had served themselves, she escorted him down the stairs and watched in silence as he dropped a great spoonful of the suspect beans on the dining-room carpet.

While Mr. Kean wove his way across the library, dropping another bean or two en route, Susanna—by force of habit—lingered in the doorway to survey the room. One of the chairs was empty, she noticed, and when she reconstructed the seating arrangement, she realized it was Lady Thornton's. Susanna could scarcely conceive that her ladyship had been so offended by Mr. Kean's conduct as to forgo supper, and her hands began to shake with rage as she conjectured a far likelier possibility. The possibility that Ned had ignored the place cards and invited Lady Thornton to sit at his table in the morning parlor . . .

She had to know, and she hurried back to the dining room, set her plate on one corner of the table, and crept up the staircase. The tables in the morning parlor were positioned in such a way that she could view them from the archway without exposing herself to the guests within, and she saw at once that Ned's chair was empty as well. In fact, two chairs at his table were empty: she had seated Ned with Lord and Lady Whitworth and their spinster daughter, but only Lady Whitworth and Lady Emma were in their assigned places. It seemed most unlikely that Lord Whitworth would be engaged in private conversation with the earl and Lady Thornton—

"Lady Langham!"

Susanna recognized Lord Whitworth's voice and spun around. She collected from his lordship's rather indelicate adjustment of his pantaloons that he had excused himself to answer a call of nature.

"I was delighted to discover that you granted us the company of your charming husband," Lord Whitworth said, giving his waistband a final tug. "We are all eager to hear more of his adventures." He peered into the parlor, squinting even through his spectacles, then looked back at her. "I expect he will be joining us shortly."

"I am sure he will try to do so," Susanna murmured. "He has been . . . been unavoidably detained."

Lord Whitworth nodded and stepped on into the parlor, and Susanna—now trembling from head to foot—flew back along the corridor. Discretion indeed! she thought furiously as she pounded down the stairs. It was obvious that Ned had taken Lady Thornton elsewhere to dine, and Susanna could only pray that none of the guests would divine the situation. Perhaps, since the missing parties were seated in different rooms, their simultaneous disappearance would not be remarked. She descended the last riser, striving to clear her face, and Percy bounded across the vestibule to meet her.

"Where the devil have you been?" the colonel demanded crossly.

His abruptness was so uncharacteristic that Susanna's eyes widened with shock, but she perceived upon closer inspection that he looked unusually nervous as well. She surmised that Mr. Kean's behavior had deteriorated still further in her absence—maybe he *had* stripped himself naked and begun to dance around the library—and she contritely patted Percy's sleeve.

"I had to attend a matter upstairs," she said, "but I shall come to the table at once—"

"No." He shook his head and resumed his familiar bland countenance. "No, I merely wished to advise you that Lady Thornton has been stricken ill. Lord Langham escorted her outside for a bit of fresh air."

"I see," Susanna muttered, half to herself. This circumstance, though far from ideal, was vastly preferable to the scenario she'd envisioned, and she drew a small sigh of relief. "I daresay they would want us to proceed without them, so I shall retrieve my plate—"

"No!" Percy repeated. "That is, I doubt Lady Thornton would want you to proceed with supper. It is my experience . . ." He stopped and emitted an embarrassed cough. "It is my experience that women's illnesses often require the sympathy of other women, and I fancied you would desire to speak with Lady Thornton yourself."

In truth, Susanna could conceive of nothing she less desired: she would not have cared a whit had she discovered Lady Thornton's comatose body sprawled across her doorstep. But Percy would not understand her attitude (indeed, she did not understand it herself), and she snatched at the first credible objection that came to mind.

"I should very much like to speak with Lady Thornton," she lied. "However, I can hardly track her and Ned all about the neighborhood—"

"They stated an intention to walk in the square," the colonel interposed helpfully. He strode to the front door, threw it open, and peered into the night. "Yes, I see them."

He beckoned Susanna forward, and she reluctantly went to his side.

"There," he said. "On the main path."

Susanna sighted along the line of his finger and discerned two figures moving toward the middle of Grosvenor Square. Shadows really; so vague that she could not determine their sexes, much less their specific identities. She started to point this out to Percy, but as she parted her lips, he nudged her over the threshold and closed the door behind her.

Susanna gazed at the square, but it had gone altogether black. She could not make out even the statue in the center, and when she glanced up, she saw that the moon had slipped behind a bank of scudding clouds. It suddenly struck her as odd that Percy had not offered to accompany her; perhaps, as a lifelong bachelor, he was extraordinarily intimidated by "women's illnesses." At any rate, he surely would not expect her to conduct her mission of mercy in total darkness, and she spun around and reached for the doorknob.

The moon, as if deliberately to thwart her, leapt out of the clouds, and Susanna looked back at the square. It was bathed in brilliant light—light much brighter than the pale glow which had illumined it before—and she could readily distinguish a man and a woman approaching the end of the path. In fact, she could distinguish Lady Thornton's headdress: a ridiculously high toque fairly dripping with bunches of artificial flowers—

"Is something amiss, ma'am?"

Susanna started and peered downward. She had been absently aware of her guests' carriages arrayed along the street, but she had not noticed the cluster of coachmen on the footpath. She couldn't tell which of them had posed the question—they were all regarding her with equal curiosity—and she felt a prickle of dismay. If Lady Thornton was seriously ill, word would get about that Lady Langham had coolly watched her suffering and declined to render any assistance . . .

"N-no," she stammered. "One of my guests is a trifle indisposed, and I wished to ascertain her condition for myself." With what she hoped to be a moue of anxiety, she hurried down the steps, across the street, and around the perimeter of the square to the gate.

Susanna had walked in Grosvenor Square hundreds of times, trudging through rain and snow and blinding fog, and she knew virtually every inch of its confusing pathways. It was fortunate she did, she shortly judged, for she had scarcely set out along the principal path when the moon once more plunged behind the clouds. She could see but a few feet ahead, and she stopped, glancing apprehensively about. She was certain this portion of the square had been deserted when she started up the path, but she now detected a flicker of movement at her right. A lone woman presented a most tempting target for a robber, she thought, her stomach knotting with alarm. A robber or . . . or worse. She wondered whether the coachmen would hear her if she screamed, would come to her rescue if they did . . .

A shaft of moonlight escaped the clouds, and Susanna obtained a clear view of her assailant: a blooming horse chestnut gently swaying in the light spring breeze. She was behaving like a child, she chided herself—conjuring up a host of monsters outside her bedchamber door. She sped on up the path, looking neither right nor left, and soon spied Ned and Lady Thornton immediately ahead.

Well, not immediately ahead, she amended, pausing at the end of the path to get her bearings. An inner pathway intersected all the others—a square within the square, bordering the statue in the middle—and the earl and Lady Thornton had walked approximately a quarter of the way around it. Susanna waved for their attention, then realized they were strolling slowly away from her. She could easily overtake them, she calculated, and she turned into the central path and strode briskly toward them.

Susanna had just passed the next intersection of pathways when the moon disappeared again, and she stumbled to a halt. She had never before had occasion to ponder the various degrees of darkness, but she now estimated that her range of vision had been reduced from a few feet to a few inches. She no longer feared attack—Ned was sufficiently close to hear her if the coachmen didn't—but she did fear she might stray off the path and grow lost in the trees. Indeed, she feared she would become disoriented if she changed direction even for a moment, and she cautiously sidled toward the middle of the square. When her ankle brushed the platform supporting the statue, she stepped away a bit and began to creep ahead, her eyes riveted to the safe, inner edge of the pathway.

Susanna was so intent on keeping to the path that she almost missed her quarry; she was still plodding doggedly forward when a murmur of conversation caught her up. She instinctively spun her head, but the darkness remained impenetrable. Nor could she detect any further sound—nothing but the whisper of the wind—and she surmised that Ned and Lady Thornton had once more moved beyond her. Or had she moved beyond them? She clenched her hands with frustration. The only certain thing was that she was most unlikely to find them if she stayed on the edge of the path and they proceeded along the center. They would pass her, she would pass them . . . She drew a deep breath and reluctantly made her way back toward the middle of the pathway.

Persuaded as she was that the earl and Lady Thornton were either ahead of her or behind, Susanna nearly missed them again: she was at the point of treading on her ladyship's slipper when she recognized it for what it was. In fact, the hems of their gowns were touching, and Susanna started to apologize for her sudden and no doubt alarming intrusion. But Lady Thornton did not appear to have registered her presence, and the words died in Susanna's throat. If she had not frightened them already, she did not wish to do so now, and she decided to retreat a yard or two and call out to them. She had taken one step backward when the moon burst out of the clouds, and her plan dissolved in an involuntary gasp of shock. Ned and Lady Thornton were locked in a passionate embrace, their lips firmly pressed together—

"Lady Langham!" Lady Thornton sprang out of the earl's arms, her amber eyes wide with horror. "How very"—she visibly groped for the right adjective—"how very awkward."

"Indeed it is," Susanna agreed grimly.

She could think of nothing more to say, and evidently they couldn't either. The three of them stood a moment, motionless, silent; she was reminded of one of Madame Tussaud's wax tableaux. The manners Mama and Lady Elwood had taught her did not encompass this particular situation, but Susanna fancied they would both have advised her to return to the house without another word. Yes, such a course would undoubtedly be the least embarrassing. But least embarrassing for whom? Ned and Lady Thornton had created this dreadful contretemps, and Susanna had no reason to spare them a single second of discomfiture. She stubbornly stood her ground.

"Well," her ladyship said at last. She was not carrying a fan, and she waved one hand energetically about her face. "If you will forgive me, Lady Langham, I must regretfully beg to be excused from supper. Excellent though I am sure it is, I find that the mere sight of food often unsettles my delicate digestion."

"Then I shall escort you back to your carriage."

The earl sounded peculiarly stiff, and when Susanna stole a glance at him, she was pleased to observe that he looked rather more distraught than Lady Thornton.

"That won't be necessary," her ladyship said kindly. "As you can see for yourself, the moon is out for good."

Susanna peered upward. A dark line of clouds hovered just above the horizon, but the rest of the sky was clear and spangled with stars. Had Lady Thornton planned the scene—Susanna's entrance, her own exit—she could not have timed it better.

"No," her ladyship reiterated, "I can readily make my way alone. Good evening, Ned. Lady Langham." She hurried round the center of the square, her elaborate toque gleaming like a beacon in the moonlight, and disappeared in the shadow of the trees bordering the main path.

"Susanna." The earl cleared his throat. "Pray permit me to explain."

"Explain?" She whirled around, once more clenching her hands. "What is to explain? You violated your promise; it is as simple as that. After pledging to conduct yourself discreetly, you left my salon with Lady Thornton—"

"At her request," Ned interposed. "She was feeling unwell, queasy, she said—"

"Which renders your behavior all the more odious! I should not have believed that even you would press your attentions on a woman weakened by illness."

"*Even* I." He sketched a bitter, crooked smile. "Then you will surely fail to believe that quite the opposite occurred."

"The opposite?" she echoed with a mirthless laugh. "If you are suggesting that Lady Thornton threw herself into your arms, you are quite right. That I do not believe you, I mean. Now, if you will excuse me, I really must see to my guests." She turned away and began to move down the path.

"No, I will not excuse you!"

The earl's roar masked his pursuing footfalls, and Susanna gasped again as he seized her wrist and spun her back to face him.

"Not until you have heard me out," he continued, resuming a normal tone. "This has gone entirely too far, Susanna."

She started to snap that indeed it had, but something in his expression froze her tongue. A certain softness round his mouth, a strange light in his silver eyes—

"I have been considering our circumstances," he said "Last night, when we were at Almack's . . ."

He stopped and raked the fingers of his free hand through his hair; she had never before seen him so uncertain.

"Last night," he repeated, "I was remembering the night we met. Do you remember as well?"

Remember? she thought incredulously. It was precisely because she remembered that she rarely went to Almack's: though she had maintained her subscription, she attended only an assembly or two each Season. The *ton* gleefully gossiped that her absences were designed to spite Lady Jersey, who had declined numerous invitations to Lady Langham's salons. The truth was that Susanna could hardly bear to return to the place where she had first encountered Ned.

But she would die under torture before she owned the truth to him, and she curtly inclined her head. "Yes, I remember."

"And then we spent the ensuing weeks trying to elude Lady Elwood." He chuckled. "Or so I fancied at the time. I later came to suspect that she pretended to be much blinder than she was."

"Probably so," Susanna murmured. "She was very fond of you."

"It was more than that." He had not released her wrist, and now he pulled her closer. "I believe she perceived at once that we were destined for each other."

He was standing so near that his breath stirred the hair at her temple, and Susanna was assailed by another flood of memories—memories of the magical night when Ned had declared his love. He reached up and gently stroked her face, and she could not repress a shiver.

"As we were." His voice had sunk to a whisper. "Lady Elwood realized that I could make you happy. And I did, Susanna; you can't deny it."

"No." Her own voice was so clogged as to be almost inaudible.

"And despite everything that has happened in the interim, I could make you happy again."

He lowered his head, touched his lips to hers, and—like a scene from some perverse fairy tale—woke her from her dream. She belatedly recollected the other matter they had discussed that night: the matter of his previous liaison with Julia Murray. She jerked out of his grasp and stumbled backward.

"What *happened*," she hissed, "is that you abandoned me for three and a half years. And then, when you finally troubled yourself to return, you launched an immediate campaign to win Lady Thornton's hand. I can only collect—appearances to the contrary—that your suit is not progressing as well as you'd hoped. Or that you've decided Lady Thornton is not sufficiently wealthy to support you after all."

"Susanna, please listen to me—"

"No!" She shook her head so violently that her toque slipped over one ear. "No, I am no longer the innocent girl you met at Almack's, Ned. Unlike the rest of London, I am not susceptible to your charms."

She whirled about and raced down the path, around the intersection, and into the broad, main pathway. She did not stop till she reached the gate, and even then she paused only long enough to straighten her headdress. She had not run so far or so fast since her childhood, and she was wheezing like a winded horse as she staggered across Grosvenor Street and—ignoring the curious coachmen—up the steps to the house.

"Susanna!"

Evidently Percy had been watching for her because she had scarcely collapsed against the door when he materialized at her side.

"You look quite distressed." The colonel frowned solicitously down at her. "Did you find Lord Langham and Lady Thornton?"

"Oh, yes," she panted, desperately sucking air into her aching lungs. "Yes, I found them. Lady Thornton was . . ." She elected to borrow Ned's word. "She was a trifle queasy. She decided to forgo supper."

"Good." Percy nodded. "It is not *good* that she is ill, of course," he hastily amended, "but I'm glad her complaint did not prove serious. As I am sure you are. You can now enjoy your own supper with a clear conscience."

He took her elbow, drew her upright, and Susanna glanced into the library. Mr. Kean was on his feet, clinging to the edge of the table for support, and she surmised from Lady Calthrop's black scowl of disapproval that he was relating another lewd joke. In years past, she would have viewed the situation as a challenge and devised some clever way to reconcile her warring guests, but tonight such an effort seemed impossibly difficult.

"No," she muttered aloud. "No, I can't face them. You will have to tender my excuses."

"What excuses?" Percy gazed around the vestibule, as though hoping an excuse or two would emerge from the woodwork. "Shall I say you've also been stricken ill?"

"Yes, that would be excellent. And not far from the truth." Susanna was dangerously close to tears, and she once more gulped for breath. "You can honestly tell my guests that I am sick almost to the point of death."

She shook his fingers off her arm and fled blindly up the staircase.

US Air
Flight 29
Arr. 6:37

6:39

Chapter 10

WHEN SUSANNA WOKE the following morning, she fancied she had had a particularly vivid nightmare. She wriggled upright in the bed, starting to draw a sigh of relief, and glimpsed the untidy heap of clothing she had flung on the Turkey carpet. It hadn't been a dream then. Mr. Kean really had behaved like a rumpot in a bawdy house, Ned had undertaken to seduce Lady Thornton, and Susanna had made a cake of herself by fleeing her own salon. Her sigh became a little moan of horror.

But it was useless to dwell on it, she decided, squaring her shoulders. If she had learned nothing else in four and twenty years, she had learned the futility of teasing oneself about the things one couldn't change. Especially since, or so she'd found, the situation was rarely as grim as one supposed. Mr. Kean had embarrassed countless hostesses in the past; no one would hold Lady Langham responsible for his disgraceful conduct. And no one knew—no one but Susanna—what had transpired in Grosvenor Square. Her guests had probably accepted Percy's report that she was ill. (Surely he hadn't repeated her hysterical pronouncement that she was "sick almost to the point of death.") And even if they had not, they would speculate about her precipitate flight for a day or two and then turn their attention to new and more interesting events—

Susanna's reverie was shattered by a great pounding on the corridor door, and she glared across the room. Ned, she conjectured, come to plead his cause again. That was another element of her distress: she could scarcely bear to recollect how close he had come to seducing *her*. It was abundantly clear, in retrospect, that he had weighed her fortune against Lady Thornton's and judged the latter wanting. But for a few humiliating moments, she had nearly succumbed to his silver eyes and glib tongue—

The pounding continued, loud enough to raise the dead, and Susanna irritably pulled the bedclothes up to her neck. "Come in," she snapped.

"Good morning, Lady Langham." Polly thrust her plump, cheerful face around the door. "I hope you're in better force today? But look what you've done!" She crossed the carpet and snatched up Susanna's gown. "Dear, dear," she clucked. "I'll definitely have to press it—"

"I do not recall ringing for you, Polly," Susanna interposed sharply.

"No, ma'am," the abigail agreed. "Mr. Putnam sent me up to advise you that Lady Calthrop is here."

Lady Calthrop. Good God. Susanna stifled another moan. She had forgotten the one guest who *would* hold her responsible for Mr. Kean's behavior. Held her responsible and had obviously come to convey her sentiments while they were still warm and fresh in her mind. Nor would that be the end of it. Sooner or later—probably the former—she would point out that Susanna had rudely abandoned her guests to Mr. Kean's none-too-tender mercies. The prospect was almost too dismal to contemplate, and she wearily shook her head.

"You don't wish to see her?" Polly rolled the discarded clothes into a neat ball and tucked the ball under her arm. "Well, of course you don't. If you'll pardon me for saying so, you're looking prodigious poor. Are you feverish? I'll bring you a pot of tea, and on my way to the kitchen, I'll tell Mr. Putnam you're much too sick to receive callers."

"No." Susanna threw the covers aside and climbed out of bed. "No, I am not sick, and I must receive Lady Calthrop."

"Then I'll help you dress." Polly bustled to the wardrobe. "I recommend you wear the rose gown; it'll put a little color in your cheeks. But I'd do without the cap if I was you. It makes your face look thin, and inasmuch as you're so haggard anyway—"

"Thank you, Polly." Susanna had not been sick half a minute earlier, but the abigail's chatter was beginning to give her a headache. "However, I should prefer to dress myself while you make certain Lady Calthrop is comfortable. Please desire Putnam to show her to the saloon and serve her some coffee. Have him tell her that I shall be down momentarily."

"Very good, ma'am." Polly bounded back to the door. "I'll also take your clothes to the laundry, and if you're not down by the time I'm finished, I'll come back and help you with your hair."

With this dire threat ringing in her ears, Susanna tore off her nightgown, rushed to the chest of drawers, plucked out a clean set of underthings, and tugged them on. Polly had removed the rose morning dress from the wardrobe, and in the interest of speed, Susanna elected not to dispute the abigail's decision. And a wise decision it had been, she conceded, studying her reflection in the cheval glass, for she looked "prodigious poor" indeed —pinched and wan, with faint, purplish shadows below either eye. She could not erase the shadows, but a liberal application of rouge did render her somewhat less pale. She hastily combed her hair and was reasonably satisfied with the final result: if not the picture of vitality, she at least appeared sufficiently healthy to survive the day. She slammed her comb on the dressing table and hurried into the corridor.

"Ah, Susanna." Ned emerged from his own bedchamber, effectively blocking her way. "You are up."

Had he been watching for her? Susanna wondered, or had he merely chanced to step into the hall at the very instant she approached his door? Whatever the case, he was dressed to go out—clad in brown pantaloons, an ecru waistcoat, and a tailcoat of cinnamon superfine. She was perversely pleased to observe that despite his handsome attire, he looked a trifle poorly as well: his sunburned skin seemed sallow rather than tan, and he, too, had slight smudges beneath his eyes.

"In your absence, I took the liberty of bidding your guests good night," the earl continued. "They all inquired after you, but I was compelled to defer to Colonel Fordyce. He stated that you'd also been stricken ill. I'm delighted to see you've recovered so quickly."

Susanna searched his face, but it was blank—an empty mask of courtesy. "Quickly enough," she said coolly. "Now, if I may beg to be excused, I was on my way to receive Lady Calthrop."

"Lady Calthrop is here?" he gasped. "It is barely half past nine."

Susanna had already brushed past him, already proceeded several yards along the corridor, but his words caught her up. No, not his words, she amended; it was his tone that drew her to a halt. She suddenly remembered that Ned—Ned alone—had created this wretched bumblebath. *He* had invited Lady Calthrop to her salon. *He* had violated his pledge of discretion. And now he was affecting to be amazed by the consequences of his conduct . . .

"Spare me your dramatics," she hissed, whirling back around. "I warned you that Mr. Kean would overset Lady Calthrop, but you chose to ignore me. As you have chosen to ignore my wishes in so many respects. You've caused one problem on another from the moment of your return." This might be a slight exaggeration, she owned, but she was too angry to be concerned with scrupulous accuracy. "You cause the problems and leave me to undo the damage—"

"It's a pity you weren't born in an earlier time, Susanna," he interrupted dryly. "You have the makings of a splendid martyr. But I shan't allow you to burn at the stake today." He strode up the hall to her side. "I shall go with you and smooth Lady Calthrop's ruffled feathers."

"That won't be necessary. I . . ."

She had started to say that she could handle the

situation without assistance, and she fancied she could. But why take a risk when none was required? Loath as she was to admit it, the earl did possess a virtually bottomless reservoir of charm.

"Very well," she muttered. "Just be certain you do nothing to vex Lady Calthrop any further."

In the event, this admonishment proved gratuitous, for it soon became apparent that Lady Calthrop *could* not be vexed any further. Susanna paused at the drawing-room entry to observe her guest, and the sight was unnerving in the extreme. As instructed, Putnam had brought a coffee tray to the saloon, but it stood untouched on the sofa table, and her ladyship was pacing round the middle of the Aubusson rug. No, not exactly pacing. To be more accurate, she was trotting— almost running—and Susanna distantly marveled that a woman of such prodigious size could move so rapidly.

But it was hardly the time to congratulate Lady Calthrop for her athletic prowess. Indeed, it was not the time to attempt any discussion at all: her ladyship's flame was clearly one of historic proportions. Susanna backed cautiously into the corridor, thinking to send word that she was too sick to receive callers after all. One step, two . . . She trod squarely on the toe of Ned's nearer boot, and he emitted a grunt of pain.

"Susanna?" Lady Calthrop spun her head and glowered at the archway. "And Lord Langham." Her scowl infinitesimally moderated.

"How good of you to call, Lady Calthrop," Ned said fervently. He hurried across the room, fairly dragging Susanna in his wake. "A less tolerant person would have counted it our duty to call on you. As we intended to do immediately after breakfast."

"You did?" Her ladyship's expression moderated a fraction more.

"Actually," the earl confided with a sheepish grin, "Susanna wished to set out *before* breakfast, but I hesitated to disturb you so early. She was most anxious to apologize for the unfortunate events which occurred last night."

"As well she should have been," Lady Calthrop sniffed.

"Though last night was not the first of Mr. Kean's appalling social performances, of course." Ned sighed and shook his head. "In fact, it was not even the *worst*. I am given to understand that he recently created an awful scene at Lady Melbourne's. With the Regent himself present."

Susanna had heard of no such scene, and she would have wagered her last groat that it was another figment of the earl's fertile imagination. But a clever one, she conceded as Lady Calthrop's eyes widened. With a few well-chosen sentences, Ned had elevated himself and Susanna—and, by association, their guests—to the loftiest pinnacle of the *ton*.

"Naturally, Susanna was in hopes that Mr. Kean would behave more circumspectly at her salon than he did at Lady Melbourne's," Ned continued. "When he did not . . . Well, you witnessed her reaction." He sympathetically patted Susanna's hand. "She was so distraught that she elected to retire without supper."

"Distraught?" her ladyship echoed suspiciously. "Colonel Fordyce stated that Susanna was ill."

"Ill with *dismay*," the earl said. "In retrospect, she well recognizes that she should not have deserted her guests. At the time, however, she was too mortified to endure Mr. Kean's horrifying conduct an instant longer."

"Umm." Lady Calthrop glanced back and forth between them. "Let me not hide my teeth, Lord Langham. I was under the impression that you and Susanna had had some sort of falling-out."

"A quarrel?" Ned's tone was one of stunned disbelief. "Susanna and I? At the risk of offending you, Lady Calthrop, I am compelled to wonder how you could possibly have arrived at such an absurd conclusion."

"Susanna looked very distraught indeed when I glimpsed her in the vestibule. You now claim that she was dismayed by Mr. Kean's behavior—"

"And mortified," the earl reminded her.

"Pray permit me to finish," her ladyship snapped. "A few minutes later, you appeared in the foyer, and you looked even more distressed than Susanna."

"I daresay I did," Ned agreed mildly. "I am invariably distressed when my dear wife is overset." He patted Susanna's hand again. "And at the moment you saw me, I was also concerned about Lady Thornton."

"Lady Thornton?" Lady Calthrop frowned, then bobbed her head in recollection. "Yes, Colonel Fordyce mentioned that she was ill as well. Is she a friend of yours, Lord Langham?"

"A very close friend," the earl replied, heaving another sigh. "I was bred up with Julia, and now she's widowed, I judge it my duty to ensure her welfare as best I can."

"A most commendable attitude," her ladyship murmured. "I am deeply sorry for my accusation—"

"I should prefer to term it a misinterpretation," Ned interposed kindly. "Your error was quite understandable in the circumstances, and there's no need to discuss it any further. As you can see for yourself, Susanna and I are in complete harmony."

He flung one arm around Susanna's shoulders, drew her snugly against him; and she willed herself not to jerk away.

"Yes, I can see that." Lady Calthrop sketched a contrite smile.

"Then we shall say no more about it," the earl reiterated. "Will you have a cup of coffee?"

"No, thank you. I was on my way to the mantua-maker for the final fitting of my gown. The one I'm to wear for Alicia's come-out." Her ladyship hurried to the drawing-room entry, stepped into the hall, turned back.

"Your salon did have one saving grace, Susanna," she said charitably. "Since Mr. Kean was much too fixed to conduct a civilized conversation, Colonel Fordyce and Lady Hadleigh began to chat with me. I found them immensely pleasant."

"Umm," Susanna muttered noncommittally. She could not suppose that Percy and Nancy reciprocated Lady Calthrop's glowing opinion.

"I collected that they are particular friends of yours," her ladyship went on. "The colonel indicated they attend your salons on a regular basis."

Particular friends? Susanna stiffened, frozen by the fear that Percy had inadvertently revealed the true nature of their relationship. But Lady Calthrop's demeanor was one of perfect innocence.

"Yes, they are." Susanna drew a shaky breath and inclined her own head. "Colonel Fordyce and Lady Hadleigh were an enormous comfort to me during Ned's absence."

"Then I shall invite them to my house party," her ladyship said.

Susanna was not inordinately surprised by this announcement. The Dickinsons' financial woes had placed them largely out of touch with society in recent years, and she had wondered whom—apart from the two families and their immediate neighbors—Lady Calthrop could recruit for her gala gathering.

"I am sure they will be delighted," she rejoined aloud. In fact, she reflected, Percy *would* be delighted, and Nancy might enjoy the novelty of a weekend in the country.

"I shall write the invitations as soon as I return from the mantua-maker." Lady Calthrop paused, tapping one gloved finger thoughtfully against her chin. "And inasmuch as Lady Thornton is such a good friend of yours, Lord Langham, I daresay I should include her as well."

Susanna detected a telltale twitch at the corners of Ned's mouth, and she was hard put to repress a giggle of her own. She wished she could be a mouse in the wall when her ladyship realized, some months hence, that she had promoted two illicit liaisons beneath her very roof. She would undoubtedly conceive some way to transfer the blame to her hapless husband—

"I haven't the time to copy their directions now."

Lady Calthrop interrupted Susanna's speculation. "Hugh will come to get them later in the day. Don't ring for your butler, Susanna; I shall show myself out. Good morning, Lord Langham."

She turned again and sped out of sight, and the slam of the front door soon echoed up the staircase.

"Did I smooth her feathers or did I not?"

The earl grinned triumphantly down at Susanna, and she swallowed a sharp retort. He had smoothed her ladyship's feathers with remarkable ease indeed, and she fancied it would be excessively ungracious to criticize his tactics.

"Yes," she mumbled, "and I appreciate your effort. I couldn't have dealt with her half so well."

"Only because you do not have half of my experience." His smile grew sardonic round the edges, then faded altogether. "I am told that the first complete sentence I uttered was a compliment to Lady Murray for the gown she wore to one of my parents' assemblies. The ball took place just before my third birthday."

"I miss your point," Susanna said.

"My point is that a child of the *ton* learns to be artificial almost as soon as he learns to talk. It is a skill you did not acquire till much later in your life." He stopped and studied her face a moment. "Does it not trouble you?" he asked. "Do you not sometimes long for the days when you could merely be yourself?"

"One can never be oneself. Even at the age of three, you could not have told Lady Murray that you thought her ball gown *ugly*.'

"That is simple courtesy," he said. "An entirely different matter. I don't wish to be deliberately unkind. It would give me no pleasure to advise Lady Emma Whitworth that she's too knocker-faced to win a husband. Or to inform Dickie that he's a mutton-head—"

"Dickie?" Susanna gasped. "Viscount Buckley is your dearest friend."

"He *was* my dearest friend," the earl corrected. "A circumstance which now astonishes me, I might add. He chanced to be home the night of my arrival because he was temporarily short of funds. A moneylender remedied that situation the following day, and Dickie has subsequently spent all his waking hours at the macao table at White's."

"He has spent all his waking hours at White's as long as I've known him," she said wryly. "He hasn't changed, Ned."

"No, *I* have changed. I've observed for myself that there is a better way to live. In Louisiana—"

"Louisiana!" Susanna belatedly became aware that Ned's arm was still around her shoulders, and she squirmed out of his grasp and stamped her foot with annoyance. "Must you forever rattle on about Louisiana? I told you long since that I'm sick of discussing it."

"When did we *discuss* it, Susanna? I related a few tales to amuse your friends, and you scarcely listened even to those."

"I listened to as much as I cared to," she snapped. "I believe I also indicated that if you were so enchanted with Louisiana, you should never have left. Since it's too late for that, I recommend you go back at the earliest opportunity."

"That was precisely my intention," he said. "I returned to England with the hope of persuading you to go back to Louisiana with me."

"Go back with you?" she echoed incredulously. "How did you think to secure Papa's consent to such a proposal? Did you fancy he would pay for another extended holiday so hard on the heels of the last?"

"It wasn't a holiday I had in mind. I should like to settle permanently in the United States."

"Ah." His whole devious plan grew clear, and she nodded. "Your actual intention was to persuade Papa to purchase property in Louisiana and appoint you to manage it."

"I shall, in fact, encourage Simon to invest—"

"And he would not have consented to that either." Susanna flew on. "He may well elect to purchase property; he has a prodigious keen eye for profit. But he will engage a local agent to handle his affairs."

"You are once more failing to listen, Susanna."

"Indeed I am," she retorted warmly. "Did you truly expect me to entertain a scheme designed to defraud my own father?"

"I—"

"Well, I should not have done so." She answered her own rhetorical question. "Not in any conditions. If you had returned from America when you promised, long before I met Percy, I should still have refused to assist you."

"I am not soliciting your assistance—"

"You struck a bargain with Papa." She waved him furiously to silence. "I was not informed of the particulars, but I presume he provided a monstrous handsome dowry."

Ned flushed, parted his lips, bit them closed again.

"In exchange for which you had only to give me a place among the peerage. And now you wish to renege even on that small offering. No"—she shook her head—"I should never have abetted your plan. My father *bought* you, and when he did, he was purchasing an earl as his son-in-law. Had he wanted a foreign bailiff, he could have hired one at vastly less expense and with infinitely less trouble."

Ned's flush deepened, and in stark contrast, white lines of anger appeared around his mouth. But when he spoke, his voice was low and calm.

"You have stated your position very well," he said. "I consequently perceive no reason to belabor the point any further."

"No, there is no reason," she agreed. "If you are so eager to return to Louisiana, perhaps you can prevail on Lady Thornton to finance your adventure."

"Perhaps I shall," he said pleasantly. "Now, if you will pardon me . . ." He bowed and strode toward the drawing-room archway.

"I trust you will caution her not to mention your journey before Alicia is wed," Susanna hissed after him. "Do not forget—forget *again*, I should have said—your pledge to conduct yourself discreetly."

"No, I shan't forget."

He stepped into the corridor, disappeared, and Susanna gazed in his wake. She had won the day, she judged, and she wondered why her victory seemed so very hollow.

Chapter 11

" . . . LADY LANGHAM?"

At the sound of her name, Susanna started, focused her eyes, and found Putnam peering down at her. He had been talking for some minutes, she calculated, but apart from the last, she had not heard a word he said.

"I am sorry," she murmured. "I fear I was not attending."

The butler heaved a little sigh, and Susanna could well surmise his feelings. He had been compelled to repeat himself on countless occasions these three days past, and he must wonder if his mistress's illness had permanently clouded her mind. She fancied that a less experienced servant would have lost his temper long since.

"I was reviewing the supper arrangements," he said, a note of impatience creeping into his voice for the first time. "I suggested that we move all the side tables to the far end of the ballroom"—he indicated the area opposite the orchestra gallery—"and draw the sofas and chairs around them. You will remember that we previously decided to place a dozen tables in the saloon."

In fact, Susanna did not remember this, but she counted it best to bob her head in agreement.

"You do concur then? That is what I was asking. I see no other way to seat everyone at once."

"Umm." Susanna pretended to ponder his plan, but she did not really care where the guests were seated. Indeed, she no longer cared if they even *came* to her assembly. "Yes, I concur," she muttered at last.

"Thank you, ma'am."

Putnam bowed and sped away, and Susanna gazed about the ballroom. Though Papa had described the London townhouse as a "wedding gift," she had always suspected that it was a principal component of her dowry. Be that as it might, Papa—and Ned, to give him credit—had permitted her to select the house herself; and after visiting a dozen available properties, she had chosen this one solely because of the ballroom.

Actually, she amended, the departed owner's solicitor had *said* it was a ballroom: it was so dark and dank and filled with cobwebs that if it had been located on the understory, Susanna would have thought it a cellar. But it was situated on the first floor, occupying the whole width of the house behind the morning parlor and the music room, and she immediately glimpsed its potential. Once the rococo plasterwork was restored, the mahogany floor repaired, the marble hearth and gilded mirrors cleaned, she and Ned could conduct one splendid assembly on another.

They had not, of course, because Ned had left before the renovation of the house was finished, and Susanna hadn't wanted to hostess a ball alone. Now, at last, her dream of a grand assembly was coming to pass. Her entire staff had been pressed into service, and they were busily stripping the protective coverings from the furniture, scrubbing the windows, polishing the lusters of the enormous crystal chandeliers. The scene was remarkably similar to the one she'd envisioned so many years before, and she supposed she should be fairly wild with excitement.

But her true emotion was more nearly one of . . . She groped for the right word and eventually selected *panic*. She had been in a daze since Friday morning, obsessed by the realization that her marriage was inexorably approaching its end. Today was Monday; in three short nights, she would bring Alicia out. The following day, she would drive to Kent for Lady Calthrop's house party, and there was every reason to expect that her sister's engagement would be announced during the weekend. After which, Papa would undoubtedly press for an early wedding. Simon Randall had never permitted the grass to grow beneath his feet for long, and when he divined the perilous state of his elder daughter's marriage, he would perceive the necessity of conducting Alicia's nuptials as quickly as possible.

Possibly as soon as July, Susanna estimated, clenching her hands. Yes, July was an excellent time to hold a wedding: though the *ton* had recovered from the rigors of the Season, they had not yet settled back into their placid rural routines. And July was so frightfully close! Alicia could conceivably be wed in a matter of weeks. Ned would then be free to introduce a bill of divorcement and, upon its passage, to emigrate to Louisiana with Lady Thornton—

"Susanna?"

She started again, spun around, and beheld Nancy striding toward her.

"I didn't mean to alarm you," Lady Hadleigh said, reaching Susanna's side. "I waved from the entry, but you seemed to be in another world. Well, I daresay the planning of a great ball requires all one's concentration."

She sounded a trifle mifty, and Susanna felt a prickle of guilt. Nancy had failed to pay her customary Friday-morning call, had failed to appear at Lord Madison's rout or Mrs. Foley's musicale; but Susanna had been too distracted by her own problems to grant more than a fleeting thought to her friend. She now collected from Lady Hadleigh's rheumy eyes and red nose that she had been laid low by a severe cold. As if in confirmation, Nancy pulled a handkerchief from her reticule, raised it to her face, and dramatically blew said nose.

"Yes, I've been quite busy," Susanna mumbled apologetically. "May I offer you some breakfast?"

"No, thank you. The one advantage of my condition"— Lady Hadleigh assumed a martyred look —"is that it has altogether destroyed my appetite. I've eaten only a few bowls of soup since your salon, and I do believe I have lost a good deal of weight."

Insofar as Susanna could determine, Nancy had not

lost a single ounce; as always, the seams of her spencer threatened to give way at any moment. But Susanna did not judge it the proper time to voice this opinion, and she issued a noncommittal grunt instead.

"However," Lady Hadleigh said, "I should be happy to sit down. If you can spare a minute or two from your *busy* schedule," she added pointedly.

She stalked away without awaiting a response, and Susanna trudged in her wake. The servants had not yet begun to move the furniture, and Nancy sank onto the Egyptian sofa just inside the entry. The furniture dealer had assured Susanna that the couch could comfortably accommodate three, but when she took the place beside Lady Hadleigh, she discovered that their knees were almost touching. She must remember to assign only two guests to the sofa. Ned and Lady Thornton maybe; they would enjoy the cozy proximity—

"Susanna!" Nancy stamped one foot with irritation. "Do you have time to talk or not?"

"Forgive me." Susanna shook her head to clear it. "I've been somewhat preoccupied in recent days as well."

"Somewhat preoccupied?" Lady Hadleigh echoed. "It would be more accurate to say that you are at the point of coma." She stopped and knit her brows. "You aren't really ill, are you?"

"No, that was merely an excuse. I had . . . had reasons for wishing to leave the salon."

"I thought as much." Nancy smugly inclined her own head. "My guess was that you and Ned had quarreled."

Her guess? Susanna wondered. Or . . . "Did Lady Calthrop say that?" she demanded aloud. "She conjectured the same thing. She came the next day to tell me so."

"Lady Calthrop." Nancy made a moue of vexation. "What a dreadful woman. I thought Cuthbert's late mother was the worst harridan I should ever encounter, but I do believe Lady Calthrop surpasses her. I scarcely know whether to be flattered or offended that she invited me to her party."

"You did receive the invitation then," Susanna said gratuitously.

"That is what I was *attempting* to tell you earlier. Yes, Percy and I both received invitations, and we have discussed the matter and determined to go to Kent together. My health permitting." Lady Hadleigh punctuated this proviso with another great honk into her handkerchief. "Percy will attend the party with or without me, of course. He is excessively eager to meet your father."

Good God. Susanna had not considered that aspect of the situation, and she narrowly repressed a moan. Papa would undoubtedly accuse her of arranging Percy's invitation—

"But Lady Calthrop said nothing to me about an argument," Nancy continued. "As we were the only guests with a clear view of the vestibule, I daresay we independently reached the same conclusion. You flew through as though the devil himself were at your heels—"

"You needn't remind me." Susanna waved her to silence. "I recollect what happened all too well. Fortunately, Ned was able to persuade Lady Calthrop that I was distressed by Mr. Kean's behavior."

"That is fortunate," Nancy agreed. "It's a pity he isn't here similarly to persuade *me*. Since he is not, perhaps you would like to tell me the nature of your quarrel."

In fact, Susanna did not like this prospect at all, but she realized that dissimulation would be futile. Like a dog worrying a bone for the last bit of marrow, Lady Hadleigh would not rest until she had extracted the truth; if her curiosity were not satisfied now, she would badger Susanna for weeks to come.

"Lady Thornton was ill," she began with a sigh of resignation. "*Genuinely* ill, and Ned escorted her into Grosvenor Square . . ." She briefly related the story of her own wanderings in the square and the scene she had literally stumbled upon at the end of her quest. "Lady Thornton raced back to her carriage," she finished, "and I returned to the house a few minutes later."

"So overset that you elected to forgo supper," Nancy said.

"Yes, I was overset!" Susanna snapped. "Would you not be overset if you observed your husband in the very act of seducing another woman?"

"To the contrary." Lady Hadleigh sketched a wry smile. "If Cuthbert demonstrated an ability to seduce *anyone*, I should conduct the grandest celebration since the visit of the Allied Monarchs."

"I was trying to be serious," Susanna said stiffly.

"Then I shall be serious as well." Nancy's smile faded. "I can seriously say that I should not be overset by the circumstances you describe. Not if I had already decided to terminate my marriage." She paused and wiped her swollen nose. "Unless I still cared for my husband. Which—or so you insist—you do not."

"No, I do not."

"Then I fancy your pride was wounded, and you've no one but yourself to blame for that. Lord Langham is a singularly attractive man, and it was your choice to set him adrift." Lady Hadleigh thrust her handkerchief back into her reticule. "Be that as it may, I have wasted enough of your valuable time—"

"I didn't tell you the half of it," Susanna blurted out as Nancy started to rise. "After Lady Thornton retreated to her carriage, Ned claimed that *she* had made advances to *him*. He then proposed that he and I should reconcile."

"Did he?" Lady Hadleigh sank back onto the sofa. "And what was your response?"

"I suspected he was primarily interested in Papa's fortune, and my suspicion was confirmed the next day. Following our conversation with Lady Calthrop, Ned admitted that he has intended from the start to return to Louisiana. He was in hopes I would consent to accompany him. At Papa's expense, of course."

"Lord Langham said that? That you should ask your father to finance the excursion?"

"No, he didn't *say* it, but it was very clear—"

"What is clear to me," Nancy interrupted, "is that you are determined to believe the worst of your husband. Did it occur to you even for a moment that he might have been sincere? That he might honestly wish to build a life with you in the United States? No, it did not." She answered her own question. "It did not because you have refused from the instant Ned arrived to give him a chance to prove his good will."

"I told you what happened *the instant he arrived*—"

"What happened, Susanna, is precisely the reverse of what happened Thursday night: your husband saw you in the arms of another man."

"Yes, but—"

"And I daresay he was at least as distressed as you were." Lady Hadleigh flew on. "Much too distressed to heed your excuses, at any rate."

"But that was two weeks ago," Susanna protested. "Since then—"

"Since then, he has suggested a reconciliation and invited you to return to Louisiana with him. And what have you done? You have resented every second of his popularity and made his existence as difficult as you could."

Yes, she had, Susanna owned. Even in the small matter of a valet, she had been deliberately perverse. She could readily have engaged a competent manservant for a month or two, but she had sought to punish Ned by saddling him with Ward. She parted her lips, but no words came, and she snapped them closed again.

"I don't mean to pinch at you, Susanna." Nancy's voice was uncharacteristically gentle. "But I could not call myself your friend if I neglected to advise you that you are at the point of committing a disastrous error. It is as plain as the nose on my face that you are still in love with Ned."

As if to emphasize her statement, she snatched her handkerchief back out of her reticule and once more sniffled into it. "You are still in love with him," she repeated, "and if your pride impels you to let him go, you will suffer for it the rest of your days."

Still in love with him. Susanna's heart began to race so madly that she could hear the blood pounding in her ears, echoing the refrain over and over. How could she have failed to perceive the truth for herself? She had loved Ned from the first moment she saw him, would continue to love him till the moment she died, and that explained everything. She experienced a brief, overwhelming rush of relief, and then her eyes widened with dismay.

"But what am I to do?" she whispered.

"Do?" Lady Hadleigh resumed her customary brisk tone. "You must tell him your feelings, of course. Unless I am badly mistaken, he will react with *considerable* enthusiasm, and you'll have a lively reconciliation indeed. Maybe you should take the precaution of procuring a new mattress before you bare your soul. Your soul and the more visible portions of your anatomy as well."

"Nancy!" Susanna chided.

But her remonstrance was an absent one; she was too happy even to generate a proper blush. It was another example of exaggerating one's problems, she reflected—of stitching a great tapestry of woe from a few strands of thread. She had only to speak candidly with Ned, and . . .

"Percy," she groaned. "We forgot Percy."

"*I* did not forget Percy," Lady Hadleigh corrected. "As I mentioned some weeks since, I am prepared to introduce him to any number of eligible women. He may be in the mopes for a month or two, but he'll eventually find a suitable wife. You needn't tease yourself about Percy."

"But I do owe him an explanation," Susanna said. "And the only honorable course is to tell him my intention before I talk to Ned."

"Perhaps so," Nancy conceded. "I shall drop you by Percy's house on my way to Leicester Square. It's early yet, but he rises at the crack of dawn."

"No!" Susanna shook her head. "I'm too busy to see Percy today. In fact, I'm too busy to see him before the assembly. I shall speak with him and Ned both while we're in Kent. The atmosphere will be much more relaxed—"

"You are a coward, Susanna," Lady Hadleigh interposed dryly. "You could offer a thousand logical reasons to delay, and I should still judge you a coward. But since a few days can't possibly signify, I shan't glump at you any further."

She closed her reticule and stood up. "I shall, instead, keep my appointment with the mantua-maker and then go directly home to rest. I should hate to miss what promises to be an excessively interesting weekend."

Nancy hurried out of the ballroom, once more dabbing at her nose, and Susanna glanced around again. Had the servants wrought a miracle? she wondered. Or was she merely viewing the scene through different eyes? Whatever the case, the windows and chandeliers seemed to sparkle, the floor to gleam; and she began to believe that her dream—all her dreams—might really be fulfilled.

Chapter 12

"I LOOK AWFUL!" Alicia wailed.

She gazed despondently into the mirror above her dressing table, and Susanna bit back a smile. She could well recollect the attack of nerves she had suffered before she and Lady Elwood left for Almack's. Her bedchamber in Papa's rented townhouse had been equipped with a cheval glass, but she had stared at her reflection in precisely the same fashion—persuaded that she was the most knocker-faced, ill-dressed girl in the British Empire. In point of fact, Alicia looked quite handsome. The graceful lines of her white muslin gown made her appear much thinner than she was; and the blue ribbon at the waist, the headdress of blue satin flowers, complemented her arresting eyes.

"You look splendid," Susanna said soothingly, patting her sister's shoulder. "I've no doubt you will be the hit of the assembly."

"I should be a greater hit in my sapphire satin," Alicia sniffed.

She turned away from the mirror and enviously studied Susanna's gown, which did, indeed, feature a corsage of deep blue satin. Below the bodice, however, the dress was white: a lace skirt over a satin slip, finished at the bottom with two satin rouleaus and—between them—a row of satin roses intermixed with garlands of pearls. Susanna had debated at great length whether to wear a toque or a simple headband and had eventually chosen the latter. Evidently she had made the right decision, she thought immodestly, because she, too, looked quite handsome—

"It is hanging in the wardrobe," Alicia said.

"Umm?"

Susanna had lost the drift of the conversation, and she frowned and spun her head. It was a familiar experience, she reflected wryly, for her daze of despair had given way to an equally impenetrable fog of joy. She had been literally counting the hours since Monday, and now, with any luck, fewer than four and twenty remained. If all went well, she would be able to speak with Percy as soon as they arrived in Kent, to speak with Ned shortly thereafter; and by this time tomorrow, all her problems would be resolved—

"My sapphire dress is in the wardrobe," Alicia reiterated. "I could change in a few minutes."

She must try to concentrate on the task at hand, Susanna chided herself. "You could, but you cannot," she rejoined aloud. "We discussed your attire before you came to London. The sapphire gown is entirely inappropriate for a young girl just coming out, and we shan't belabor the matter any further. Come along now. It's a quarter to nine, and the first guests will be here at any moment."

To say the truth, Susanna owned, she was a trifle nervous herself, and as she ushered Alicia into the ballroom, she glanced apprehensively about. But everything appeared to be in order: none of the florist's potted palms or bouquets had expired since she went upstairs to dress; the orchestra, seated in the gallery, were energetically tuning their instruments; and a veritable battalion of footmen—armed with trays of champagne—was poised to march into battle.

"Ah," Ned said. "What a wonderful sight for tired eyes. The two loveliest women I know standing side by side."

The earl had crept up behind them, and when Susanna whirled around, her knees weakened. During the days just past, viewing him through eyes undimmed by prejudice, she had been compelled to admit that he *had* grown handsomer over the years. Though his tan had faded a bit, he had not regained any of his lost weight; and in his wasp-waisted coat, his smallclothes and silk stockings, he seemed even taller and leaner than he was.

"Loveliest?" Alicia echoed with a grimace of distaste. "Susanna wouldn't allow me to wear my favorite gown. She insisted I rig myself out like . . . like . . ."

"Like a vestal virgin?" Ned supplied dryly. "I don't subscribe to that particular custom either. But since it *is* the custom, permit me to say that you're the most fetching vestal virgin it has ever been my privilege to encounter."

"Really?"

As if by magic, Alicia's pout vanished, and her own eyes began to sparkle. Indeed, it *was* magic, Susanna thought—the magic of Ned's charm—but she no longer resented it.

"Really." The earl nodded. "As I told you earlier, it is fortunate for Hugh that he won your heart before you could enchant every other young buck in England. In fact, were I not so *happily* wed to your sister, I should undertake to court you myself."

He cast Susanna a sardonic smile, and she clenched her hands. That had been the most difficult aspect of the preceding days: keeping her raging emotions to herself. She had repeatedly been tempted to forget Percy and blurt out her feelings, but she had come to believe that the honorable course was also the best. When she did confess her love to Ned, he would naturally ask whether she had terminated her relationship with the colonel, and she wanted to be able to say she had.

"Susanna!" Lady Calthrop brushed past Putnam and bustled toward them, her husband and son trailing in her wake. "It lacks but five minutes to nine, and we must form a receiving line. Good evening, Lord Langham. Alicia."

She paused for perhaps half a second to incline her head in greeting, then returned her attention to Susanna. "I fancy," she said grudgingly, "that inasmuch as it's your home, you should be at the head of the line. And since Alicia is your sister, she should probably be positioned beside you. I shall stand at the end, and Walter and Hugh and Lord Langham can mingle with the guests."

Susanna had planned for herself and Alicia alone to welcome the guests at the ballroom entry, but she perceived at once that objection would be futile. At least, she observed with relief, Lady Calthrop looked relatively presentable. Her smoke-colored gown emphasized her one redeeming feature—her fine gray eyes—and the cut of the dress minimized her multiple chins and dumpy little body.

"You should step back a foot or two, Susanna," her ladyship continued. "And Alicia should move here . . ."

She arranged and rearranged them—tugging them about, standing away to evaluate the effect—until, at last, she was satisfied. And not a moment too soon, for even as she nodded her final approval, Putnam announced the first arriving party. Lady Calthrop was hard pressed to scurry to her self-appointed place at the end of the line, and she was still panting with exertion when Sir Cecil and Lady Rowe strode into the ballroom.

According to Susanna's list, some two hundred guests had consented to attend the assembly, but it seemed that the arrivals numbered in the thousands. She had been in a receiving line twice before, first at her engagement ball and later at the banquet following her wedding. But Lady Elwood had been the official hostess on those occasions, and Susanna had been required only to react —to greet the guests she knew and acknowledge the introductions to those she didn't. She soon discovered that it was immensely more tiring to manage the proceedings: to register the names Putnam intoned, welcome each arriving party, present them to Alicia and Lady Calthrop. To make matters worse, her ladyship insisted on chatting with each guest at prodigious length; and by half past nine, there was an ever-growing, and ever more impatient, throng awaiting entrance to the ballroom.

By a quarter past ten, however, the flood of arrivals had dwindled to a mere trickle; and fifteen minutes after that, Susanna counted it safe to disband the receiving line. Lady Calthrop stalked toward her husband—no doubt to berate him for some real or imagined breach of conduct—and Hugh bounded forward to claim Alicia's hand for the next set. Alicia had performed splendidly, Susanna reflected with satisfaction, even remembering to curtsy to the Duke of Cambridge and the Duke of Cumberland and address them as "your highness." Indeed, it appeared that *everything* was progressing splendidly: the floor was clogged with dancers, and those not dancing were engaged in lively conversation.

But it wouldn't do to rest on her laurels, Susanna counseled herself; exhausted as she was, she must recheck the supper arrangements. She could see from where she stood that the tables in the ballroom were properly set, and she rapidly inspected the remainder of the first story. The morning parlor, music room, and saloon looked to be in order as well, which—in view of the caterer's exorbitant fee—seemed little enough to ask.

Susanna descended the staircase and stepped into the dining room. The caterer's employees were to serve the meal (one of many excuses he had used to justify his outrageous bill), and the table had been extended to its full length and laid for twenty. After much deliberation, Susanna had abandoned the notion of assigning every guest a seat and elected to provide place cards only in the dining room. Ned would occupy the head of the table, she the foot; and they would be joined by Hugh and Alicia, Lord and Lady Calthrop, her ladyship's relatives, their royal highnesses, and the members of the cabinet. She had put Lady Calthrop next to the prime minister, and she wryly suspected that Lord Liverpool— the most powerful man in England—would emerge the worse from the encounter.

Susanna walked to the rear stairs, tilted one ear toward the kitchen, and judged it best to proceed no further. After years of complaining that she could not prepare supper for two dozen, Mrs. Putnam had flown into the boughs when informed that *outsiders* would be engaged to feed the two hundred guests expected at the assembly. As nearly as Susanna could determine, she was now venting her wrath on the caterer and his assistants: though her words were indistinguishable, her tone was unmistakably one of fury. Susanna could not quell a wicked grin; maybe the caterer would earn his outlandish fee after all.

Susanna crossed the vestibule and peered into the library. It had been necessary to place four tables here rather than the two she normally utilized for her salons, but the room did not look as crowded as she'd feared. She started to step back to the main staircase, but as she turned her head, she noticed that the corner table was improperly set. No, not misset, she corrected, studying it more closely; someone had left a fan squarely in the middle, beside the floral centerpiece. She hurried forward, thinking to transfer the fan to the Pembroke table, which had been moved against the front wall.

"Ah, Susanna." Percy's voice caught her up just as she reached the supper table, and she spun around. "How convenient that I should find you here."

"Convenient?" she repeated shrilly.

"I meant that . . . er . . ." As had been the case at her last soiree, the colonel seemed peculiarly nervous, and he stopped and cleared his throat. "I meant that I wanted to speak with you in private, and it's unlikely anyone will disturb us here. I believe you indicated that supper would not be served till midnight."

"No, it will not, but I . . . I . . ."

Susanna sputtered to a halt as well. Perhaps Nancy had been right, she thought; maybe her "honorable course" was nothing more than cowardice. Whatever her true motives, she was in no humor to talk to Percy tonight, and she cast about for a credible means of escape.

"I must return to the ballroom," she concluded in a rush. "I really shouldn't have left at all, but I felt I ought to check the supper arrangements—"

"The assembly is proceeding without a hitch," the colonel interposed. "Indeed, the guests are remarking that yours is by far the most entertaining ball of the Season."

"I . . . I'm delighted to hear it," Susanna stammered. "But you know how quickly things can go amiss without the hostess's personal supervision—"

"And I was wondering how our other project is progressing." Percy flew relentlessly on.

"Our . . . other project." Susanna's mouth had gone quite dry, and she tried in vain to moisten her lips.

"The dissolution of your marriage."

The colonel closed the library door, strode to her side, and set his *chapeau bras* next to the fan. The deuced fan! Susanna ground her teeth. Were it not for the fan, she would be safely back in the ballroom by now.

"Since the assembly is such a success," Percy continued, "I daresay your sister's engagement will be announced during the weekend."

"Yes, I'm sure it will!" Susanna's voice had once more risen to a screech. "And I was thrilled to learn that you'll be in Kent to enjoy the festivities. Now, if you will excuse me . . ."

She snatched the fan off the table and attempted to walk past him, but his fingers snaked around her elbow.

"I am more interested in the events which will follow the engagement festivities," he said. "That is the subject I wished to discuss. Does Lord Langham still plan to introduce a bill of divorcement as soon as Alicia is wed?"

"He might reconsider," Susanna mumbled, easing her arm from Percy's grasp.

"Excellent." The colonel bobbed his head. "Anxious as I am to resolve our dilemma, I have come to believe that annulment is preferable to divorce. More . . . more *honorable*. I've written to my cousin in Yorkshire, and he is prepared to assist us."

She could put him off no longer, Susanna realized; at this juncture, further dissimulation would become an outright lie. She squared her shoulders and replaced the fan on the corner of the table.

"There will not be a divorce or an annulment either one," she said as levelly as she could. "I have determined to reconcile with Ned."

"You have told him so?" Percy said sharply.

"Not yet. I counted it my duty to advise you of my intentions first."

"Then perhaps I can persuade you to change your mind."

The colonel withdrew a watch from his waistcoat pocket, opened it, glanced at the face; and Susanna felt a stab of pity. Did he honestly suppose that matters of the heart could be scheduled with the precision of a military campaign? That a few extra minutes of conversation might serve to modify her decision?

"I'm afraid not, Percy," she said gently. "My mind is quite made up."

"If you are concerned about my financial circumstances, permit me to assure you that I shall come into my inheritance very shortly." He returned the watch to his pocket. "Uncle Charles grows weaker with every passing hour. His physician does not expect him to survive another month."

Susanna did not know whether to express condolences or congratulations, so she did neither. "The money doesn't signify," she said instead. "Nor the title. I admit that the title might have won my father over, but it never signified to me."

"But you loved me, Susanna!"

"No, I did not." She reached out and awkwardly patted his shoulder, but she recognized that no amount of kindness could blunt her words. "That is the whole point, Percy. I'm enormously fond of you, and I hope we can continue to be friends. But I perceived earlier in the week that I'm still in love with Ned. I shall *always* be in love with Ned; and if it is any consolation, I fancy our marriage—yours and mine—would have been wretchedly unhappy."

She paused and obtained the impression that his attention had wandered; his eyes were darting between her and the door. But maybe that was for the best, she reflected, and she once more patted his sleeve.

"There is nothing further to discuss," she finished, "and I've been away from the ballroom much too long already. I shall consequently ask again to be excused."

Susanna took a step or two toward the library door, but after that, things happened so rapidly that she could not reconstruct the precise sequence of events. The clock in the foyer began to chime eleven, she recalled, and she recollected that she had left the fan on the supper table. But she could not have said whether she started back to retrieve it or Percy moved forward; she remembered only that the colonel suddenly seized her in his arms and smashed his mouth down on hers. His action was so uncharacteristic, so unexpected, that Susanna was temporarily paralyzed. At length, however (it might have been seconds or minutes), she realized that his assault had thrown both of them dangerously off-balance and put them in imminent peril of falling to the carpet. Until that moment, she had been desperately trying to squirm out of Percy's embrace, but she now flung her arms around his neck in an equally desperate attempt to regain their mutual equilibrium. And it was at *that* moment—or so she calculated—that the library door creaked open.

"Pray forgive my intrusion," Ned snapped.

"Lord Langham!" The colonel thrust Susanna away so abruptly that she almost lost her balance again. "How exceedingly embarrassing."

"Ned!" Susanna choked. "I can readily explain—"

"Do not trouble yourself," the earl interrupted frigidly. "I obviously arrived at an inopportune time. At *another* inopportune time, I should have said. Julia requested me to search for her fan, and she thought she might have left it here. Yes, I see it."

He stalked across the room, plucked up the fan, and marched back toward the library entry.

"Ned!" Susanna raced after him and succeeded in

capturing the tail of his coat. "This is all a dreadful misunderstanding."

"I told you not to waste your explanations on me," he hissed. He whirled around, dislodging her tenuous grip on his coat. "Save them for someone who might believe you. Someone like—"

"Lord Langham!" Lady Calthrop, her plump face beaming, loomed up behind the earl. "And Susanna! How fortunate that I should find you together! I wanted to tell you both that—"

"I must beg you to pardon me, Lady Calthrop," Ned said savagely, spinning round again. "I am not at my best just now."

He bowed past her, galloped up the staircase, and her ladyship frowned after him. "Dear, dear," she clucked. "Is Lord Langham ill?"

"Yes!" Susanna eagerly snatched at this excuse. "Yes, he has a . . . a dreadful headache. So I trust you will also pardon me—"

"Dear, *dear*." Lady Calthrop's cluck became a moan. "I hope he will recover in time to attend my party."

"I am sure he will," Susanna said. "Well, actually I'm not *sure*," she amended. "Which is why I must try to cure him without delay—"

"Is that Colonel Fordyce?" her ladyship interjected, peering over Susanna's shoulder. "Yes, it is! I am excessively pleased that you consented to come to my party as well, colonel."

"No more pleased than I was to receive your invitation." Percy sketched a gracious smile, picked up his *chapeau bras*, and strode to the library door. "I shall look forward to seeing you in Kent tomorrow."

He executed a splendid bow of his own and retreated into the vestibule, and Lady Calthrop sighed with approval.

"What a charming man," she said.

"Yes, he is," Susanna muttered, resisting the inclination to scrub her mouth with the back of her hand. "But I really should see to Ned—"

"Indeed," her ladyship continued, "*all* your friends are charming. I am compelled to own that my previous criticisms were most unjust. The company this evening are behaving with perfect propriety."

"I'm happy you feel so." Susanna backed into the entry hall.

"And Alicia's conduct has been *flawless*," Lady Calthrop went on. "That is what I wished to tell you and Lord Langham. I have firmly resolved to announce the engagement during the course of my party."

"Excellent," Susanna said. "I shall really that welcome intelligence to Ned at once—"

"However"—her ladyship raised an admonitory finger—"I should like to postpone the announcement till the end of the ball on Saturday night. Make it the grand finale, so to speak. You and Lord Langham must not drop a *hint* of it before then."

"No, we shall not. I shall warn Ned immediately—"

"Nor your father," Lady Calthrop added. "But I daresay I shall speak with Mr. Randall before you do. We plan to depart for Kent at eight o'clock . . ."

She chattered on, describing the schedule for the weekend in excruciating detail, until—as the clock struck quarter past eleven—Susanna could bear her endless discourse no longer.

"I am certain your party will be lovely," she said, cutting her ladyship off in mid-word. "And I should hate to think that Ned's . . . ah . . . indisposition might cause us to miss it. So if you will excuse me, I must determine whether he requires the services of a physician."

"Well, of course, dear. I . . ."

Susanna fled up the stairs without awaiting the rest of Lady Calthrop's reply and peered into the saloon, the music room, and the morning parlor. A number of guests, evidently tired of dancing, had repaired to the chairs and sofas to sip champagne, but Ned was not among them. Susanna hurried across the parlor, smiling as cheerfully as she could to the guests within, and stopped at the ballroom entry. The floor was still quite jammed, but the earl's excessive height and pale blond hair normally rendered him visible even in a crowd. Susanna surveyed the scene for several minutes and—when she did not see him—speculated that he had chosen to retire from the assembly altogether. She rushed back through the parlor, up the staircase to the second story, along the corridor to his bedchamber and frantically rapped on the door.

"You!" Ned growled, yanking the door open. "I was expecting Ward. But I fancy any such expectation was wildly optimistic. I rang for him only fifteen minutes since, and it generally takes him an hour or more to respond to the bell."

"I am sorry for that," Susanna murmured. "I shall instruct Putnam to engage an accomplished valet tomorrow."

"That won't be necessary." The earl turned away and walked briskly to the open doors of his wardrobe. "Not unless you intend to set up housekeeping with Colonel Fordyce, and *he* requires the services of a valet. I shan't be here tomorrow."

"Ned, please permit me to explain—"

"That won't be necessary either." He walked back to the bed. "Your actions spoke quite eloquently for themselves. You and your colonel are obviously so consumed by passion that you can no longer behave with even the *slightest* discretion."

"Please, Ned—"

"But I daresay no irreparable harm was done." He fastened his silver eyes on her face. "No one saw you except myself, and that was my fault, was it not? The library door was closed, and I should have knocked before I blundered inside."

"You don't understand," Susanna pleaded. "Percy . . . Percy *attacked* me."

"Attacked you." The earl emitted a mirthless chuckle. "You disappoint me, Susanna. You've become so entangled in your lies that you can't remember who said what to whom. You're parroting the very words I used when you discovered Julia and me in Grosvenor Square."

"Yes!" Susanna agreed. "And if you were saying the truth then—"

"Whether I was saying the truth or not, you elected not to believe me. As I do not believe you now."

He shifted his eyes to the bed again, and Susanna belatedly noticed that his trunk lay open on the counterpane. It was better than half full—the contents extended well above the top of the lower section—and she further observed that Ned had carried another armload of garments from the wardrobe to the bed. He dropped his burden on the counterpane, jerked the uppermost garment from the stack, folded it, and shoved it into the trunk.

"You are packing," she said gratuitously.

"Yes, one usually packs when one plans to embark upon a journey. I should be finished by now had Ward come when I rang."

"You . . . you are going back to Louisiana?" she whispered.

"Not immediately." He stuffed his white pantaloons into the trunk. "I shan't leave you in the lurch again, Susanna; I shall secure our divorce before I go. In the interim, I'll reside with Dickie."

"Will Lady Thornton go with you?" Susanna could not seem to raise her voice above a whisper. "Has she consented to finance your adventure?"

"No, she has not!" He flung his gray waistcoat into the trunk and whirled once more to face her. "For the simple reason that my *adventure*, as you call it, requires no financing. Which you would have known long ago had you ever spared a moment to listen to me. Why do you suppose I went to America in the first place?"

"You said it was to assist Papa—"

"That was a factor." He nodded. "I did wish to help Simon, but I also recognized that I couldn't accept his charity for the rest of my life. The United States seemed to afford the best opportunity to make my own fortune, and after I arrived—as I advised you in my second letter—I learned that Louisiana was a particularly promising area. And so it proved to be. Shortly after I reached New Orleans, I purchased a sugar plantation not far from the city."

"But how—"

"I used a portion of your dowry; I shan't deny that. However, the plantation has profited beyond my fondest expectations, as have the other properties I subsequently acquired. I am not yet so wealthy as Simon, and perhaps I never shall be. But before I return to America, I shall refund every groat he spent to *buy* me, with accumulated interest."

"I . . . I . . ." But she had misjudged him so completely that she could compose no adequate apology, and she lapsed into silence.

"There was one complication I did not foresee, of course," he continued. "I intended to come back for you as soon as I was established, but I reckoned without the war. Well, *c'est la vie*, as my Creole friends would say." He flashed a bitter, crooked grin. "I was detained, and you met Colonel Fordyce, and that is that."

He snatched the next garment from the heap on the bed, thrust it into the trunk; and Susanna's mind churned in calculation. It was clearly pointless to pursue the conversation tonight: Ned was too angry to entertain explanations, apologies, or any other soothing words she might offer. And who knew what might happen during the weekend? Though the earl had stated an intention to remain in England for a time, he might decide, upon reflection, to set out for Louisiana at once. He could leave it to Lord Wrentham to introduce the bill of divorcement and notify him of its passage. If she traveled to Kent alone—sorrowfully claiming that Ned's "illness" had prevented his attendance at the party after all—he might be gone when she returned . . . He transferred his charcoal tailcoat from the counterpane to the trunk, and she glimpsed a ray of hope.

"You have forgotten Alicia," she said. "We are to go

to Calthrop Hall tomorrow for the announcement of her betrothal, and Lady Calthrop has assured me that the announcement will be made. You pledged to affect a reconciliation until Alicia's future is assured. You said that inasmuch as you'd created our bumblebath—"

"I recollect what I said, Susanna." He irritably added his brown pantaloons to the growing pile of clothing in the trunk. "My memory is not as selective as yours. It is you who conveniently *forgot* that my promise was one side of a bargain. And since you have abrogated your part of the agreement, I perceive no reason to abide by mine."

He folded his cinnamon coat and placed it beside the pantaloons. "No, if I may borrow an expression used at White's, I have redeemed all my markers. We are dead even, my dear, and I won't play your adoring husband for months and months to come."

"I am not asking for months!" Susanna desperately grasped this final, slender straw. "I'm only asking you to continue our charade till Monday. Until Lady Calthrop's house party is over and Alicia's engagement has been formally announced."

"Monday?" Ned was sufficiently intrigued to stop folding his ecru waistcoat and turn his head in her direction. "Four days? What will that accomplish?"

With any luck, Susanna thought, it would give her a chance to persuade him of her love. But she couldn't own to that, and she groped for an alternative explanation.

"Once the engagement is announced, Lady Calthrop will begin planning the wedding," she replied at last. "My guess is that she and Lord Calthrop will stay in Kent; they can't possibly afford to spend the rest of the Season in town. She will therefore be unaware of our separation."

"Perhaps so," the earl conceded. "But she'll certainly hear the *on-dit* that I have introduced a bill of divorcement."

"Not if we seek an annulment instead. As I told you before, Nancy is connected to a high official in the

Church, and I'm confident Bishop Addison will act on our petition with maximum speed and the utmost discretion. Lady Calthrop will never discover what we're at."

Susanna well realized that her plan—if it could be dignified by such a term—was riddled with holes. She held her breath, waiting for Ned to point them out, but at length, he nodded.

"Very well," he said. "Pray understand, however, that my cooperation is solely for Alicia's benefit. I am still of the opinion that I owe *you* nothing. I shall accompany you to Lady Calthrop's house party, but on Monday, I shall remove to Dickie's. And before I do, we shall dispatch a letter to Bishop Addison."

"Yes, I understand."

Susanna expelled her breath in a great sigh of relief, but even as she stepped back into the corridor, she wondered how she was to salvage her marriage in four short days.

Chapter 13

SUSANNA'S TRAVELING CARRIAGE rattled to a stop, and she peered out the window on her side of the coach. She initially fancied that Tennant, the coachman, had misunderstood her instructions and taken the turn to Randall Manor, for the servant hurrying toward the carriage was Papa's first footman. But the crumbling *porte-cochère* behind him was unmistakably that of Calthrop Hall, and Susanna recollected that the Dickinsons' meager staff was scarcely adequate to operate the household from day to day. Faced with the simultaneous demands of a house party and a ball, her ladyship had obviously been compelled to borrow some of Papa's servants.

Fowler pulled the coach door open and beamed inside. "Good afternoon, Miss Susanna. Miss Alicia. And Lord Langham! What a pleasure it is to see you, sir!"

"It's a pleasure to see you again as well, Fowler," Ned growled.

Insofar as Susanna could recall, these were the first words he had spoken since their departure from Grosvenor Square, and his waspish tone was hardly encouraging. He was in prodigious poor humor indeed, and though she had lain awake most of the night, she had yet to devise a solution to her dilemma—

"Mr. Randall is eager to see you too," the footman went on. "He is just inside, in the entry hall."

Alicia had been fidgeting with impatience throughout this interchange, and as soon as Fowler handed her out of the carriage, she raced into the house to search for Hugh. The footman assisted Susanna to the drive, and she smoothed the wrinkles from her black bombazine carriage dress, straightened her hat, and drew a deep breath. She had realized she would have to deal with Papa before the day was over, but she had desperately hoped to be granted a few hours' grace. More specifically, she had hoped to warn Ned—*beg* him, if it came to that—to hide his hostility from her father.

But Alicia's presence in the coach had prevented any such conversation, as did Fowler's presence now, and Susanna could only rely on her own addled wits. The earl clambered out of the carriage and strode stonily past her, and she was hard put to catch him up before he stalked through the front door.

"Ned!"

Papa bounded forward to meet them, and in the relative gloom of the foyer, it briefly appeared that he was bearing a lance in his right hand. As he transferred the object to his left hand, however, Susanna identified it as a cue stick; and when she glanced toward the side of the entry hall, she spied Sir Reginald Milton—similarly armed—bending over the billiard table. Papa had taken up this gentlemanly pursuit during Susanna's early childhood, and she well remembered Mama's vociferous protests when he had installed a table in the foyer of Randall Manor. Papa had explained that no other room in the house afforded sufficient space for the table and the requisite area around it, whereupon Susanna had vowed that if she ever built a country home of her own, she would instruct the architect to design a room exclusively for billiards.

"Ned," Papa repeated. He extended his freed right hand, and the earl politely shook it. "It's a delight to see you again, my boy. And to see you looking so well! I collect that North America quite agreed with you."

"Yes, sir."

"I am excessively anxious to hear your adventures. I trust you discovered numerous new investment opportunities?"

"Yes, sir." Ned cast Susanna a sardonic sideward look, and she bit her lip.

"You returned not a day too soon," Papa said

jovially. "Susanna was growing most impatient, weren't you, my dear?" He released Ned's hand and patted her shoulder. "Had you tarried much longer, you might well have found yourself replaced."

It was the worst thing he could have said, and from the corner of her own eye, Susanna saw the earl's jaw harden. Fortunately, Sir Reginald chose that moment to emit a whoop of triumph, and Papa spun his head.

"You scored?" he gasped. "I did not fancy you could." He turned back to Ned. "I fear we shall have to delay our discussion till the game is over; I've a hundred pounds at stake. We should be finished by the time you refresh yourself, and then you and I shall play a game or two. Rosemary will show you to your room."

He waved peremptorily toward the staircase, and Susanna noticed one of his chambermaids standing at the bottom. Rosemary had been in Papa's employ but a few months, and her reaction upon being introduced to Ned was much the same as that of Susanna's servants: an astonished gape which suggested that she had heretofore believed Lord Langham a figment of Lady Langham's imagination. At length, she recovered herself, dropped a curtsy, and withdrew a sheet of paper from the pocket of her skirt.

"Lord and Lady Langham," she muttered. She consulted the paper, and Susanna perceived that it was a rough map of the first story with names scrawled beside the boxes which represented each bedchamber. "You're in the blue room, and that is . . ."

She began turning the paper, attempting to align the drawing with the actual layout of the house; and when she had rotated it twice around without success, Susanna decided to assist her.

"These are the stairs," she said, pointing to a crude series of lines. "If you put them at the bottom, you'll easily be able to get your bearings." She turned the map ninety degrees and pointed again. "You see? The blue room is to the left of the landing, the second bedchamber on the far side of the corridor." She absently noted that Lady Thornton had been assigned the room immediately adjacent to theirs and Percy the first bed-chamber on the other side of the landing.

"Yes, I see. Thank you, ma'am."

Rosemary bobbed her head and led them up the staircase and left along the first-floor corridor. Lady Calthrop's map had not been drawn to scale—all the boxes were more or less the same size—and Susanna prayed that her and Ned's room would prove to be large. A large room would probably include a sofa among its furnishings, and a sofa would serve as a reasonably comfortable second bed . . .

Rosemary threw the door open, and when Susanna stepped across the threshold, she stifled a moan of dismay. The bedchamber (true to its epithet, it was decorated entirely in blue) was, in fact, a spacious one, but it was furnished with only the bare necessities: a narrow bed, a battered wardrobe, a dilapidated chest of drawers, and an ancient, sagging washstand. Evidently the latter was intended to double as a dressing table, for a shield-back chair stood in front of it, and a mirror—cracked squarely down the middle—was suspended from the wall above.

"Here you are then." Rosemary returned the map to the pocket of her skirt. "I'll go down and show Mr. Fowler where to bring your luggage."

She sped away, and Susanna gazed despondently round the room again.

"I shall sleep in the chair, of course," she murmured.

"Do not be absurd," Ned snapped. "I shall sleep in the chair."

"No, I truly don't mind. I'm smaller than you, and I did ask you to come—"

"For God's sake, Susanna! Must you argue with me even when I'm attempting to be courteous? I shall sleep in the chair, and we'll say no more about it."

He flung his beaver hat on the counterpane and stumped to the washstand, poured water into the basin and began to splash his face. As he reached for a towel to dry himself, Rosemary reappeared, Fowler and one of Papa's footboys in tow.

"Here's your baggage," the maid announced brightly. "And I've a message for you from Mr. Randall, sir." She shifted her eyes to Ned. "He desired me to tell you that his game is over, and he's waiting to play with you."

"Thank you, Rosemary."

The earl tossed his towel on the washstand and marched into the corridor, and Susanna once more bit her lip. His black mood quite prohibited any constructive discussion, and time was fast running out—

"Lord Langham is very handsome," Rosemary said with a sigh of approval. "I daresay you're happy as can be to have him home."

"Yes," Susanna mumbled.

"And isn't it a lovely day!" Fowler and the footboy had deposited the luggage on the bed, and Rosemary crossed the threadbare carpet, opened Ned's portmanteau, and plucked out his evening coat. "I was all on end about helping at a grand house party, I can tell you." She went to the wardrobe, hung the coat inside, trotted back to the bed. "Especially Lady Calthrop's house party; she can be a fearful dragoness, you know." She removed Ned's smallclothes from the case and carried them to the wardrobe. "And I was thinking to myself when I woke up this morning that if it *rained*, her ladyship would be cross as crabs." She returned to the bed. "So I was monstrous relieved to see sun and a blue sky . . ."

She rattled on, and Susanna felt the first sharp twinges of a headache. Rosemary sounded remarkably like Polly, she reflected, but she glimpsed no convenient avenue of escape. It was imperative to avoid Papa as much as she could, and she was too dispirited to undertake a conversation with any of her fellow guests. Unless . . .

"Nancy!" she blurted aloud. She had forgotten that Lady Hadleigh did not yet know what had happened at the ball; perhaps she could tender some advice. "Has she arrived?"

"Nancy." Rosemary frowned. "Who might that be, ma'am?"

"Lady Hadleigh. A—"

"The tall, red-haired lady!" Rosemary nodded. "Yes, she and Colonel Fordyce arrived about an hour ago. She's in the bedchamber next to his, on the other side of the stairs."

"Excellent." Susanna removed her bonnet and gloves and set them atop the chest of drawers. "If you will excuse me, I shall see whether she's in her room—"

"She is," Rosemary interposed, "but she requested not to be disturbed. She wasn't feeling well, she said, and she wanted to rest from the journey. It looked to me like she's just getting over a cold."

Susanna sank glumly into the chair. Though the back as well as the seat was upholstered, decades of use had squashed the padding nearly flat, and the chair was wretchedly uncomfortable. She did not suppose Ned's humor would improve after he tossed and turned in rock-hard misery all night.

"And I do believe spring colds are the worst." Rosemary bore Ned's cinnamon tailcoat to the wardrobe, sorrowfully shaking her head. "The worst except for *summer* colds, that is. My mama always fretted that we only got sick in the warm months. My brothers and sisters and me, I mean. There were nine of us, and by the time we finished passing our colds around, the summer was over. We weren't all well till the *cold* months came, and then we were cooped up in the cottage, driving poor Mama mad. The things we did!" She walked back to the bed, giggling in recollection. "My brother Bill—he's the oldest—Bill was the ringleader . . ."

She described their wickedest prank (loosing a frisky piglet in the parental bedchamber), then hastily added that Bill, for all his "deviltry," had turned out "splendid": he was now tenanting a large farm in East Sussex and had four children of his own and another on the way. Maggie, the eldest sister, was in service in

London; maybe Lady Langham knew her; she worked for a Mr. Danvers, a banker . . .

It soon became clear that Rosemary planned to relate the entire life history of each and every one of her eight siblings, and the twinges of pain at Susanna's temples expanded to a dull, relentless throb. Any alternative was preferable to the maid's endless discourse, she decided; and as Rosemary moved from Sally, the second-eldest sister, to Jamie, the second-eldest brother, Susanna leapt to her feet.

"You're excessively lucky to have such a large and compatible family," she interrupted, affecting an envious sigh. "I wish we could talk about them all. However, I have a bit of a headache, and I believe I shall take a walk in the garden."

"A headache?" Rosemary echoed with alarm. "Are you catching Lady Hadleigh's cold?"

"I'm afraid I might be." Susanna eagerly seized upon this explanation. "But country air seems to have marvelous restorative powers—"

"So it does." Rosemary sagely inclined her head in agreement. "Mama always said we'd be even sicklier if we lived in the city . . ."

She withdrew Ned's brown pantaloons from the case, cheerfully chattering all the while; and when she turned back toward the wardrobe, Susanna slipped into the hall. She proceeded along the corridor to Nancy's bedchamber and laid one ear to the door, hoping to detect some hint of activity within. She heard, instead, the soft but unmistakable sound of snoring, and she retraced her way to the landing and crept down the staircase. Ned and Papa were absorbed in their game—their eyes riveted to the billiard table—and she scurried to the opposite side of the foyer, crossed the library, and stepped out the French window.

Susanna hadn't seen the garden of Calthrop Hall for many years, and she now noted that it had deteriorated even more shockingly than the house. The shrubs and hedges were untrimmed, the gravel pathways choked with weeds, the rose bushes long since dead. Indeed, were it not for the grimy statues bordering the central lawn, a first-time visitor might well collect that he had exited by the wrong door and blundered into the woods.

But the guests gathered round the crumbling fountain in the middle of the garden were not first-time visitors: Susanna recognized Sir Reginald and Lady Milton; Mr. Tanner, the local vicar; and Hugh and Alicia. If she ventured in their direction, she would inevitably be drawn into their conversation, and before they could spy her, she hurried to the nearest of the outer pathways. The vegetation was so thick, she calculated, that she could walk around the perimeter of the garden without being observed.

Susanna did not remember the lake until she reached the end of the path and saw it sparkling in the sunlight some hundred yards ahead. A lake was one of the few amenities Randall Manor did not have, and as children, Susanna and Alicia had often ridden their ponies to Calthrop Hall and (despite Mama's express instructions to the contrary) waded in the water. In fact, she further recalled, they had been sitting in the thatch boat house attempting to dry their stockings when they first encountered Hugh. Susanna squinted into the sun and discovered, to her considerable surprise, that the boat house was still standing; it had seemed at the point of collapse a dozen years since. It would be an ideal retreat, she thought: she doubted any of the other guests even knew of its existence.

Susanna struck out across the park, noticing that it, too, had been left to grow wild. The entrance to the boat house was on the water side, and she stepped gingerly around the little structure, avoiding the dampest patches of ground as best she could. She was approaching the front corner when she heard a murmur of voices inside the boat house, and the sound so startled her that she narrowly repressed a gasp. Had she stumbled upon an illicit lovers' tryst? She started to steal away, but the next words caught her abruptly up.

"If you are correct"—it was Lady Thornton's voice —"I do not comprehend why they are here together."

"You are sorely deficient in patience, Julia, and you are beginning to try mine."

Percy! Susanna stiffened with shock. Why was Percy alone with Lady Thornton, casually addressing her by her Christian name? Insofar as Susanna knew, they had exchanged no more than a few polite words.

"I explained the situation at the outset," the colonel went on. "Susanna made it clear that they would maintain the fiction of a reconciliation until her sister is wed. Our objective, as I told you then, is to be certain they do not change their minds."

"But if Ned was as angry as you say—"

"I assure you that he was very angry indeed. Susanna was insisting that the incident was a *misunderstanding*, and he quite refused to listen."

"But they must have discussed it later—"

"If they did," Percy interjected, "nothing was resolved. You will recollect that Susanna claimed he was too ill to come to supper. And when I watched their arrival this afternoon, it appeared to me that they are not speaking at all."

"I hope you're right," Lady Thornton said peevishly. "I should hate to have to lure them into Grosvenor Square again. Indeed, I cannot conceive why I consented to such an absurd scheme in the first place."

"It was not an absurd scheme," the colonel snapped. "I couldn't predict that the sky would cloud over. And you must own that it worked out very nicely."

"It worked out only because I felt her skirt brush mine and threw myself into Ned's arms. Had it not been for that, we might have wandered round the square all night."

Good God! Susanna's eyes briefly widened with amazement, but as she thought on it, she wondered how she could have failed to perceive the truth for herself. She had remarked Percy's peculiar nervousness, had counted it odd that he did not offer to accompany her into Grosvenor Square. In fact, she recollected, she had even entertained the fleeting notion that Lady Thornton could not have planned a more dramatic scene. Never dreaming that she and Percy *had* planned it—

"Do you fancy I had an easy time of it last night?" the colonel said plaintively. "*Your* performance was not dependent on the clock."

She had missed the significance of that as well, Susanna reflected. He had removed his watch from his waistcoat pocket, and she had drawn entirely the wrong conclusion.

"I should rather depend on the clock than the weather," Lady Thornton sniffed. "You had only to keep Lady Langham talking till eleven."

"Which was no easy task," Percy reiterated. "Particularly inasmuch as I couldn't be sure Lord Langham would *come* at eleven. He might have stopped to search elsewhere for your fan or chat with one of the guests . . . But, again, it worked out splendidly."

"It worked out splendidly if we succeeded in driving them farther apart," Lady Thornton said. "I am not yet convinced we did."

"Your problem, as I indicated a moment ago, is that you have no patience." The colonel heaved a martyred sigh. "One learns, when one is in the army, that ninety percent of a successful campaign is careful preparation. Another five percent is good luck, and it was prodigious lucky for us that Susanna didn't reveal her feelings to Lord Langham before last evening."

"But she still could," Lady Thornton protested. "Her sister won't be wed for several months."

"They will not be together in several months." Percy emitted a smug chuckle. "Susanna and Lord Langham, I mean. That is the beauty of my strategy: we have sown so much ill will that he'll leave her at the earliest opportunity. Quietly, of course; Susanna will persuade him not to risk any breath of scandal. But he'll leave her nonetheless—as early as next week, I surmise—and secretly seek a dissolution of their marriage."

"*Secretly!*" Susanna heard a thump and conjectured that Lady Thornton had stamped one tiny foot with vexation. "I am sick to death of prowling round in *secret*."

"Do you have a better idea?" Percy asked coldly.

"I . . . ah . . ."

"No, you do not." The colonel answered his own question. "And until you do, I trust you will continue to follow our plan. At this juncture, if I may refresh your memory, the plan is simply to wait. I am confident Susanna will shortly advise me that she and Lord Langham have separated."

"And if she does not?" Lady Thornton demanded.

"Let us cross that bridge when we must."

"Very well," her ladyship muttered.

"For the present, we must take great care to create the impression that we are barely acquainted. We dare not chance another private conversation during our visit here. Should I perceive a need for further action, I shall call on you in town, and we can . . ."

Susanna was intensely curious to know at what point he would contemplate "further action" and just what form such action might take. But the discussion was obviously drawing to a close, and she, for her part, dared not chance being discovered on the listen. She whirled about and raced across the park, not stopping till she had again reached the garden pathway. She realized then that she had made a drastic error: if Percy and Lady Thornton had witnessed her flight, they would collect at once that she had overheard them. She turned fearfully back round and saw, to her relief, that the park behind her was deserted. She hurtled on up the path and through the French window and literally collided with Nancy.

"Good God!" Lady Hadleigh yelped. "Is country air really so healthful? Rosemary said you had gone to the garden in hopes of walking off your headache, and now you are *running*."

"I'm sorry," Susanna panted. The impact of the collision had driven the last bit of breath from her body, and she staggered to the nearest wall and sagged against it. "I . . . I . . ."

"Are you all right?" Nancy frowned with concern. "You look as though you've seen a ghost."

"I didn't . . . didn't see anything," Susanna gasped. "I *heard* . . ." She paused, desperately gulping for air. "I heard Percy and Lady Thornton . . ." Her voice expired in another wheeze.

"Percy and Lady Thornton have conceived a *tendre*?" Lady Hadleigh clapped her hands with delight. "Did I not tell you he would find a suitable wife? It's an ideal solution, and I wish I had thought of it myself. I daresay Percy sensed which way the wind was blowing and elected to waste no time. Naturally, you're somewhat wounded that he recovered so very *soon*—"

"No, that isn't it." Susanna shook her head. "I heard Percy and Lady Thornton . . ." She stopped again, and at length, she was able to draw a full breath. "They have been plotting to keep Ned and me apart. Scheming to be sure there is no reconciliation. They arranged the incident in Grosvenor Square and also the one last night."

"Last night?"

Nancy once more knit her brows, and Susanna remembered that she still did not know what had transpired during Alicia's ball. She described the awful scene in the library, her subsequent discussion with Ned, the gist of the conversation in the boat house. When she had finished, Lady Hadleigh's frown deepened.

"I cannot imagine that Percy would employ such dishonorable tactics. Are you sure you heard aright? Perhaps you misinterpreted—"

"I heard them quite clearly," Susanna insisted, "and there was no room for misinterpretation. But that is neither here nor there. I've only to tell Ned what they've been at . . ."

Her voice trailed off again. Nancy's instinctive reaction had been one of skepticism, and Nancy had no reason to doubt her. The earl—who had *every* reason to doubt her—would probably conclude that she had fabricated the entire story. She gazed despairingly at Lady Hadleigh.

"What am I to do?" she moaned. "Ned will not believe me without proof, and I have no proof to offer."

"Not at the moment." Nancy tapped one long fingernail thoughtfully against her teeth. "But you'd have ample proof if Ned observed Percy and Lady Thornton in suspicious circumstances."

"But he will not!" Susanna wailed. "Percy warned her that they mustn't risk another private conversation. Not while they're here, and Ned will remove to Lord Buckley's on Monday."

"*Highly* suspicious circumstances." Lady Hadleigh did not appear to have registered a single word of Susanna's objection. "Circumstances which leave no question that they are engaged in a secret and nefarious enterprise." Her green eyes began to sparkle. "Yes, Ned would readily believe you if he discovered Percy and Lady Thornton conspiring in her bedchamber in the middle of the night."

"Her bedchamber!" Susanna screeched. "Percy would *never* go to her bedchamber—"

"He would if he thought he was to meet you there," Nancy interposed.

"Meet . . . meet me." Susanna once more lost her breath.

"Yes. You said that Percy is confident his scheme has succeeded. He fancies you and Ned will separate before the week is out. What if you slipped him a note confirming his opinion? Men adore to be proved right. You could claim that Ned has stated an intention to leave you as soon as the house party is over."

"Which is true," Susanna said grimly.

"You could then say"—Lady Hadleigh flew on—"that in view of the imminent separation, you and Ned have agreed to pursue your alternate pleasures without delay."

Susanna was too fascinated to blush.

"After that," Nancy continued, "you will explain that Ned has invited Lady Thornton to share his bedchamber tonight."

Susanna distantly noted that her phraseology had changed from *could* to *will*.

"Then," Lady Hadleigh finished triumphantly, "you need but inform Percy that you will be occupying Lady Thornton's room in her absence. Ask him to join you there an hour after the evening's festivities have ended."

"It won't work." Susanna shook her head again. "When Lady Thornton answers his knock, he'll realize something is amiss."

"Tell him not to knock," Nancy said. "Point out that it wouldn't do to disturb the neighboring guests."

She and Ned were the neighboring guests, Susanna recalled, but she doubted Percy was aware of that. "And then?" she asked aloud.

"And then you waken Ned. Wake him the instant Percy enters Lady Thornton's bedchamber. Pretend you heard a mysterious noise in the corridor and insist he investigate. Percy will shortly recognize that something *is* amiss, and Ned will see him creep back out of Lady Thornton's room. You will then relate the conversation you overheard, and Ned will be absolutely persuaded of your honesty."

It was a good plan, Susanna conceded. Not perfect, but no plan was perfect; Percy and Lady Thornton had nearly been tripped up by the weather and the clock.

"Write the note immediately," Lady Hadleigh urged. "If you hurry, you can deliver it to Percy's bedchamber before he returns to the house."

Susanna nodded and sprang away from the wall, then remembered that there was no writing table in her bedchamber. She peered around the library and spotted a scarred *bonheur-du-jour* desk in one corner.

"I must do it here," she said, racing to the desk. "Watch the garden and warn me if anyone approaches."

Nancy scurried to the French window, and Susanna sank into the chair in front of the desk, jerked the drawer open, snatched out a sheet of paper, and plucked the pen from the inkstand. In the interest of speed, she abbreviated the message to its barest bones, but when she reread the words she had composed, she decided that one embellishment was required. Percy might question her sudden change of heart, and she dipped the pen in the inkstand again. "I trust there is no need to add," she inserted, "that my husband's odious conduct last evening destroyed the lingering vestiges of my affection." She hoped the colonel had forgotten her declaration that she would *always* be in love with Ned.

Susanna reviewed the revised message and feared it was all wrong. The final sentence should be first, and the general tone much resembled that of a business communication—

"They are coming!" Nancy hissed. "Lady Thornton is coming, that is; she's at the end of the pathway. Are you finished?"

She would have to be finished, Susanna thought. She scrawled her initials at the bottom of the note, jammed the pen into the inkstand, yanked an envelope from the drawer, and jumped to her feet.

"Hurry!" Lady Hadleigh pleaded. "She's halfway up the path. I shall engage her in conversation as long as I can."

Susanna dashed across the library and into the entry hall. Fortunately, Ned and Papa had completed their game—she could hear the rumble of masculine voices in the saloon on the opposite side of the foyer—and she galloped on up the staircase. She stopped when she reached the first-floor landing, looking cautiously left and right, but the upper corridor was deserted as well. She folded the note, shoved it in the envelope, sealed the envelope, and crossed the hall to Percy's bedchamber.

Susanna stared at the colonel's door, then gazed apprehensively at the envelope. She and Nancy had devised their plot in a monstrous rush, she reflected; perhaps they had overlooked some fatal flaw. But what flaw? At worst, Percy would fail to respond to her summons, and the situation would remain unchanged.

Susanna drew a deep breath, stooped, and pushed the envelope under the door.

Chapter 14

THE DINING ROOM looked astonishingly well, Susanna reflected, peering through the archway. The draperies had been drawn, and in the soft, kind light of the chandelier, the crumbling plasterwork was almost invisible. The table was *entirely* invisible—shrouded from top to floor in a lace cloth and laid with gleaming china and sparkling silver. Susanna suspected that Lady Calthrop had borrowed Papa's tableware as well as his servants, but when she ventured forward for a closer look, she did not recognize the patterns. Apparently the tableware had been passed along from previous, more prosperous, generations of Dickinsons. At any rate, no one was likely to notice the rickety, mismatched chairs—

"Susanna?" Lady Calthrop bounded through the rear door of the dining room. "Is it half past seven already?"

"No," Susanna murmured. "I finished dressing a few minutes early."

She elected not to add that she had dressed early at Ned's express insistence. He seemed determined to behave as though they were two strangers compelled to share a room at an overcrowded inn.

"With Ward's assistance, it takes me half an hour to dress," he had said when he returned to their bedchamber late in the afternoon. "*Without* his help, I daresay I can be finished in fifteen minutes. I should consequently appreciate it if you would complete your own toilette and vacate the room by a quarter past seven."

He had stalked out then, leaving Susanna to wonder

whether Nancy's plan—*any* plan—would enable her to penetrate his hostility. Perhaps their marriage was beyond salvation. Maybe she had wounded him so deeply that he would never forgive her—

". . . satisfactory?" Lady Calthrop said.

"I'm sorry?"

Susanna started and glanced up, and her ladyship scowled with vexation.

"I was remarking how very handsome the table looks," Susanna explained hastily.

"How good of you to say so, dear." Lady Calthrop sketched a forgiving smile. "I asked if you approve the seating arrangement. I placed Colonel Fordyce immediately across from you, with Lady Thornton at his left and Lady Hadleigh at his right."

The flaw, Susanna realized with a stab of panic: there was the fatal flaw. If Percy and Lady Thornton sat together during dinner, they would inevitably have an opportunity to exchange a few whispered words. The colonel would smugly comment on the success of their scheme, her ladyship would question his statement . . .

"No, that won't do." She frantically shook her head.

"Whyever not?" Lady Calthrop frowned. "Colonel Fordyce and Lady Hadleigh appear to be quite friendly."

"*They* are friendly," Susanna agreed, "but he and Lady Thornton do not get on at all."

"Do not get on?" Lady Calthrop repeated. "I was under the impression that they are scarcely acquainted."

As was I, Susanna thought grimly. "That is true," she concurred aloud, "but they formed a . . . an instantaneous dislike. I'm sure you have experienced the same feeling."

"Indeed I have." Her ladyship nodded, and Susanna suspected she experienced the same feeling every day of her life. "I fancy the easiest alternative is to put you at Colonel Fordyce's left—"

"No!" Susanna screeched. If she were situated next

to Percy, he would engage *her* in whispered conversation, and she was far too nervous to deceive him.

"Have you and Colonel Fordyce fallen out?" Lady Calthrop knit another frown.

Susanna swallowed an hysterical giggle, visualizing her ladyship's reaction if she were suddenly to reveal the scandalous events of the preceding days and weeks. But that was unthinkable, of course, and she shook her head again.

"No, it's just that . . . that . . ." She groped for a credible explanation. "I believe Colonel Fordyce and Lady Thornton would welcome the chance to make new friends. You will recall that she was recently widowed—"

"What a splendid idea!" Lady Calthrop interposed. "Mr. Tanner lost his own dear wife not long ago." She scurried along the table and snatched up one of the place cards. "I shall switch Lady Thornton with Lady Milton. Perhaps we shall shortly have *another* engagement to announce."

Susanna did not suppose Lady Thornton would be much interested in a second elderly husband—particularly not an impecunious clergyman—but she judged it best not to criticize the seating plan any further. Lady Calthrop hurried round the table, substituted Lady Milton's place card for Lady Thornton's, bore the latter back, and carefully set it on the cloth. As she stood away to evaluate her effort, Hugh and Alicia entered the dining room, and Susanna drew a shaky sigh of relief. She remained far from certain that she could win Ned back, but at least she had overcome the first obstacle.

She had predicted the composition of the house party quite accurately, Susanna observed when all the guests were seated and she gazed around the table. Lady Calthrop's sisters and their husbands were present, and though her ladyship had mixed them up—placing Mrs. Adcock next to Sir Alfred Fry and Lady Fry beside Mr. Adcock—the sisters apparently felt as free to correct their brothers-in-law as they did their own spouses. Sir

Alfred was positioned at Susanna's right, and she clearly heard Mrs. Adcock snap that he was to rest his soup spoon on the *plate* and not in the *bowl*. Lady Fry and Mr. Adcock were seated too far away for Susanna to overhear them, but she collected that he had been similarly reprimanded when she saw Lady Fry jerk his left arm off the table and shove it into her lap. Poor Lady Calthrop had no one to torment: Lord Calthrop was situated at the opposite end of the table, and she could only glower at him in helpless frustration.

At any rate—Susanna rapidly counted heads—there were eleven family members in attendance, and Percy, Nancy, Lady Thornton, and Mr. Tanner made fifteen. The remaining guests, as she had expected, were neighbors: Sir Reginald and Lady Milton, Viscount and Lady Eustace, and the Earl and Countess of Walmer. *Impoverished* neighbors; despite their titles, not a one of them had sixpence to scratch with. Susanna wondered if Papa appreciated the irony of the situation. She tried to catch his attention, but he was valiantly conversing with Lady Calthrop.

The footmen removed the soup bowls and served the entrées, and Susanna detected at once that Lady Calthrop had not borrowed Papa's cook. Simon Randall had always prided himself on setting an impeccable table, and tonight's roast beef was tough and stringy, the cauliflower cooked to a mush, and the potatoes nearly raw. Not that it signified; Susanna had altogether lost her appetite. She pushed the food around her plate and glanced at Sir Alfred, but Mrs. Adcock was now instructing him how to cut his meat. She turned toward Lord Walmer, who was seated at her left, but he was also occupied: discussing Napoleon's latest depredations with Lady Eustace.

Susanna turned back to reach for her wineglass, and as she did so, her eyes brushed Percy's. She wondered how a woman should greet her soon-to-be lover across the dinner table, but as she debated between a cool nod and a warm smile, the colonel hastily dropped his eyes and busied himself with one of his potatoes. Which might mean that he had decided to accept her invitation and did not trust himself to look at her. Or—equally and conversely—his reaction could indicate that he had decided *not* to join her in Lady Thornton's bedchamber and was too embarrassed to meet her gaze. Dear God, Susanna thought, how she wished she knew! She picked up her glass and noticed that her hands were trembling.

Following the dessert—a soggy currant tart—Lady Calthrop led the ladies to the drawing room for after-dinner tea. This proved to be nearly as unpalatable as the meal: a brew so weak that it looked, and tasted, like warm beige water. Unfortunately, Susanna was seated beside Lady Calthrop on the tattered Hepplewhite sofa and thus compelled actually to *drink* the awful concoction. She sipped from her cup as slowly as she could and had just forced down the final drop when Lord Calthrop ushered the gentlemen into the saloon. Their cheeks were flushed with brandy, and Susanna bitterly regretted that she could not have consumed a fortifying dose of spirits in lieu of the dreadful tea.

Lady Calthrop—her own cheeks flushed with what she evidently fancied to be a social triumph— brightly suggested that the men and women play cards together for a time. As Papa's footmen set up the tables, the guests divided themselves into groups: some wanted to play casino, others Pope Joan, and still others preferred piquet. Susanna, for her part, did not wish to play at all; but when everyone else was seated, it became clear that a fourth was needed at one of the casino tables. Susanna was recruited to serve as Mr. Tanner's partner, and she soon had reason to be thankful that they were playing for only a shilling a game. Had there been hundreds of pounds at stake—as was generally the case at White's—she would have lost a substantial portion of Papa's fortune, for she made one blunder on another. At the end of three rubbers, the affable vicar was so livid with rage that he could scarcely hold his cards.

"Well!"

Lady Calthrop rose and beamed around the drawing room. She had been playing piquet with Viscount

Eustace, and Susanna surmised from her joyful expression that she had won.

"Well," her ladyship said again. "I trust you have all enjoyed the evening as much as I have."

There were polite nods and murmurs of agreement.

"However," Lady Calthrop continued, "we must remember that there are many activities to come. Breakfast will be served at nine o'clock, and after that, Walter will conduct a fishing expedition for the gentlemen."

She looked pointedly at the casino table next to Susanna's, but the game there had ended some minutes since, and Lord Calthrop was sound asleep in his chair. "Walter!" she shrieked.

He jerked his head up, shook it, and blearily focused his eyes. "Yes, dear?"

"I was saying that you will take the gentlemen fishing tomorrow!"

"Yes, dear."

The viscount obediently bobbed his head, then began to nod again, and Lady Calthrop essayed another smile.

"I daresay Walter is as tired as the rest of us," she said, casting him a murderous, sideward glare. "And the rest of us shall be very tired indeed if we don't sleep while we have the chance. When the men return from their fishing tomorrow, we shall have a picnic in the garden, and by the time the picnic is over, we shall have to start dressing for the ball. Which is the *principal* event of the weekend, of course."

She directed her smile to Hugh and Alicia, who had played Pope Joan with Mr. and Mrs. Adcock.

"If we are to be fully refreshed for the assembly," Lady Calthrop concluded, "I fancy we should retire without delay."

This proposal elicited another murmur of agreement. The majority of the party had traveled down from London, and though none of them seemed quite so exhausted as Lord Calthrop—who had laid his head on the table and was audibly snoring—they all appeared eager to repair to their beds. As they rose from their chairs and trooped out of the drawing room, Susanna peered at the clock on the mantel. It was twenty-eight minutes after eleven, but even Percy, precise as he was, would ignore a few odd seconds. If he came to Lady Thornton's room, he would come at half past twelve.

Susanna hurried into the foyer, still looking over her shoulder at the clock, and promptly collided with the billiard table. That was the worst thing about them, she thought grouchily. Mama had eventually owned that Papa's billiard table was quite handsome, but she had never ceased to lament that it was always *in the way*. Susanna stepped back, straightened her dress, glanced around the entry hall, and saw Ned and Papa at one end of the table.

"Good evening, my dear," the latter said cheerfully. "Would you care to watch our game?"

"You intend to play *now*?"

This was one complication Susanna had not anticipated. Lady Thornton was already ascending the staircase, and Percy was standing at the bottom, evidently expressing his compliments to Lady Calthrop. The colonel would judge it most peculiar if Ned postponed his romantic rendezvous in order to play at billiards.

"Yes." Papa plucked a cue from the rack on the foyer wall. "Your husband took three hundred pounds from me this afternoon, and I'm anxious to win it back. Unless you've some objection."

"In point of fact, I do." Susanna eagerly seized the opening he had provided. "If you are to be at your best for Alicia's engagement ball, you must have a good night's sleep."

"I shan't stay up more than an hour or two." Papa bent over the table and slid the cue expertly through his fingers.

"But . . . but . . ." Susanna cast about for another objection. "But you will disturb the other guests."

"Nonsense," Ned said. "The bedchambers are all on the floor above."

He began studying the remaining cues in the rack, but Papa laughed and drew himself up.

"Never mind, my boy. I fancy your wife has other plans for you this evening." He winked at the earl, and Susanna's cheeks flamed. "And perhaps she's right in any case. I am a trifle tired, and it's possible we might keep someone else awake. We'll play tomorrow, when I'm rested, and I daresay I shall have three hundred pounds of *yours* before the day is over."

He replaced his cue in the rack and strode across the entry hall to the staircase. He could yet change his mind, Susanna thought, and she sped after him, nearly treading on his heels, and trailed him up the stairs. They were halfway to the landing when she heard Ned's footfalls behind her and felt his silver eyes boring angrily into her back. Papa turned at the top of the steps, bid them both a jovial good-night, and made his way down the long, dim corridor to the right of the landing. Susanna raced in the opposite direction, and the earl caught her up just as she opened their bedchamber door.

"What the deuce are you at?" he snapped, closing the door behind them. "You certainly have no *other plans* for me this evening."

"I simply . . . simply felt—"

"And I shan't obtain any sleep either. Not in that wretched chair."

He glowered toward the washstand, and Susanna perceived that he, too, had given her an opening.

"That is it exactly!" she said. "The chair, I mean. I plan to read for a while before I retire." By a stroke of good fortune, she had packed Miss Austen's latest novel in her portmanteau. "And it occurred to me that you could use the bed while I'm reading. When I get tired, I shall wake you, and we can exchange."

Ned knit a brief frown, then apparently concluded that even a few minutes in a relatively comfortable bed were better than no minutes at all.

"Very well," he growled. "If you will step into the hall a moment, I shall undress."

Susanna reluctantly complied, wondering what she could say if she encountered one of the other guests. She could say she had lost something, she decided, and she hastily removed her left earring and clutched it in her hand. Should anyone venture into the corridor, she would fall to her knees and pretend to be conducting a search.

But no such ruse was necessary: the earl, now clad in his dressing gown, soon opened the door and curtly advised Susanna that it was her turn to change. She dashed past him, stripped off her clothes, tugged on her nightdress and her own dressing gown, and bounded back across the room. Evidently Ned had eluded detection as well; he was standing alone in the hall, looking—except for his attire—much like a sentry guarding a remote military outpost.

"I am finished," she whispered.

The earl spun around, stepped over the threshold, closed the door again, and stalked to the bed. It had been turned down for the night, and he crawled under the covers without removing his dressing gown.

"Your book was on the chest," he said, "but I moved it to the washstand."

Damn! Susanna ground her teeth. She desperately wanted to know the time, and she could see the tantalizing gleam of Ned's watch atop the chest of drawers. But she had been excessively lucky thus far, and it wouldn't do to tempt fate at this late juncture.

"Thank you," she murmured.

She walked to the washstand, sank into the chair, picked up the book, and opened it to the first page. She had stared sightlessly at the print for a considerable interval before she realized that it was much too dark to read, and when she pulled the candle closer, she discovered that she had been holding the book upside down.

Susanna closed the book and tried to calculate the hour. She had talked with Ned and Papa for five minutes, she estimated. Ten minutes at the most. The three of them had then come upstairs, and her and Ned's undressing had taken fifteen minutes more. Maybe twenty. After that . . .

But there was the rub: she had no idea how long she had been sitting in the chair. She glanced at the chest of drawers, then shifted her eyes to the bed. Though she could barely discern the earl's form beneath the bed-clothes, she could see—and hear—that he was still tossing fitfully about. If he had fallen asleep, he was sleeping very lightly and would wake again the instant she moved.

Susanna sat as quietly as she could, scarcely permitting herself to breathe, and began to count the passing seconds in her mind and the minutes on her fingers. When the latter count reached fifteen, she decided she could afford to wait no longer. If Percy went to Lady Thornton's room, discovered her ladyship inside, and returned to his own bedchamber, the plan would fail in any case.

Susanna laid her book cautiously on the washstand, rose, and crept toward the chest of drawers. She was approximately halfway across the room when one of the floorboards emitted a great creak, and she stopped and peered fearfully at the bed. To her immense relief, Ned did not stir; and she quickened her pace, snatched his watch off the chest, carried it back to the washstand, and thrust it into the candlelight. Her luck had held, she saw: it was twenty-nine minutes past midnight. She laid the watch beside the book, stole to the door, and cracked it open.

Susanna had judged it most fortunate that Lady Thornton's room was situated immediately next to hers. She could wake Ned the instant Percy entered, she'd reasoned, and there would be no opportunity for the colonel to escape without detection. She had abandoned Nancy's notion of reporting a "mysterious noise" in the hall and determined, instead, to claim that she smelled smoke. The possibility of a burglar was so remote that the earl might well refuse to investigate, but he couldn't ignore even the smallest chance of fire.

The hitch, Susanna now perceived, was that Lady Thornton's door was at the wrong angle; though it was located only a few feet away, it was quite invisible. But that didn't signify, she assured herself, for she could readily see the corridor in front of the door. She would waken Ned the moment Percy *appeared*, and if her luck continued to hold, the earl would be sniffing round the hall as Percy left Lady Thornton's bedchamber.

Susanna was no longer counting the minutes, but she fancied some five or six had elapsed when she began to grow alarmed. The colonel was punctual to a fault, and it seemed prodigious unlikely that he would be late for such a critical meeting. Which must mean that he had elected to decline her invitation. Unless Ned's watch was wrong. Yes, that was it. The earl had never much cared about time, and his watch could easily be five or ten minutes fast. Susanna started to draw another sigh of relief, then realized that Ned's watch could as easily be *slow*. Perhaps Percy had gone to Lady Thornton's room and already returned to his own bedchamber.

Susanna had watched the corridor for several minutes more before she recognized the basic fallacy in her and Nancy's plan: they had both assumed that as soon as Percy discovered the wrong woman in Lady Thornton's room, he would frantically retreat. But why should he? He would initially collect that some unforeseen circumstance had prevented the exchange of bedchambers and express his disappointment to Lady Thornton. Her ladyship would naturally be confused, and she and the colonel would begin to discuss the situation . . .

So perhaps the flaw was to her advantage, Susanna realized; perhaps Percy and Lady Thornton actually *were* conspiring in the privacy of her bedchamber. If so, Susanna could wake Ned and insist he listen at the door, and there would be no doubt whatever that they were at some sort of mischief. But first, of course, she must be certain the colonel and Lady Thornton were together.

Susanna stepped to the center of the hall and looked from one end to the other. As she had hoped, the corridor was deserted, and she scurried to her ladyship's door and pressed one ear against it. She heard nothing —no murmur of conversation, no hint of movement— and she wondered if Percy had come and gone after all.

Or had he and Lady Thornton reached a lull in their discussion? Maybe they were independently pondering their next move. Or maybe they were speaking so softly that their voices could not penetrate the thick oak door.

Susanna clenched her hands with frustration, raised her head, backed away from the door; and at that moment, she was seized from behind. She stifled a shriek and whirled about.

"Percy!" she gasped.

She attempted to squirm out of his grasp, but the colonel's arms tightened round her.

"Susanna," he whispered. "Are you just arriving as well? I feared I was late, but I couldn't be sure how long you had chatted with your father."

"I . . ." Oh, dear God. "I . . ."

"I trust you can conceive how delighted I was to receive your note." The colonel smiled fondly down at her. "Delighted, but not inordinately surprised. I was confident you would soon come to see that you no longer care for Lord Langham."

"But I . . . There has been a dreadful misunderstanding—"

"No," Percy said soothingly, "I understand very well. I quite comprehend how you could be misled by the memory of your previous feelings. I assure you that I do not—shall not—bear you any grudge."

"But you *don't* understand," Susanna croaked. "I never intended—"

"Never intended to wound me? I know that, my dear, and you needn't apologize any further. Your marriage is behind us; let us look ahead."

He drew her closer, lowered his head, laid his mouth on hers; and Susanna jerked desperately away.

"Please, Percy," she pleaded. "You must listen to me—"

"I've all night to listen to you," the colonel interposed huskily. "Well, not *all* night; there will be other . . . ah . . . activities to occupy our time. I'm mad for you, Susanna." He bent his head again.

"Stop!" she screeched. "Please—"

"What the devil is going on?" Lady Thornton snapped. She had opened her door and was glaring across the threshold.

"Julia?" The colonel's eyes widened with puzzlement. "You have not yet gone to Lord Langham's bedchamber?"

"Why should I be in Ned's bechamber?"

Susanna heard the squeak of rusty hinges, and when she glanced over Percy's shoulder, she saw Sir Reginald and Lady Milton peering curiously into the hall. Nor were they the only guests to have been awakened: Lord and Lady Walmer were standing in a doorway at the end of the corridor. Susanna could but pray that none of them had overheard the conversation. They would undoubtedly mention the midnight disturbance to Lady Calthrop, but if Susanna returned to her room at once, perhaps she could persuade her ladyship that she had, in fact, smelled smoke, left her bedchamber to investigate, encountered Percy in the hall—

"What is amiss?"

Lady Calthrop emerged from the door opposite Lord and Lady Walmer's, and Susanna's knees weakened. Her ladyship rushed up the corridor, her nightcap fairly quivering with alarm, and ground to a halt when she reached Lady Thornton's door.

"Susanna? Colonel Fordyce? Lady Thornton? What is wrong? Surely someone told you the location of the sanitary facilities."

If she was ever to use her excuse, Susanna thought, she must use it now, and she moistened her lips. "I . . . I fancied I smelled smoke—"

"I can tell you what is wrong," Ned drawled.

The earl's voice came from behind Susanna, and when she spun her head, she saw that several other guests had wakened as well. Lord and Lady Eustace had moved into the hall for a better view of the proceedings; Mr. Tanner was discreetly observing the scene through his half-open door; and even as Susanna watched, Mrs. Adcock opened her own door and thrust her head into the corridor.

"What is wrong," Ned continued, "is that Colonel Fordyce is attempting to seduce my wife."

"Colonel Fordyce!" Lady Calthrop shot him a look of horrified reproval.

"No!" Susanna protested. "The truth is . . ." She belatedly noticed that Percy's arms—though they had gone quite slack—were still around her, and she dodged out of his embrace. "The truth is—"

"The truth is," the colonel interjected, "that Susanna was trying to seduce me."

"Susanna!" Lady Calthrop's jaws sagged with shock.

"But there were mitigating circumstances," Percy added hastily. "Lady Thornton was to go to Lord Langham's bedchamber—"

"Lady Thornton planned to seduce Lord Langham as well?"

Lady Calthrop started to sway, but Sir Reginald Milton had the presence of mind to bound forward and throw one arm around her shoulders. She sagged against him a moment, then drew herself up.

"I now perceive that my original suspicions were all too justified," she said stiffly. Her eyes darted from Susanna to the colonel to Lady Thornton, then fastened again on Susanna. "London has always been a hotbed of sin, and I should never have credited your claims of morality."

Susanna did not believe she had made any claims of morality, but before she could say so, Lady Calthrop flew on.

"However, we shall discuss that tomorrow. For the present, I shall merely remind you where you are. You may conduct yourself as you will in town, but I won't countenance your lascivious behavior in *my* home."

"Nor will I," Ned said.

Susanna spun her head again and saw that the earl had ventured down the hall; he was situated just behind herself and Lady Calthrop.

"Lord Langham," her ladyship murmured. "Forgive

me. I'm sure this lamentable situation embarrasses you far more than myself."

"No." Ned shook his head. "I lost my ability to be embarrassed the first time I stripped myself half-naked and cut sugarcane side by side with my slaves."

Lady Calthrop blushed.

"Shortly after that," the earl went on, "I recognized that *lamentable situations* are often opportunities in disguise."

"Yes," her ladyship said. "Your adventures in Louisiana were most exciting—"

"And I glimpse a golden opportunity now," Ned interrupted. "Susanna is in a mood to be seduced, and I fancy no one can satisfy her as well as I."

"Lord Langham!"

Lady Calthrop's face turned from pink to purple, and Susanna feared she was at the point of an apoplectic seizure. But she was not to know, for Ned's fingers had snaked around her elbow, and he was fairly dragging her along the hall. Their audience had increased, she noted: Mr. Adcock had joined his wife at the door of their room, and Sir Alfred and Lady Fry stood in the doorway immediately across the corridor. With a pleasant nod, the earl tugged Susanna into their bedchamber, slammed the door behind them, and dropped her arm.

"Ned," she choked. "You must permit me to explain—"

"No." He shook his head again. "There have been far too many explanations already." He untied his dressing gown, tore it off, and flung it on the floor.

"What . . . what are you doing?" Susanna stammered.

"I am preparing to fulfill my promise to Lady Calthrop. Getting ready to do what I should have done long ago. I am going to seduce you, my dear."

"But I haven't yet told you—"

"I won't talk about it now, Susanna. Talk has nearly been the death of us."

He reached forward, pulled her into his arms, and took her mouth with his. She instinctively struggled a moment, but then she was overwhelmed by all the old sensations, and she strained against him and wound her own arms round his neck. His lovemaking was subtly different, she reflected distantly. As she had surmised, he was stronger than he'd been before: his neck and shoulders were like steel, and his hands on her body—though gentle—were hard. He moved his lips to her ear, her throat, and she moaned with pleasure.

At length, Ned scooped her up and carried her to the bed; he had never done that before either. He lowered her to the mattress and stripped off his nightshirt, then carefully removed her dressing gown and nightdress. He climbed into the bed and took her in his arms again, and she felt the wild, familiar thrill of his bare flesh touching hers. They had sometimes lain this way for many minutes, she recalled—kissing and caressing and teasing until their desire could not be denied. But she had been without him too long; she had to have it finished.

"Please," she whispered. "Please."

"Yes," he murmured. "Oh, yes."

And now it was exactly as she remembered: the exquisite shock of his possession, the pleasure growing until it became almost unbearable, the final explosion of ecstasy. She nestled against him, as she had that first night so many years before, and tumbled into oblivion.

Chapter 15

WHEN SUSANNA WOKE, she lifted her head from the pillow and peered about in puzzlement. She was not in her bedchamber—the angle of the sunlight was wrong —but where was she? Calthrop Hall, she remembered, dropping her head back to the pillow; and the delicious ache in her limbs further reminded her what had transpired during the night. She turned her head and found Ned, propped on one elbow, grinning crookedly down at her.

"Good morning," the earl whispered. "I trust you'll agree that my seduction was at least as satisfactory as Colonel Fordyce's would have been?"

He ran one finger lightly down her nose, and Susanna started to return his grin. But he had not permitted her to tender any explanations last night, she recalled, and too much had been left unsaid. She wriggled upright in the bed, drawing the bedclothes modestly up to her armpits, and moved the pillow behind her back.

"You are laboring under a dreadful misapprehension." She drew a deep breath and turned once more to face him. "I can only beg you to believe me when I swear that Percy and I did not . . . not . . ."

"Did not have an affair?" Ned supplied. He sat up as well and shoved his own pillow against the ancient headboard. "I knew that."

"You knew?" Susanna echoed indignantly. "Then why the devil did you accuse me—"

"Because I didn't know at the outset," the earl interposed. "When I reached your house and saw you kissing Colonel Fordyce, I naturally leapt to the obvious conclusion."

"The *wrong* conclusion," Susanna sniffed.

"So it proved. At the time, however . . ." He stopped and raked his fingers through his hair. "Try to put yourself in my place, Susanna. I daresay it was unreasonable of me to expect that you'd patiently be awaiting my return; I'd been gone for three and a half years. But I *did* expect it. I'd thought about you every day of all those years, and I assumed you were longing for me in the same fashion. Imagine my distress when Dickie informed me that—far from pining away—you'd become the premier hostess in London."

He paused again and rearranged the covers round his waist. "I had barely swallowed that affront to my pride when I discovered you were involved with another man. More than *involved*: you announced that you were at the point of *wedding* him. I was . . . Well, at the risk of sounding melodramatic, I was devastated."

"You hid it very well," Susanna said dryly. "The next morning, you consumed enough breakfast for three."

"You noticed!" Ned sketched a lopsided smile of triumph. "Yes, I fancy I did eat enough for three, and since I had no appetite at all, it's lucky I didn't sicken and die on the spot. But I wanted to persuade you that I didn't care a damn whether you married Colonel Fordyce or not."

"Which you did," Susanna said. "But in the event there was any lingering doubt in my mind, you hastened to call on Lady Thornton and invite her to my next salon."

"No." The earl shook his head. "I truly have changed, Susanna. Well"—he flashed another crooked grin—"I *hope* I've changed. At any rate, I had no intention of using Julia as a weapon against you. You'd rejected me, and when I called on Julia, I honestly thought to rekindle our *tendre*. I believed you were sleeping with Colonel Fordyce, and it seemed only fair that I should have a . . . ah . . . a companion of my own."

It *was* only fair, Susanna owned, but she couldn't bear the vision of Ned and Lady Thornton entwined in passion. "Did you?" she croaked. "Make love to her, I mean?"

"Good God, no! I recognized within the space of five minutes that I didn't care a whit for Julia. Didn't care then and never would, but by that time, it was too late."

"Too late?" Susanna frowned.

"I had already invited her to your soiree." The earl winced with the memory. "That was the excuse I had devised for calling in the first place. Dickie had told me that Julia was widowed, but he knew nothing more of her circumstances. I judged it quite possible that she was at the point of remarriage as well, and if that was the case, I didn't wish to create an awkward situation. So as soon as we had exchanged greetings, I blurted out my invitation, and she . . . she—"

"Leapt to the obvious conclusion?" Susanna suggested wickedly.

"Exactly. And after that, I could not be rid of her. Not even when I realized you *weren't* having an affair with Colonel Fordyce."

"And when was that?" Susanna asked.

"Two days later; the morning after your salon. The first time I met the colonel. When I observed the two of you together, I perceived at once that you had never . . ." His voice trailed off, and he waved vaguely round the bed.

"Why did you so quickly draw that conclusion?" Susanna was genuinely curious.

"Because you didn't look at him the way you're looking at me now. There's an unmistakable glow in a woman's eyes when she's been well loved."

His own eyes softened, and he touched her nose again, and then her cheek, and Susanna willed herself not to melt against him. It would be terribly easy to ignore the past—to thrust the preceding weeks and years entirely out of her mind. But if she did so, every hour would inevitably come back to haunt her.

"And then?" she demanded aloud. "When you recognized the true nature of my relationship with Percy, why didn't you speak?"

"I tried to," he reminded her. "I tried to talk to you in Grosvenor Square."

"But that was nearly a week later," she protested. "You wasted all those days—"

"Would you have listened to me?" he countered. "You hadn't up till then, and you didn't listen to me that night either."

"I thought you'd *abandoned* me, Ned! And then I thought you'd come back only to get another slice of Papa's fortune—"

"Hush." He laid one finger gently over her lips. "You've told me before what you thought. Consider for a moment what *I* thought. You weren't engaged in an affair with Colonel Fordyce, but I feared you could begin one at any moment. In fact, I fancied you might turn to him solely to spite me. Which is why I enticed Lady Calthrop to invite herself to your next salon."

"You *did* encourage her then!" Susanna jerked her mouth away from his finger. "I knew I was right."

"Indeed you were. I adore Lady Elwell; had she been fifty years younger, I should probably have married her instead of you. But Lady Elwell was a very poor chaperon. Lady Calthrop is another matter. I calculated that you'd have to be on your best behavior if she was breathing down your neck."

"But what of *your* behavior?" Susanna said. "You asked Lady Thornton to that soiree too."

"No, Julia also asked herself. Well, to be more accurate, she made it clear after the first salon that she expected to attend every week. However, I must confess that I didn't attempt to dissuade her; I perceived no harm in such a plan. To the contrary, I thought a bit of jealousy might further my cause. I never dreamed, of course, that Julia would lure me into Grosvenor Square and throw herself into my arms. You must believe *me* on that head, Susanna. She took me entirely by surprise—"

"Good God!" Susanna gasped. She had forgotten that he did not yet know of Percy and Lady Thornton's machinations or her own counterplot, and she related both as quickly as she could. The earl began to chuckle as she described the note she had written to Percy, and by the time she had finished her story, he was roaring with laughter.

"It is not amusing, Ned," she said sternly. "I was appalled when I encountered Percy in the corridor."

"I daresay you were, but it's fortunate for us that you *did* encounter him. I was wakened by the sound of your conversation, and I reached the door just as you were screeching at him to cease his attentions. It was obvious he had forced himself on you, and I realized he must have done so the previous night as well."

"It would have been even more fortunate had you realized it then." Susanna could not keep a note of bitterness out of her voice.

"Yes." Ned sighed. "I'm sorry I acted so harshly. But try, again, to imagine my feelings. I had attempted to effect a reconciliation, I had asked you to return to Louisiana with me, and you had continued to reject me at every turn. No, worse than merely *rejecting* me, you'd accused me of scheming to steal Simon's money or lay my hands on Julia's fortune—"

"And I'm sorry for that," Susanna whispered.

"It no longer signifies." He took her hand. "But that night, when I discovered you in the library with Colonel Fordyce . . . Well, I altogether lost my temper. I was so angry that I wouldn't have believed you had you told me the sky was blue."

He raised her hand to his lips, and Susanna shivered, but there was one more thing she had to know.

"Would you really have gone back to America without me?"

"Never." He laced his fingers through hers. "As I indicated to Lady Calthrop, I worked like a slave— *harder* than a slave—for three years. But I was always working for *us*; my success wouldn't matter a deuce if I couldn't share it with you. No, if you had married

Colonel Fordyce, I should have sold my holdings in Louisiana and become a wastrel again, no doubt."

He hesitated, then crushed Susanna's hand in his. He had no conception of his strength, and she was hard put not to wince.

"I . . . I do love you, you know. Or do you? I was often afraid you didn't. I contracted a fever in Louisiana, and for two days I thought I was going to die. And my worst fear wasn't of death itself. My worst fear was that you'd go to your own grave believing I'd wed you for your money."

Susanna wanted to say that that didn't signify either, but she couldn't speak around the great, swelling lump in her throat.

"I did decide to *court* you for your money," the earl went on. "I shan't deny that. I was a callous young man in those days, Susanna. I fancied myself in love with Julia, but I was quite prepared to put her aside for Simon Randall's fortune. But once I met you—as I told you at the time—I recognized that my feelings for Julia were nothing more than a childish infatuation. I loved you then, and I love you now, and I'll love you as long as I live."

"Oh, Ned." She emitted a great, indelicate sniffle and buried her face in his shoulder.

"And I fully expect to live another forty or fifty years." He tugged her chin up, grinned down at her, then sobered. "But perhaps you don't want to go to Louisiana. If you don't, I'll sell my property and invest in some enterprise here in England. But I won't allow Simon to support us; make no mistake about that. We shall have to survive on whatever I can earn."

Louisiana! Susanna thought. It was thousands and thousands of miles away, and abounding in pirates and Indians and fevers . . . But she would follow Ned to the ends of the earth if that was what he wanted.

"I'll go with you," she said, dabbing her eyes with the back of her hand. "Perhaps Papa and Alicia will visit from time to time—"

"And perhaps we'll eventually return to England. When I'm as rich—or *almost* as rich—as Simon."

He slid down in the bed, flung the bedclothes impatiently aside, and took her in his arms. His attentions were beginning to grow most serious when she recollected a final complication and drew away.

"When we arrive in Louisianna," she said, "shall I be compelled to meet your mistress?"

"My mistress?" he barked. "What mistress?"

"You admitted that you weren't altogether faithful during your absence, and I assumed—"

"Are you really that naive, Susanna?" He shook his head. "Men have certain . . . er . . . needs, and there are women who make it a business to . . . ah . . . fulfill those needs. I visited such women on occasion, but I do not even remember their names. Indeed, now I think on it"—he frowned—"I do not believe I ever *knew* their names. And one of them was a remarkably handsome redhead—"

"Never mind," Susanna interrupted hastily. "You'll have no chance to pay similar calls in future."

She pulled his mouth back down to hers and blanked her mind. His hands on her body were ever more urgent, and in just a moment—"

"Susanna?" There was a sharp, commanding rap at their door. "Ned? I must talk to you."

"Papa!" Susanna hissed.

She squirmed out of Ned's embrace, sat up, and gazed with dismay at the rumpled bedclothes. Papa would perceive in an instant what they'd been at. But they were legally married, Susanna reminded herself, and there was no reason to be embarrassed—

"Susanna!" Papa bellowed. "Open the door at once!"

She leapt out of the bed, plucked her dressing gown off the floor, and frantically tugged it on. In the interim, Ned had raced across the room to retrieve his own dressing gown, and when she reached his side, he pulled the door open.

"Well, you have done it now," Papa said heavily.

"Done . . . done what?" Susanna's cheeks warmed, but she soon saw that he was not looking at the bed.

"To say the truth, I don't *know* what. Lady Calthrop only gave me to understand that you had committed an unforgivable sin. You and Ned."

He glared back and forth between them. "I collected that Colonel Forsythe and Lady Thornton were involved as well, but—as I indicated—the details were unclear. Lady Calthrop was fairly hysterical when I reached her bedchamber."

"Her bechamber?" the earl echoed. "She summoned you to her *bedroom*?"

"She claimed that last night's horrifying events had rendered her physically ill. No, permit me to rephrase that: she said she was *mortally* ill. But not too ill to inform me that in view of your disgraceful conduct"—Papa scowled again—"she will not permit Hugh to marry Alicia."

"She won't permit it *now*," Susanna said soothingly. "But when she understands what happened . . ." Her voice trailed off. It would be no easy task to explain the situation to Lady Calthrop's satisfaction.

"After that," Papa continued, "she ordered me out of the house."

"Do not tease yourself about it." Susanna patted his shoulder; she would somehow devise a way to talk her ladyship round. "She'll soon come down out of the boughs—"

"Me and all my relatives," Papa went on. "But I daresay we're in excellent company." He shrugged her hand away and essayed a brave smile. "Lady Calthrop is now speaking with Hugh and Alicia, and upon the conclusion of their conversation, she intends to summon Colonel Forsythe and Lady Thornton and order them to leave as well. If I've figured aright, that's nearly a third of the party . . ." His smile collapsed, and his own voice expired in a little whimper.

"Let me think on it, Papa," Susanna said weakly. "I

doubt even Lady Calthrop is sufficiently brazen to instruct your own footmen to pack your bags."

"I fear she is," he muttered. "Well, we shall soon find out."

He trudged disconsolately down the corridor, and the earl closed the door behind him.

"What are we to do?" Susanna moaned.

"Inasmuch as Lady Calthrop has commanded us to leave, I fancy we should pack *our* bags," Ned said cheerfully. "However, we first have some unfinished business to attend."

He drew her against him and lowered his mouth to hers, and she struggled away.

"I was asking what we should do about Alicia. You heard Papa: Lady Calthrop has forbidden Hugh to marry her."

"I do not perceive that we should do anything." The earl's jaws hardened. "If memory serves me correctly, Hugh is above one and twenty years of age. He does not need his mother's permission to wed."

"No, but—"

"And if he doesn't care for Alicia enough to defy Lady Calthrop, she should count herself lucky to be rid of him."

She had recently entertained a similar notion, Susanna recalled. Alicia would be temporarily crushed, of course, but a few months of misery were better than a lifetime of unhappiness. Ned propelled her toward the bed, stopping at frequent intervals to kiss her lips and her throat, and her knees began to tremble. He untied his dressing gown, and at that moment, there was another frantic pounding at the door.

"Susanna?" It was Alicia's voice. "Please let us in."

"Hell and the devil!" the earl hissed.

He fastened his dressing gown again and stalked back across the room. Susanna hastily rearranged her own attire and hurried after him.

"I daresay Papa has told you the news," Alicia said as Ned jerked the door open. "That Lady Calthrop has refused to approve our engagement, I mean." She glanced up at Hugh, who was standing beside her.

"Ah . . . yes." Susanna realized that she couldn't possibly express her opinion in Hugh's presence, and she groped for some innocuous words of comfort. "But you mustn't be too overset. She may yet change her mind—"

"It doesn't signify," Hugh interposed. "Alicia and I discussed the matter as soon as Mama dismissed us, and I assured her I shall marry her with or without Mama's consent."

"That is wonderful!" Susanna beamed at him and Alicia in turn. "Papa will be so relieved. And I'm sure he'll be entirely fair with you, Hugh. He won't reduce Alicia's dowry by a groat, and you can live at Randall Manor rather than here—"

"No." He shook his head. "Alicia and I discussed that as well, and we've decided to settle elsewhere. We should prefer to emigrate to Louisiana, and I was in hopes Lord Langham would agree to assist us." He transferred his eyes to Ned. "Perhaps you'd be kind enough to provide some letters of introduction, sir."

"*Sir?*" the earl growled. "I'm not even ten years older than you; you needn't call me *sir.*"

"Yes, sir," Hugh agreed. "But about the letters . . ."

"As it happens, no letters will be required." Ned was still growling a bit. "Susanna and I have determined to return to Louisiana ourselves. If you like, you can go with us."

"We should like that very much," Hugh said happily.

Poor Papa, Susanna thought. He was shortly to achieve his fondest ambition—two titled daughters—and neither title would do him the slightest speck of good.

"We shall inform Mama of our plans at once."

Hugh tugged Alicia into the hall, and Susanna shut the door.

"Was that wise?" She frowned at the earl. "I'm immensely pleased that Hugh has elected to oppose

Lady Calthrop, but I wonder if he has the gumption to make his way in America."

"I wonder as well," Ned confessed. "But as I indicated earlier, he's a grown man, and it is not my place to advise him. Nor am I much interested in other people's problems just now. If I recollect aright, I was trying to complete a project of my own."

He pecked her nose, brushed his lips against her temple, then took her mouth again. A long, deep kiss, but as he began to fumble with the sash of her dressing gown, there was a light tap on the door.

"Susanna?" Nancy whispered. "Are you still here?"

"Good God!" The earl stamped one foot with vexation. "Can we not be granted a moment's peace?"

He flung the door open, and Lady Hadleigh nearly tumbled over the threshold.

"You *are* still here!" she said brightly. "Good morning, Lord Langham. Susanna."

"Where the devil did you think we'd be?" Ned snapped.

"I thought you might be slinking back to London. The servants are circulating the most incredible rumors. When Rosemary brought up the water for my basin, she told me Lady Calthrop had canceled the ball and intended to order everyone out of the house."

"Not *everyone*," Susanna corrected. "She did order Papa to go and to take all his relatives with him. She also intends to evict Percy and Lady Thornton, but insofar as I know, you are safe."

"Well, she can't order Percy and Lady Thornton to leave," Nancy said.

"Why not?"

"Because they have left already. That was the other thing Rosemary told me. Lady Calthrop desired Rosemary to summon Percy and Lady Thornton to her bedchamber, but when Rosemary tried to knock them up, she got no answer. She entered their rooms and found them gone. Them and all their personal effects. She consulted the head groom, and he informed her that Percy and Lady Thornton had departed in her carriage at the very crack of dawn. Perhaps they *will* conceive a *tendre*," she concluded.

"Perhaps so." Susanna wryly fancied that the colonel and Lady Thornton were prodigious well suited.

"But that is of little consolation, of course." Lady Hadleigh contritely dropped her eyes. "It's all too clear in retrospect that my plan was an excessively poor one. I observed the end of the . . . ah . . . incident last night, and even *I* can understand Lady Calthrop's shock. I'm sorry, Susanna."

"That is all right," Susanna murmured. "It worked out for the best."

"It's good of you to say so, but . . ." Nancy raised her eyes, and they fell on the untidy bed. "Well!" She grinned. "Maybe it *did* work out for the best."

"Thank you for your concern, Lady Hadleigh," Ned choked. "Now, if you will excuse us—"

"Yes, I daresay you've better things to do." Her smile broadened. "And while you do them, I shall go down to the dining room and have a scone. You may or may not be aware, Lord Langham, that I've been ill. I have scarcely eaten these eight days past, and I fear I've wasted quite to nothing—"

The earl slammed the door unceremoniously in her face. "She's right on one account." He was growling again. "We do, indeed, have better things to do."

He kissed Susanna's neck, touching his tongue against her skin, and she shuddered with pleasure.

"And at last"—his tone softened—"there is no one left to disturb us."

His lips moved to her chin, her mouth, and as she wound her fingers in his hair, another fist began to beat upon the door.

"Good *God*!" Ned thrust Susanna away and gazed incredulously over her shoulder.

"It must be Rosemary," she whispered. "I shall tell her we're not yet ready to pack—"

"Susanna?" Lady Calthrop said. "Lord Langham? I have to speak with you immediately."

She opened the door without awaiting a response, and Susanna judged it most fortunate that she and Ned were not in the very process of consummating their "project."

"Lady Calthrop!" The earl affected an expression of delight. "Dare I hope you've recovered from your *mortal* illness?"

"I . . . er . . . I do feel a trifle better," she owned. "But I have been extremely ill indeed," she added severely. "I . . . Well, let me not hide my teeth. I was horrified by the events which occurred last night."

"As were we." Ned sorrowfully shook his head. "Susanna and I had regarded Colonel Fordyce and Lady Thornton as dear friends. Imagine our dismay when we recognized the true nature of their . . . their *indecent* designs."

"Well put, Lord Langham." Her ladyship sympathetically bobbed her own head. "Their designs certainly were indecent, and I trust you'll be pleased to learn that they departed for London some hours since. They will trouble you no further."

"I am *extremely* pleased to learn that." The earl drew a sigh of relief. "It was quite right of you to request them to leave."

"Ahem." Lady Calthrop cleared her throat. "In point of fact, I did not have an opportunity to . . . ah . . . request them to leave. When Rosemary went to fetch them, she discovered them already gone. A clear sign of guilt." Her lips thinned with indignation. "Though I'm still somewhat confused—"

"Let us not dwell on the past," Ned interrupted hastily. "Am I to collect that you no longer blame Susanna and myself for last night's . . . er . . . *horrifying* events?"

Lady Calthrop nodded.

"Then I hope you are prepared to withdraw your opposition to Hugh and Alicia's engagement."

"I have already done so," her ladyship said.

"And I am prepared to facilitate their emigration to

Louisiana. So, as I indicated, there's no reason to tease ourselves about the past—"

"Louisiana." Lady Calthrop moistened her lips. "That was what changed my mind, Lord Langham. When Hugh and Alicia returned to my bedchamber, and he said they'd marry without my consent and go with you to America . . ."

Her face crumpled, and for the first time in all their long acquaintance, Susanna felt a stab of pity. Lady Calthrop was human after all.

"I love my son," she whispered, "and I've always wanted the best for him. But if he went to Louisiana . . . Walter and I couldn't possibly afford to travel so far, and I might never see Hugh again. Might never know my own grandchildren . . ."

She squared her shoulders and rearranged her face. "At any rate, I struck a bargain with Hugh. I agreed to bless his marriage to Alicia, and they agreed to stay in England. Though not necessarily *here*." She made a moue of annoyance. "Since he isn't going to America, Hugh thinks to invest a substantial portion of Alicia's dowry in some silly mill near Birmingham."

"It's hardly *silly*, Lady Calthrop," Ned said. "I may well invest in a mill myself. I recently acquired partial interest in a cotton plantation—"

"You young people." Her ladyship rolled her eyes with despair. "You are far too obsessed with money." She glanced past him and knit her brows. "When we receive Alicia's dowry, I really must replace the curtains."

She turned, stepped across the threshold, then turned back round.

"I still haven't puzzled out exactly what happened last night," she said. "Colonel Fordyce and Lady Thornton were obviously the guilty parties, but . . ." She frowned again. "How did you chance to be in the corridor, Susanna?"

"I . . . I smelled smoke. Did you leave the fire burning in the drawing room?"

In fact, there had never been a fire in the saloon, but Lady Calthrop eagerly inclined her head.

"Yes, I daresay I did. I knew no breath of scandal could attach to *your* conduct. Everything has worked out splendidly—"

"Not quite everything," the earl interposed.

"What do you mean, Lord Langham?"

"No one will grant me five minutes to make love to my wife!" he roared.

"Lord Langham!"

Lady Calthrop scurried down the corridor, and Ned kicked the door closed and drew Susanna firmly—most decisively—into his arms.

About the Author

Though her college majors were history and French, Diana Campbell worked in the computer industry for a number of years and has written extensively about various aspects of data processing. She had published eighteen short stories and two mystery novels before undertaking her first Regency romance.